Beginning of the End

Alane Hotchkin

Affinity
eBook Press
NZ

Beginning of the End

© 2013 Alane Hotchkin

Affinity E-Book Press NZ Ltd.
Canterbury, New Zealand

ISBN: 978-1-927282-13-7

1st Edition

This is a work of fiction. Names, character, places, and incidents are the product of the author's imagination or are used fictitiously and any resemblance to actual persons living or dead, businesses, companies, events, or locales is entirely coincidental

Editor: Nat Burns
Cover Design: Nancy Kaufman

Acknowledgments

Life is a journey that all must travel. It is an emotional filled road. My words are, for the most part, about everyday people you could pass on the street, know nothing about them and yet you say hello on the way for a latte.

From the first to the very last moment, be prepared for a rollercoaster of emotions. At times, you will laugh so hard you will cry; while others your heart will ache. I invite you to share with me... a journey into life and perhaps you will even see a little piece of yourself within.

None of this would have come to be if not for my dear friend Lori pushing me into starting to write again. She's a true inspiration to all.

So, please grab a snack, some tea and relax. The lives contained within should be read slowly and contemplated, as you, the reader, step into their lives.

Dedication

As I celebrate the happiness of bringing my words to you, I bow my head in sadness at the loss of a life-long friend. She was the first to read my words many decades ago and was overjoyed when I started writing once more. The moment I was done with a chapter, she was itching to take a look at it. This book is for her.

Donna, there's a hole now that you're gone. Thank you for being in my life.

Table of Contents

Introduction 1

Chapter One *Tangled Webs* 2

Chapter Two *Emotions Make Us Human* 56

Chapter Three *Ramifications of War*
101

Chapter Four *The Gifts of Love and Trust* 154

Chapter Five *Humanity Comes Calling* 195

Chapter Six *Liars, Cheaters and Life* 249

About the Author 295

Introduction

By
Lillith Blackhawk

Welcome to the Blackhawk Chronicles. Within the pages of these books are people whose lives I've crossed. I've touched all their lives. Some thank me while others curse my name.

This first book in the series tells the beginning of the story of the woman who gave me the light. She wanted only to be loved. Loved as much as I needed redemption.

In the end, we all stand alone in judgment of our souls. Nikki makes me worthy.

This is her beginning and when the call for help came, I fell into those eyes and I knew….

I would do *anything* for her.

LB

Chapter One

Tangled Webs

The two-story, red brick house had been the home of Charming Advertising for the past eleven years. Red and blue flashing lights atop police cruisers alerted the employees arriving to work at Charming that this would be far from a normal day. They found themselves turned away and told to go home after the police officer obtained their personal information.

The smells created by death permeated the offices.

Unfortunately for Nikki McLoud and her co-worker Mike White, they'd both arrived at the advertising agency early that day. Detective Scott Jackson requested they remain in Nikki's office until he and his partner returned for their statements. The detective stood protectively in the front doorway to await Detective Canton, the lead detective.

Mike bumped shoulders with Nikki. "What do you think the boss died from? Oh my God, he was naked. And did you see the purple condom he had on?"

Nikki couldn't believe her ears. She looked at Mike as if he had grown a horn in the middle of his forehead. He was her best friend but sometimes what spewed from his mouth made her question his IQ. She laughed nervously, shaking her head in disbelief, causing her wavy, auburn hair to fall into her eyes. "Mike, he's our boss! You're gross. I can't believe you can sit there—"

Mike cut her off in mid-sentence. "My bet is that his little twenty-something ho was here last night going down on him and that's when he kicked it. Then his little chick-on-the-side just left him where you found him this morning. I'll bet you twenty bucks."

Nikki sat on the corner of her desk, glaring at him. After meeting Mike on her first day with Charming Advertising eight years before, they had, strangely enough, soon become best friends.

Nikki, though she loved being a graphics designer at Charming, did not like how Mike had been treated —as the office lackey— and she immediately set about to defend him.

Nikki knew that Mike was intelligent and not a lackey, just immature. And, sure enough, he had confided in her, several weeks after they'd met, that he only acted clueless so his uncle, who co-owned the agency, wouldn't expect him to take control some day. Mike didn't want to be tied down to a desk job. He enjoyed the freedom to come and go as he pleased and liked being everyone's boy Friday, as he called himself.

That true Mike had been the only one to break through the walls she had erected about herself. Her trust issues always affected every relationship in her life, especially the few lovers she'd had.

Several years ago, after knowing one another a little more than a year, Nikki realized Mike wanted more than just friendship with her. Nikki told him bluntly she wouldn't date him. She told him she could never feel that way about him. At first, he had thought it meant she thought he wasn't good enough for her.

He sulked for two weeks before she decided enough was enough.

"Look, you shithead, I love you like a brother. That is all there ever will be. Don'tcha get it? I'm gay. In case you don't know, that means I only sleep with women."

Nikki had laughed when she saw the light bulb click on in his brain.

"Oh," he had said as a sly grin crept across his face.

Knowing him well enough, Nikki could imagine what he was thinking. "And no you can't watch, you sicko."

Nikki had just shaken her head, knowing it wouldn't be the only time Mike would suggest such a thing.

"How do you do that? What are you? A psychic?"

She knew it always drove him crazy when she knew exactly what he was thinking. It was as if he thought she was inside his head looking around.

✝

"Wow, that was eight years ago and you're still demented." She realized too late that she had said the thought aloud.

"What was?" Mike turned to her, but then glanced past her into the hallway. "Damn! Boy, would I like to wake up to that every morning."

Nikki turned, wondering what had caught his attention. It had to be good to leave him flustered. The hair on her arms suddenly stood up.

Her office walls were made of glass, which gave her the opportunity to observe everything. Now, Nikki watched as a woman stopped to speak with the waiting detective. Seeing the shiny badge attached to her belt, she concluded the beautiful woman must be Detective Canton. Her stride spoke of confidence and power.

Nikki saw the detective look into her office as she slowly walked by the windows. She felt like the detective was looking right through her. It gave Nikki an eerie feeling. Then she saw it. The corner of the detective's mouth turned upwards and her eyebrow arched. Nikki watched as the woman's eyes traveled down then slowly back up her body.

Was she misreading the detective or was she indeed checking her out?

The thought made her want to bolt from the room and Nikki told herself to get a grip. *Not every woman you become interested in is going to break your heart.*

She and Mike watched as the detectives slowly made their way down the hall.

"Wow, is she hot! Do you think she'd like to join me and the wife for some bedroom fun?" Mike said, laughing.

"Mike, you are way too much." Nikki rolled her eyes. "I know you're joking around, but you'd better not say anything like that in front of her."

"Oh come on, everyone loves my sense of humor."

"I know, but she's a cop and might not take too kindly to it. I'm so used to it that it doesn't faze me anymore."

Nikki straightened a stack of papers on her desk and sat behind the desk.

"Fine…I'll behave. She is hot though."

Nikki gave him a wicked grin. "You're not her type."

"Oh, come on, how can you freakin' tell that just by looking at her?" he asked.

Nikki laughed. "Because my gaydar is screaming dyke, that's why."

"Then why don't you ask her out while she's here?" He wiggled his eyebrows.

"Yeah right, just what I need…to ask a cop out. Especially one working the crime scene concerning my boss's death. Besides… she doesn't exactly look approachable."

There was no way Nikki was going to get involved with a cop. They liked to dig into areas where they were not welcome. Everyone had ghosts in their closets that were best left where they were.

Leaning over her, Mike put his hand on her shoulder.

"Come on, Nikki, it's the twenty-first century. Ask her out. You're a good woman and a great catch. Now, dig deep and find that courage, 'cause I know you have it. You sure tell me off enough, so I know it's there somewhere."

She pulled her focus back to her friend.

"Screw you!" she snarled, even as she secretly found him amusing.

"Anytime, anyplace, baby."

He seemed happy that, for once, he got in the last word.

†

Detective Alex Canton came from a long line of cops and she had been trained to investigate everything in a habitual, efficient fashion, overlooking nothing. Some of her co-workers even described her as having extreme OCD. Because of this, she radiated arrogance without trying. Officers working with her knew better than to interrupt her train of thought but, if they were foolish enough to try, it took only one contemptuous look from Alex to change their minds. She knew they hated her for her arrogance, but probably hated themselves more for backing down from her. Her ruthless reputation was well known and she was famous for getting answers out of the most tight-lipped suspects, no matter how long it took.

Chiseled features gave her a hard, aloof air but appearance mattered little to her. Today she knew her blonde hair was in dire need of a haircut and the light streaks from the summer sun would soon disappear, darkening the color once more.

The detective's clothes hid her physique. She liked it that way. Even though working out every day, alternating between the gym and the dojo, kept her in top physical shape.

Being fit was important. It paid off when she saw the looks of admiration she received from her numerous female conquests.

Arriving at the scene, Alex was pleased to see her favorite tech already there. Dominic Mancini had started on the force the same time she had. She liked working with him whenever possible and considered him one of the best in his field.

Dom even knew her routine. He had started snapping pictures from the hallway into the office. Now, stepping into the office, he took more from inside the doorway.

Alex pointed to a rookie tech standing nearby. "You stay here for a minute."

Her partner Scott moved next to her.

"Scott, it's been what, a year since we had a naked one?"

"Yeah, I think that's about right," he said after a moment.

"Who was here before us?" she asked.

Turning to look at her, he answered. "The dead man's assistant, Ms. Nikki McLoud, found him. She says she didn't step into the room. Another worker, Mr. Mike White, was standing behind her when she opened the office door. Mr.

White went in and checked for a pulse. Finding none, he called 911 on his cell phone."

He checked his notes.

"Next was Mitchell, the first officer on the scene. He re-checked for a pulse. He also kept everyone else out of the building and made sure the two inside stayed put. When I showed up, I informed Mr. White and Ms. McLoud that we would take their statements shortly."

"Who was the last one here yesterday?" Alex opened her leather portfolio.

Alex loathed wasting the time on taking notes. She could remember everything in detail months later. Her photographic memory came in handy when she compiled her reports at the end of each day. She very seldom had to refer to what she had written during the investigation.

Scott consulted his notes once more.

"Ms. McLoud was. She left a little after eight, locking up behind her. She said the door was locked when she arrived this morning. It's a keyed entry lock with a panic bar on it and shows no sign of forced entry."

"Four possible options here that I see right away, Scott...."

Alex ticked them off on her fingers.

"One, he let someone in. Two, an employee came back. Three, the person is still here. Or four, Ms. McLoud is lying."

Alex turned to the young man who had remained standing quietly nearby. "You're the rookie Dom's been raving about, right?"

"Yes, Ma'am, it's Peterson."

"Well, put on gloves and come in here."

Alex watched a moment as Dom photographed the body. Pulling on latex gloves, she knelt next to it. Scott followed, kneeling next to her. "Well Scott, not much of a chance of finding a wallet on him. Get extra close-ups of the cuffed hands. No visible wounds on the front side of him. You see anything, Dom?"

Carefully, they rolled the body onto its side.

"Not a thing," Dom said as he stood, taking more pictures of the victim's back.

Alex studied the condom as they laid him back down. "I'll look at the rest of the office first. I want to leave his desk for last."

"Okay. I'm finished here. I'll do some close-ups of his desk and the perimeter. Then it's all yours." Dom moved onto his next task.

"Good. Scott, get the medical examiner in here. That's an interesting condom he has on…did you take a good look at it?" Alex was fishing but Scott wasn't biting.

Scott seemed to notice that she had inspected it closely, but he obviously couldn't figure out why.

When he didn't respond, she continued. "Bag it and I want those results as quickly as possible."

She had noticed something interesting on the condom, but didn't want to mention it. For Alex, being a good detective meant constantly learning.

She was trying to teach Scott to keep his eyes and mind open to all possibilities.

Scott motioned for the medical examiner to give them an estimated time of death with his thermometer. Afterward, the techs put the body in a bag on a gurney and removed it from the room.

"All right. Peterson put on fresh gloves. Put your old ones in this bag," Alex said.

This was one of Alex's quirks. She insisted that anyone who touched the body put on fresh gloves when finished. The contaminated gloves were then sent with the body to be examined on the off chance one of them had picked up any trace evidence.

Slipping on fresh latex gloves, Alex went through the room with Peterson, leaving the desk for last. Fast food wrappers were strewn around the room. She also noticed candy wrappers in the trash can along with more condom wrappers.

"Bag each of those separately. Understand? Separately," Alex said, pointing to the wrappers on the desk. "Put the trash can in one of the bigger bags. Scott…we have an awful lot of candy wrappers here. You find anything interesting?"

Knowing Alex's line of thought, Scott was already looking for particular evidence. He didn't mention aloud what he was looking for because he knew Alex was testing the rookie's knowledge. "Nope, I haven't seen any at all."

Alex turned to Dom. "You see any evidence?"

"No." He never stopped clicking his camera while talking to her.

Peterson had a puzzled look.

"Drugs, Rookie Peterson, drugs. Study up on them tonight. Certain drugs cause sugar cravings. That could be one of the reasons for so many candy wrappers here."

Dom patted the rookie on the shoulder. "Don't worry, kid. These two talk in code. Once you've worked a few cases with them you'll know exactly what they're talking about. It can sometimes be scary. Ms. Big Bad there is especially scary."

"Dom …." Alex glared at him.

Dom smiled. He had known Alex for years and she knew he would do anything for her if she requested it.

Alex, standing at the decedent's desk, flipped through his day planner, looking for any names, initials, numbers or strange notes. Anything that repeated itself. "Peterson, don't forget the time, date, and initials, and get it back to me once it's photographed."

Scott picked up a cell phone that was lying on the desk. Flipping it open, he made notes of the numbers called. "Looks like the final call was at 9:32 last night. There's no name attached to the number."

Alex looked at the number as well. "We'll call it when we're done."

She wiped her glove-covered finger across a dusty lampshade. "You can leave this alone. No one's touched it in months."

Seeing the tube of lip balm, Alex pointed it out to the rookie. "Peterson, bag it and mark it priority."

Scott glanced at it. "Curious. True Shimmer Botanical Berry. Young girl?"

Alex raised an eyebrow. "Maybe...."

Opening the top drawer of the desk, Alex called out and asked Dom to take a picture. Then she pulled a bottle out, holding it up for Scott to see.

"Nitroglycerin...looks like he already had a bad heart. Add other factors and boom, the Reaper's a-knocking on your door."

Scott studied the lamp on the desk. "Looks like this guy wasn't much for cleanliness."

"Yeah. Look at this," Alex said after opening the bottom drawer. "Obviously the old man entertained here often."

Looking at the contents, Scott laughed. "Oh, yeah, dirty old man. Hey, isn't that like the strap-on your ex bought for you the year before last?" he asked, low enough so that only Alex could hear.

"Looks like it. It was the best thing I got out of that relationship," she replied, laughing. "I made sure she left it behind."

For that brief moment, Alex had let her guard down. Then the wall was back up. Scott was the only person she allowed to see those rare moments.

Alex stood, surveying the room one more time before turning to Scott. "Okay, where's the woman who found him?"

Relationships. All it took was a simple reminder and thinking about her last girlfriend to bring back the loneliness. Alex knew what she needed. A night of good sex was all it would take. It had been a year since the Donna fiasco. The blues still settled around her at the thought of Donna. Wondering if the hurt would ever go away, Alex tried to control her thoughts, envisioning a bloody crime scene.

Unfortunately, her mind wandered down the path on its own. Alex thought back to her latest failed relationship. Alex had known it was finished for some time. She just couldn't bring herself to send Donna packing. That was, until she came home very early one day to surprise Donna with dinner. Immediately she spied someone else's clothing strewn across the living room floor as she entered the apartment.

Walking quietly down the hall, she looked into the bedroom. There was Donna in bed with a woman Alex had never seen before. The next thing Alex knew she had her gun muzzle pressed to Donna's head.

Donna was obviously so terrified she couldn't move her head from between the other woman's legs. "Alex, I—"

Alex had looked down at her. "I suggest you both get out now!"

✝

"Alex, you okay?" Scott asked in a concerned, quiet tone.

Hearing Scott's voice snapped her back to the present. "Yeah, the mind's wandering. Is she in the office you were standing outside of when I first came in?"

It had been a long time since Alex had lost concentration while working.

"Yep…two doors down. Mr. White is with her. Her name is Nikki McLoud, age twenty-nine. She was our dead man's assistant."

Alex's curiosity was piqued. It must be the woman she'd seen earlier. She shook her head to clear her thoughts. "Do you think she's the missing piece of puzzle? What's the gut tell you?"

As detectives, it was their job to be open to all possibilities. During the past few years, they'd learned to bounce ideas off one another, no matter how weird or outrageous. Alex's gut instinct had never failed her. This time it was telling her there was more to this than met the eye.

From what Alex had already pieced together, she knew the decedent hadn't spent the weekend with his assistant.

Scott chuckled. "I don't think so."

Sighing, Alex rolled her eyes. "Oh, come on, share."

Alex knew Scott loved it when he could get one up on her. It happened very rarely. When it was of a personal nature, he positively basked in it. If it was business, he usually shared right away, not wanting her to think he was withholding evidence from her.

"Nope, no way am I breaking this time. You'll know soon enough."

Stopping in front of the door, Alex shook her head. "Spoil sport. I can always break you. What are you playing at?"

Scott had piqued her curiosity.

Alex paused for a moment, collecting herself, fighting the distracting thoughts. "All right then, let's get this done."

Alex stepped inside Ms. McCloud's office and paused again. Upon first glance, Alex found the assistant adorable.

Trying to regroup herself, she looked around the office. Alex noted the large oak desk and the matching credenza. The furniture was nothing ornate, more of a mission style. Two large black lateral files sat to the right along one wall, while the desk and credenza sat in the middle of the office. Two matching visitor chairs with black leather seats sat in front of the desk, inviting one to sit and talk with this woman for hours. She looked anywhere but at the woman sitting behind the desk.

She glanced at Scott.

"Oh, this is going to be fun," she whispered,

Scott smiled. "Yep...."

Alex wondered if the woman was gay. She would love to show her a thing or two. Yet as much as she craved company for the night, Alex realized that she was too tired. All she wanted to do right then was go home to a tall, ice-cold beer.

Turning her head, she sighed. *Shit Alex, do your job.* Alex's thoughts were still running amok. Slowly she approached the couple, observing them closely as she pushed all unprofessional thoughts from her mind.

†

Studying the detective, Nikki was intrigued. The detective wore a black T-shirt under a Yankees jacket, along with black jeans. Black western boots finished the dark, menacing appearance. The designer in Nikki quickly took control. She pictured the detective wearing a silk blouse under a tailored jacket and pressed trousers.

Nikki's stomach flipped as the woman walked toward them. She blushed when steely-blue eyes locked onto her own green ones. The detective's eyes were like none she had ever looked into before. She could only describe them as blue sapphires.

Suddenly, Nikki wanted to know more about this woman. All the reasons she had for not letting a cop know her better melted away. *Maybe it's time to get back in the game,* Nikki thought to herself, Nikki knew it was rude to stare but she was unable to look away. How could she be this attracted to a stranger so quickly?

†

"Ms. McLoud, I'm Detective Canton, are you the one who found the body?"

As Nikki stood, she noticed she had to look up, way up. The detective's height *and* good looks only added fuel to Nikki's fire.

"Ms. McLoud?" The right corner of Alex's mouth raised in a smirk as she watched Nikki appraise her.

Nikki was startled to have been caught staring. As the detective came closer, Nikki could see a hint of grey around the blue in her eyes.

It took her a second to find her voice again. "Y…yes, I found Mr. Williams in his office when I came in. I got here at seven-thirty and started the coffee. I was here early, so I went to his office to boot up his computer and start printing his reports. "

Nikki sat down abruptly. She was feeling queasy and she was sure her face had paled. Mike put his hand on her shoulder trying to soothe her.

Detective Canton turned to Scott, whispering to him. He left the office. A moment later, he came back with a cup of water from the water cooler. Nodding her head in thanks, Alex handed it to Nikki. "Here this might help. So, you walked into his office and…."

Alex waited for her to continue.

Nikki felt foolish. "I opened the door to his office. Mike was talking my ear off about his honeymoon. I looked down and there he was on the floor. I just stood there, thinking it was some kind of nightmare. Mike was behind me. He went into the office and saw Mr. Williams. He checked for a pulse then called 911. I've been here in my office since then."

Alex nodded, seeing color returning to Nikki's face. "I just have a couple of questions for both of you and then you can go home. Ms. McLoud—"

"It's Nikki, please. The other makes me feel old."

Alex looked at Scott, who had a smirk on his face.

Nikki was appalled at herself. Had she just tried to flirt, and with a cop no less?

Nikki knew a woman like this detective would never be interested in her. Besides, blondes were not Nikki's type. Those she had met were like bubbles, with only wind blowing between their eardrums. The mere thought that she found Detective Canton attractive sent cold shivers through her body. Everything about her was wrong.

"Ms. McLoud, did you touch anything in the office when you found him?"

Nikki didn't understand why that would matter. "No, I only touched the door knob and the light switch. I hate going into dark rooms. After that, I didn't go any farther into the room. I...I, um...I froze. I couldn't go any farther."

She was embarrassed to admit that she couldn't go into that room.

†

Alex was reluctant to ask the next question.

"The other question I have for you is personal, so if you would like to speak with us in private—" Alex glanced at Mike.

Nikki obviously didn't want to be alone; not when cops were questioning her. "No, here is fine, he's like my big brother."

Alex's lip curled a little. Nikki's statement answered one of her questions. The next however, was the big one. "Okay, that's fine. Were you romantically involved with Mr. Williams?"

With a look of horror on her face, Nikki looked at each of them.

Alex grinned. "I take that as a no then?"

"Yes, I…mean no. I mean, no I… yuck." Nikki was flustered and repulsed. She looked as though she were having trouble putting together a coherent thought.

Mike stood off to the side. He chuckled as he watched the scene play out.

"Detective, I can guarantee you that he was nothing more than Nikki's boss. I might be able to help you with who he was seeing on the side. Rumor has it he's seeing some little twenty-year-old. I think someone said her name was Cindy something. It's probably in his book in his briefcase. Now if that's all, I would like to take Nikki home, she's had a rough morning and I really don't think she should be driving."

Both of the detectives nodded their agreement. Nikki looked as if she were either going to pass out or toss her cookies.

To Alex, Nikki looked fragile and sweet. And, oddly, no woman Alex had ever met caused her heart to race as it was now.

After Donna, Alex vowed to change before she self-destructed. Letting her eyes roam across Nikki, she wondered at the possibilities of having this woman in her life. It would be pure pleasure.

Scott broke the silence. "If we need anything else, we have your information. We would like you to come to the station tomorrow morning. At that time, we'll have you examine your statement to verify that it is correct. We'll give you a call then and have you come down."

Nikki stood. Slowly they walked to the door. Stopping, she looked back at the detective. After smiling shyly at Detective Canton, Nikki walked out of the office.

✝

Mike started on her again as they left the building. "She's good-looking and I didn't see a ring on her finger. I think she was checking you out when she walked in. I really think you should ask her out."

Nikki closed the door. "Oh please give me a break. Why would anybody that h-o-t be interested in someone like me? I'll never have women throwing themselves at me. Did you see her height? God, she has to be six feet tall."

Mike laughed. "Yeah, you're a munchkin compared to her. Course at five-four you're from Oz compared to most people we know."

"Very funny! Not! I can't even entice her with being a bubbly blonde. I'm positive someone like her wants some tall, skinny, leggy bombshell. The only things I have that would interest any woman at all are big boobs. However, one can dream, can't she? Damn…she was so hot." Nikki smiled.

Mike returned the smile. "You sure you're not interested. Then why are you rambling? A little flustered, are we? Want to get in her pants, do we?"

Nikki shook her head. "No. Take me home."

Gazing out the window on the drive home, her thoughts told a different story. Nikki had to admit to herself that there was something about Alex she liked and felt drawn to.

"Hey, I almost forgot. Cathy has to work tonight so we'll come tomorrow night instead to show you the honeymoon pictures."

"Sure, no problem. I really don't feel up to it tonight. I just want to go home and crash for the day."

Nikki chuckled. She wanted to go home and dream about tall, dark and deadly.

✝

The phone rang at seven that morning, rudely awakening her and she had been having the most erotic dream she had experienced in years. She

22

remembered the woman's eyes the most. They had been an amazing blue color.

Frustrated, Nikki slammed the receiver in the cradle.

Had the past twenty-four hours really happened? Then she remembered the phone call. Nope, no dream, just a pain in her ass. She had way too much work to get done.

The president of the agency had informed her that the office would be closed the remainder of the week. Due to the circumstances, everyone would get full pay for the missed days but he requested Nikki call a meeting with mandatory attendance for Monday morning at nine.

Nikki knew that meant one thing, reorganization. The thought scared her. Reorganization usually resulted in people losing their jobs. She had nothing better to do so though so she might as well make the phone calls getting everything set for Monday.

Finished phoning everyone, Nikki needed to find something to do for the rest of the week. She hated sitting around the house as much as going on vacation. Neither was productive in her mind. That was the reason why she had most of her vacation banked from the past four years.

As she pulled her hand from the phone, the doorbell rang. Nikki nearly jumped out of her skin. "Shit! That took a year off my life."

Nikki looked down at what she was wearing. Realizing it showed way more than was probably legal in public, she panicked a little.

"One moment please, I'll be right there," she yelled to the person on the other side of the door.

Running upstairs, she grabbed her robe from the back of the bathroom door. Trying not to trip, she pulled on the robe while she raced down the steps. Nikki hoped she didn't look too disheveled. She could not imagine who would be at her door.

Breathing hard from running, she opened the door a little. Nikki couldn't believe who was standing on her doorstep. Her heart rate sped up as she looked up into blue eyes.

"Hello. Detective Canton." Nikki was confused.

"Oh, I'm sorry. I've caught you too early."

Nikki looked down at her robe. She chuckled. "No place to go today, seeing as they've shut down the office for the week. So, I'm just hanging out, relaxing."

"Uh…May I come in Ms. McLoud? It's a little chilly out here this morning. I think the thermometer in my truck said it's only about five degrees."

Nikki loved the cool weather. "I was just listening to the news. They say winter is going to be a long bad one, filled with record low temps and snowfalls. I was hoping that stupid little groundhog was wrong."

Seeing the detective shiver, she opened the door, motioning her to step in. "I'm sorry, please come in. I haven't had my coffee yet this morning, so I'm not quite awake yet. Would you like a cup?"

She closed the door behind the detective and led the way into the kitchen. Turning, she found the detective leaning against the doorframe. The sight surprised her, rendering her speechless. It was as if the detective belonged in the house. She looked so at ease, as if she were part of the structure.

Alex broke the spell.

"Please call me Alex. Actually, I'll take a coke if you have one."

Pushing away from the doorframe, she stepped into the kitchen.

Smiling, Nikki wrinkled her nose. "Okay, I think I have some. Soda so early in the morning though?"

Alex shivered, thinking of putting the vile coffee into her system. "I don't like hot drinks. Never have. I've especially never understood the need to drink jet fuel."

Nikki tilted her head slightly, giving Alex a strange look.

Alex laughed. "I know, I know. How could I be a cop and not like coffee to go with my donuts?"

This made Nikki laugh.

Alex looked around the kitchen, obviously admiring it. "This is a nice place you have here."

Nikki nervously studied the tile floor. She hated to admit that this was her sister's place. It sounded like such a turn-off that she still lived with a family member.

"Actually, it's my sister Millie's. I entered college when I was seventeen and skipped right to classes for second year students. I took classes while in high school so I could get ahead of the game. I studied for two degrees at the same time. As a result, it put me way behind in money, trying to repay everything. I'll be finished paying off my loans by the end of next year. In the meantime, I'm living here while I save enough money to get a house of my own. This place isn't exactly my style. It's a little too boring. Millie's on a cruise in the Caribbean right now."

Nikki was puzzled. Why would she tell the detective something like that? She gulped her coffee, trying to calm her nerves. She found irony in standing in front of the woman from her dream in her nightshirt. Nikki's heart raced once more remembering the erotic dream, especially the orgasm that woke her in the wee hours of the morning.

Alex was amused. She realized Nikki was flustered. "Well it has a nice kitchen. It looks like one of you can really cook."

"That would be me. I can cook dishes from just about any nationality. Nothing beats a good old-fashioned down to earth home cooked meal. Her idea of a good meal is some fru-fru size of a quarter meal that cost her fifty dollars." She poured herself more coffee.

"Why are you here, by the way? Detective Jackson said yesterday he would call me to come down there."

✝

Alex followed Nikki into the living room. How did she explain why she was here? Alex's mind asked herself. She knew it had nothing to do with the case. Alex had just wanted to see Nikki. That caused her to pause. She never chased women, they chased her. Alex chastised her libido for taking charge. She had to stop or she might do something she would later regret.

"I just wanted to make sure you were okay after what you saw yesterday. Most people go through their whole lives without seeing a dead person. If you want, we have a couple of therapists we usually recommend."

Nikki sat in the rocking chair and motioned Alex to sit on the couch. "Actually, I'm kinda used to death. Almost all of my family is gone now. When I was a child, it seemed as if we were always going to a funeral. Thank you for the offer though. Did you find out anything more?"

Hearing sadness in Nikki's voice as well as seeing it in her eyes troubled Alex. She felt an overwhelming need to protect her. Alex had to back off. She was letting Nikki get to her.

"I'm very sorry Ms. McLoud. I had no intention of upsetting you. Please forgive me. As far as the case goes, I can't really give you any details. What I actually came for was to escort you down to the station." Alex sat her empty glass on the coffee table.

"Did I do something wrong? Am I being arrested?"

"No...I..."

"Then why would you come here when I said I would willingly come to the station? Maybe I've watched way too many cop shows. However, I know cops don't just show up at your door step for no reason."

Alex stuttered. She had to think fast. "I just…well, I… I knew you had a rough time of it yesterday. I felt you might be more comfortable with a female around."

Alex knew the words sounded lame even as they left her mouth.

✝

"I see." Nikki could not look Alex in the eyes. Instead, she picked at the edge of the sleeve on her robe. Alex was lying, Nikki was sure of it. She decided to let it slide.

Nikki looked down at her hands holding her empty coffee cup. She couldn't understand why she became so upset when she thought about her family. It was not as if they were worth anything. Most of them were spam-sucking, trailer-park trash. She had to forget about them and pay attention to what was in front of her.

Her body twitched thinking of spending a few more moments with the detective. "Yes, thank you. That would be very nice. I'll just go grab a shower and I'll be ready to go." Nikki flew up the stairs.

In record time, Nikki was ready to go. As she came down the steps, she ran her fingers through her hair to bring the unruly mess under control.

Alex laughed. "Wow, that was quick. It takes me forever to get my hair to dry in the morning. It seems like I'm in there for hours. I was actually thinking of getting it all cut off someday real soon."

Nikki looked at her in bewilderment. "Please don't, I like it like that. I'm just used to getting ready fast. Usually Millie is chomping at the bit to get into the bathroom in the morning."

✝

Silence filled the truck as Alex drove them to the station. It was almost unbearable for Nikki. She hated quiet, even as a child growing up. It wasn't until her mother remarried and they moved to Pittsburgh that she felt calmer. She loved the noise and speed of a city.

At heart, Nikki was a city girl. On the farm, she would never have been able to be herself. They could never have understood why she loved women; it would've been unnatural. Hiding within herself, Nikki hid her desires until much later. Knowing at a young age that she was different Nikki knew she didn't want a life like any of them.

Alex looked at Nikki. She looked lost in thought. This time, though, Nikki was half smiling. Alex turned her eyes back to the street.

"It's amazing. You should do that more often." Alex cringed, hoping she hadn't really spoken the words aloud. Alex knew she had because Nikki was gaping at her. She wondered what a full smile would be like.

"Do what?" Nikki saw a distressed look upon Alex's face.

Alex debated with her inner self. Should she tell her what Nikki was thinking or should she lie? She didn't need any distractions in her life.

Alex could think of many reasons not to get involved with Nikki. She worked eighteen-hour days; they would never see one another. The icing on the cake though was everyone knew how she sucked at relationships. All of them would tell Nikki to run away very fast. Alex was up for a promotion. She didn't have time to deal with having a girlfriend. Alex had no idea where the idea of having Nikki as a girlfriend had come from.

"I, um…I…you should smile more. You have a nice smile." There, she had said it. Did Alex feel better...no. Alex rationalized if Nikki were gay; her face wouldn't look like someone just killed her cat. What she didn't need was a sexual harassment charge against her.

Alex was sweating. This was one of those times that she just didn't know when to keep her mouth shut. She looked out her side window, muttering under her breath, "Shut your mouth Canton."

Alex knew she was fighting a losing battle.

She turned back to Nikki. "Sorry, that was out of line. I shouldn't have said such a thing. Please accept my apology."

Nikki was silent. She looked at Alex as if she had a third eye. Nikki found herself at a loss for words. The truck was suddenly getting warm to Nikki.

"Please?" Alex asked. She did not know why this woman affected her so much. Alex never apologized, let alone begged for acceptance.

Nikki smiled again.

There was the smile again. Alex could get used to having it aimed at her. It was just wishful thinking. Nikki was probably just being nice.

"No apology necessary. That was a very kind thing to say. Thank you. If you're not doing anything this weekend, would you like to go out for a drink, maybe dinner?" Nikki studied her fingernails, as if embarrassed to have asked Alex out.

Alex's mind raced with the confirmation that Nikki was gay. This opened up a new world of possibilities.

Nikki struck her as naive and perhaps inexperienced. She didn't care to go down that road again. She liked them somewhat naïve, but not too vanilla... nor virgins. Several years ago, she'd picked up a girl in a bar who told her she was twenty-four. Alex was unpleasantly surprised when she found out the girl was not only too vanilla for her own tastes, but an eighteen year old virgin as well.

Alex hastily made her exit when she realized she had just taken the girl's virginity when she thrust into her. To say the girl never saw Alex again was an understatement.

Alex thought carefully for a moment. She didn't want to hurt Nikki or lead her on. Alex liked her, but that didn't mean she was the right person for Nikki.

"I don't think that would be a good idea. You seem like a wonderful woman. I'm sure you could have anyone you wanted. I can guarantee you that I'm not the one for you. I'm not exactly relationship material. Besides anyone around here can tell you I'm a mean mother of a bitch most of the time. I guess what I'm trying to say is…I don't exactly date."

Alex made sure to put emphasis on the word date.

Nikki was embarrassed. "Oh…Okay..." She then blushed when she realized what Alex meant.

Nikki didn't want their time together to end. It didn't matter to her that Alex had been around the block a few times. She remembered something she needed to tell the detective. "Oh, before I forget. I told Gwen, the ad exec we had put up in the company apartment, it was okay to leave. I hope that's okay."

"I wish you would've talked to me first before doing so. In case we do need to speak with her, please provide me with her information once we arrive at the station."

"I don't have the information with me. I have it at home. I'll have to call you with it later."

✝

Alex pulled her truck in next to the station. As always, she parked in the No Parking Zone, as if daring anyone to say a word to her. Sitting for a moment, Alex buried the personal thoughts and feelings that where driving her to distraction.

She was all business when on duty. Lately, that seemed to be slipping.

"Ms. McLoud, the detective will finish your statement. Then he will return you safely home." Alex closed the door after Nikki exited.

Nikki watched the transformation. One moment she was talking to Alex the person. Then in the blink of an eye, Alex the aloof cop was back, placing an icy wall between them. The abrupt change left Nikki reeling.

Scott, Alex's partner, met them on the steps of the station. He stood admiring Alex's truck, with the personalized license plates that read-The Best. "Damn, that truck is nice. Looks like you went for the extended cab this time. You can carry what, four more in it? When did you pick it up?"

"Yesterday… Shall we?" Alex motioned them inside, wanting to get this finished fast. She wanted to get away from the smaller woman who affected her so much.

"Ah, yes, all business." Scott mumbled to himself.

"Did you say something Jackson?"

"No, Ma'am, not at all." He shook his head walking through the doorway into the chaos they called home.

Halfway up the steps, Alex remembered she wanted to check on the phone number from the previous day. If she was correct, it belonged to a male prostitute they'd picked up almost a year ago who had a penchant for older men. She had found the final four digits familiar and it had stuck with her since.

Alex turned on the steps in front of Scott. "I need to check on something. Go ahead to Room three. I'll meet you there in a minute."

Scott returned to the station after escorting Nikki home. Finished with his report already, he now waited on Alex.

"Come on, aren't you done yet? You've been putting the finishing touches on your notes for the past half hour. We have a date with a burger."

"Finished...." She handed the papers to Scott, waiting for the fur to fly.

Alex knew he always read her reports. It didn't matter if they were going to the Captain or into the investigation binder. Scott was obsessed with spelling errors.

He looked up from the report. His face was scarlet. "What the…!"

Alex looked up at him innocently. "What?"

Scott leaned over his desk so they wouldn't be overheard. "Don't what me, Alex. Sometimes you can be such a bitch. How could you not tell me this?"

"Aren't you a detective, Scott?"

"What the fuck are you getting at?" Anger showed on his face.

Alex stood and walked around her desk. She sat on the edge of his as if she owned it. She looked relaxed, as if she had not a care in the world. "You examined the evidence, correct? Didn't I ask you if you noticed something about the condom?"

"Yeah, and I didn't notice anything other than the color." He was frustrated.

"Well then, my friend, you missed a big clue. If you'd seen the feces on it, you would've thought anal sex. That, along with the number of condom wrappers, was a little fishy. Now, add to that the two different types of condoms found. Plus the size medium men's polo shirt—"

Scott held up his hand. "How do you know it's a man's polo shirt? These days it's so damned hard to tell the difference."

"I know because I shop at the same store. Actually, I have one identical to it. I take it you don't remember me ever wearing it." Alex shrugged her shoulders. "What can I say? I like most of men's clothing better than the lacy crap they make for women. However, we're getting off topic."

He threw the papers on his desk. "Yeah, you could say a few things are off about this! Why didn't you tell me?"

Alex ran her fingers through her hair. "Like I said, you're a detective. You should've found the same things I did. What's your conclusion now that you do know?"

Scott lowered his voice. What happened between partners stayed that way. "What I am is pissed. Do you know what, Alex? You can be a real fucker sometimes. I thought we were partners and friends. You've pulled shit before but never anything like this."

"We are both. That doesn't mean you ever stop learning. Neither of us does for that matter." Alex sighed.

"Fine! I would have to say he was with a young man, not a girl." Scott was so angry he wouldn't meet her eyes.

Alex could tell he was really pissed. Rubbing her hands on her face, Alex said to herself *Why do I do shit like this? Shit, guess I pushed too far this time.*

Alex ran her hand through her hair again. She then did something she had never done before in her life. "Scott...I'm...I'm sorry. Okay?"

Scott looked up at her. She saw astonishment on his face. "What?" He felt his anger deflating.

"I said I'm sorry okay. I wanted to teach you a lesson to pay attention to everything in the room. You have to look even at the most bizarre things. Even though we have these shields, we never stop learning. Remember that. By the way, did you remember to look into that phone number?"

"I was going to do that this afternoon."

Scott looked at her in puzzlement. Alex's words had just sunk into his brain. "Oh my God, woman. Did you just apologize to me? Wow. There's a first for everything. Did hell freeze? It must have if you just said you're sorry. Did it kill you to say that?"

"Okay enough. Let's move on. I got a feeling about that apartment that the company keeps. I think that is where they were normally meeting. Nikki said they had an ad executive in town and they put her up at the apartment two days ago. That would tell me they couldn't go there. Also the phone number belongs to our junkie working boy, Paulie."

Scott smiled. "Shit, that's not good. Nikki…huh?"

Alex glared at him. "What?"

"You called her by her first name. I find that fascinating. You like her, don't you?"

"Scott, stop trying to play matchmaker. We have a job to do. Let's go grab those burgers. I'm starving. When we get back, we should have the rest of the reports from Dom."

✝

Seventy-two hours after apologizing to Scott, the two detectives finished their final reports. An analysis of the deceased's blood showed an abnormally high amount of an oral drug for erectile dysfunction in his system. The condoms showed two sets of DNA, one belonging to the dead man.

The second belonged to a young man with a record of drugs and prostitution.

"Ooh, Alex. This is not going to be good if the press gets wind of it. His daughter is the head prosecutor downtown. She's not going to want any of this to come out."

Alex sat on the corner of Scott's desk, grinning. "Yep, good Catholic, wasn't the old man?"

Scott closed the binder. "When she finds out her father was paying to bonk a druggie boy-toy, she is going to blow a cow. Maybe you should take her out on a date first, soften her up a little."

Alex laughed at the thought. "As if! Please, she's probably still pissed at me from before."

"I told you not to get involved with her. That she was looking for a relationship."

"Come on Scott, I told her up front that all I was looking for was a quick screw."

"I ran into her a few months ago. She thought she could change you, make you want a partner, not a quickie."

Getting antsy, Alex stood. "I know, she told me that a week later when I ran into her after the incident. I tried telling her again but she was too pissed to listen. Oh well. Okay, then this pretty much sums up this case. It was an accidental death due to an overdose of erectile dysfunction meds and a weak heart. What an idiot. Doesn't anyone read the side effects on meds anymore? This is why beer is my vice of choice. You have the interview with our boy Paulie in the binder, right? The only thing we can charge him with is fleeing the scene. There's no crime against kinky sex."

"Yep…and I triple checked everything. Then when I thought everything was good to go, I checked again."

Taking the binder from Scott, Alex started for the Captain's office. "Okay let's go give the good news to the Captain. I'm sure he's going to be more than overjoyed at this one." Alex couldn't keep the sarcasm from her voice.

✝

Nikki knew she would probably never see Alex again after leaving the police station. Three long weeks had passed since the morning she had spent with the aloof detective.

Nikki shook her head in frustration. She felt like such a fool for asking her out. Well, at least Alex hadn't laughed in her face. Geez, how could she have been so stupid? Now she was without a job too. How could her life get any worse?"

Events had caused Nikki to grow increasingly cranky. After attending the office meeting Monday morning, she found herself out of a job. The owners had decided not to replace her boss. His workload was to be absorbed into other positions already in place. They informed her that her services were no longer required and Nikki found out later that one of the owners brought in his daughter to do the artwork for the company.

To make matters even worse, Millie had returned from vacation to find Nikki upset and jobless. Millie added to her frustration by continuously berating her.

"Ah yes, dealing with my irate sister. What a mess. Can't anything go right lately? Oh God…now I'm talking to myself too."

Nikki sighed. She knew she'd better find a job soon. If she wished to keep her sanity.

Nikki tried to blame Millie's behavior on being twelve years older than her and only looking out for herself. In Millie's eyes, Nikki messed up everything she touched. When Nikki told her she had lost her job, Millie asked her what *she* had done to get herself fired. Millie never offered support for anything her younger sister did. They lived in two very different worlds. This was one of several reasons that she hadn't told Millie she was a lesbian.

What bothered Nikki most was that it had been weeks since she had had any contact with the tall, blonde-haired detective. Nikki's erotic dreams returned almost every night, interspersed with dreams of the detective arriving on a black stallion to save her from a dragon. She found it ironic the dragon's face always took on Millie's features.

Nikki lost track of the number of resumes she'd sent out. She had even called in several favors of people she had worked with previously. She had feelers out everywhere. Nikki hoped it wouldn't be long before she caught a break.

Frustrated, Nikki threw her checkbook on the table.

Christmas was about a month away. Luckily, she had only a couple of gifts to buy that year. She would have to curtail going to the clubs with Mike until she found a job. If she calculated correctly, she could go three months without work before she had to worry. Plus, the unemployment only stretched so far—not even half of her normal weekly pay.

Nikki knew Millie wouldn't give her a break, either. Her sister would still expect her to pay rent and half of all the other household expenses. As long as no extra expenses came up, the money in her savings account would cover those items along with car payments and insurance.

She wasn't dating, which helped. Mike often called and asked Nikki to go out with he and his wife. Hanging out with Mike and Cathy was her only form of entertainment. She found trying to date was more work than it was worth. She could not even find the heart to try. The way Ann had used her only confirmed Nikki's feelings of inadequacy.

Unless of course the interesting detective asked me out, then things would be looking up.

Nikki let her mind wander, staring out the window. She couldn't understand why she was so attracted to the detective.

The phone rang and she absently answered it. Speak of the devil. It was Mike. Nikki held the phone on her shoulder, not really listening as Mike droned on for more than twenty minutes..

"Nikki, yo Nik, you still there? You seem to be muttering to yourself quite a bit."

Mike was trying to talk her into a night on the town. They hadn't been bar hopping in weeks and he was having withdrawal symptoms. She wasn't sure she wanted to waste the money even though it would be nice to go out. Nikki rolled her eyes when she knew she'd been caught

"Yeah, I'm here. I was just thinking about something. I'm trying to come up with a game plan on how long I can survive without a job. As much as I truly want to go out, I don't think I should spend money right now. Christmas is coming and I have car insurance due in two weeks. I'm hoping it won't be much longer before something comes through. How's your new job going?" Nikki felt like she just wanted to hide out until she found a job.

Nikki was trying to change the subject but Mike wasn't about to let her.

"Nikki, don't go giving me, of all people, that shit! I know what's going on. You're upset that you haven't had any bites yet and you are letting it get to you. Well, don't! You need a break. You work too hard as it is. You've been working twenty-four-seven for the past five years. Don't worry, everything will fall into place."

Mike knew he'd gotten his point across when he heard a barely audible agreement come through the phone line.

"So, on that note, we're taking you out tonight. The entire night is on us. How about it? Huh?" There was silence once more.

Nikki sighed. "Fine, if I do, will you lay off for a while?"

"Yes, for a little while. Then look out, 'cause I'll start harassing your ass once more."

"Okay, okay, I got it. Actually, it would be nice to get away from Millie for a while. She's driving me up the damn wall. You know how it is with her."

"Nikki, I remember exactly what your sister is like. I've tangled with Millie a few times. Don't listen to a thing she says. She's a bitter, nasty woman. You know we are going to Florida in three weeks with Mom and Dad. Why don't you come with us? It would get you away from her for a while. It'll do you good."

"I don't think so. I already told you I don't have any extra money right now, but it would really be nice to get away. Especially after what Millie pulled the day before. She actually tried to get me to agree to go out with the brother of a friend of hers. Can you believe it? As if I don't already have enough shit to deal with, she had to go and pull this on me. Just what I don't need is fending off some creep, yuck!"

A shudder ran through her as she thought about it. She felt ill. "I'll think about the Florida thing."

"Nikki, don't worry about money. You know Dad always pays for the hotel and all our dinners. Do you remember how much fun we had a couple years ago? Come with us tonight and we'll talk about it. Okay?"

Finally, Nikki gave in. "Stop harping on me. What time are you picking me up and where are we going?"

Nikki sighed when she heard him laugh.

"Let's go to Fairy Tails. There will be lots of good-looking women there. What do you say, how about it? If nothing else, you'll have eye candy all night."

She laughed before she could stop it. "Why is it that you always want to go to the gay clubs? Are you sure Cathy's not just a front? And how does she feel about hanging out with all the gay boys and dykes?"

"She doesn't care as long as she can have a good time. And… ha ha, very funny! You know my interests only lay with my wife. That is unless of course you want to join us?"

She snorted into the phone. "Pig!"

"Can't hurt to ask. Anyway, we'll pick you up at nine. Okay?"

"Fine, see you then and, Mike, take a cold shower."

Hanging up the phone, she couldn't believe it. She had let him talk her into it. "Hell, it might be fun to have a few beers, see a little eye candy and dance."

Why not, she was young, alive and somewhat willing.

✝

Nikki stood in front of her closet. She was trying to decide what to wear when she heard Millie come in the front door and start up the steps. Physically cringing, she heard Millie's voice. "Nikki, did you put dinner in the oven?"

"Yes, and your clean clothes are on your bed."

Millie stopped at the top of the steps, looking into Nikki's room. Nikki could see the frown as it crossed Millie's face.

"Going out tonight? Do you think you can really afford to? Don't you have bills due?"

Nikki felt her hands tightening around the jeans she was holding. Now was not the time for a confrontation. "Yes, I'm going out and no, I'm not paying. Mike and Cathy are taking me out."

Millie looked skeptical. Nikki pretended to study the pair of shoes in the bottom of her closet.

"Why would they pay your way? Did you get a job? I didn't think you even had any return calls from anyone. I assumed that no one had showed any interest in you. You haven't mentioned any phone calls." Millie started in on her without a moment's hesitation.

Nikki never knew for sure if her sister realized how she treated her. If it wasn't one thing, it was another. Right now, it was that she was jobless, not dating and a little pudgy and not in any particular order.

"We're celebrating because he got a job, that's all." Nikki's temper bubbled just below the surface.

It had been many years since she had come close to losing control. Now she was a heartbeat away from that moment. At times she felt like a tightly wound coil, ready to spring at any second. Since childhood, Nikki had worked very hard at keeping reign on her temper where Millie was concerned.

"Well, good for him, maybe he can get you a job where he works. Where is he working?"

"He's the manager of a drug store." She saw the look on Millie's face. She knew that look well. It was the *manual labor is beneath me* look.

"He likes what he is doing. On top of that, it pays the bills. I think that's all that matters. Don't you? Of course you don't. He's too blue collar for you." It sounded mean but she didn't care.

"There's no reason to get nasty with me. I'm just concerned, that's all. I'm looking out for what is best for you. If I don't do it, no one else will. It's my job. At the rate you're going you'll never find a man to take care of you."

Now the guilt started, just as it always did. Millie was a master at it. She used it to get what she wanted every time. She used it to control Nikki's life, to try to mold her into what she thought Nikki should be. It worked every time.

"I'm sorry. I shouldn't have been so short with you. I guess I'm just a little upset about some things and I didn't realize it. Maybe I *should* stay home tonight. I just thought maybe my luck would change a little if I went out and relaxed for a while." Nikki sighed.

"Yes, I think that would be for the best. You could search the job sites again tonight, sending out resumes to any new ones you find. Then all you would have to do tomorrow is go through the paper. You have to be diligent and search every day."

Hanging the jeans back in the closet after Millie left her room, Nikki let out a frustrated breath. She knew she would not be going out that night. Why did she even bother? She resigned herself to calling Mike.

For every step forward that Nikki took in gaining her self-confidence and independence, it seemed she was thrown back two at every turn.

Someday…someday I'll be in charge of my own life.

Mike didn't give her a hard time. And she was glad. It was something she just couldn't deal with right then. They made plans to go out two nights later instead. Nikki knew Millie wouldn't be around to say anything because she was going to a concert that evening.

✝

Mike and Cathy arrived at nine to pick her up for their night out. Nikki had decided on black jeans, black leather boots and her favorite lavender shirt. She thought she looked good.

Getting into the back seat of his truck, she closed the door behind her. "So, where are we going as if I don't already know?"

Mike turned and grinned at her. "I thought we could go to Fairy Tails if that's okay with you?" It was more of a statement than a question.

"That's fine with me. I could use a good night out."

The bar was only half-full when they arrived. Mike went to the bar to get their first round of beer, while Cathy and Nikki managed to grab a table by the dance floor.

The three friends were there for a little more than an hour, having already downed several beers each when Mike decided he wanted to dance. As always, Mike grabbed Nikki's hand, physically dragging her onto the dance floor. Unfortunately for Nikki, Cathy was a unenthusiastic dancer so Mike always wanted to dance with her instead. Usually half way through the night, Nikki would get frustrated then demand he dance with his wife and leave her alone. That was one of the nice things about this particular club, even though it was a gay club everyone felt comfortable there.

✝

Nikki and Mike had been dancing for a while when Mike saw *her* walk in, with Nikki's evil ex on her arm. He was thankful that Nikki had her back to the door and that the couple continued on into the other side of the bar.

Mike's mind raced. What was he going to do? Nikki would freak if she saw her, and she would never fall for the, it's time to go home line. Not being able to come up with a way to keep Nikki from seeing them, Mike needed to get her out of the bar somehow.

He tried to get Cathy's attention, but as usual, she was oblivious to everything around her. He motioned to Nikki that he was thirsty and needed a break.

Making their way to the table, he kept her talking and facing him. Knowing Nikki hated sitting with her back to the door, Mike took the chair facing the doorway anyway. It was better than the alternative.

"Babe, can you get us something more to drink?" He leaned close to Cathy's ear, even though he knew Nikki couldn't hear him because of the loud music. "I'll keep Nikki entertained, so she won't wander around. I saw that detective come in a couple of minutes ago with Ann on her arm."

She nodded. "Okay, I'll be back in a few."

Cathy wound her way through the crowd to the bar. While waiting for service, she observed the couple through the fish tanks serving as a wall between the two bars. Picking up the beer, Cathy turned around to head back to the table. Then she saw them walk through the doorway into their side of the club. Cathy raced back to the table, catching Mike's attention. When he saw her, Cathy nodded to her right.

Mike saw it all happen in slow motion. Nikki stood as she mouthed the word 'bathroom,' then turned, laying eyes upon the couple.

✝

Nikki froze. She didn't know whether to continue to the bathroom, sit back down or just leave. Staring at the couple, she moved toward the bathroom, thinking she would hide in there for a while. Nikki didn't realize Cathy was following her until, once in the bathroom, Cathy laid her hand on Nikki's shoulder.

"Nikki you can't hide in here. We'll just leave after we finish our drinks. Okay?"

Seeing the hurt in Nikki's eyes, Cathy squeezed her shoulder to reassure her.

"You're right, I just had to get out of there for a minute, plus I was going to the bathroom anyway. I'll be fine, Cath, really."

She saw the concern on Cathy's face.

"Don't worry, I'm okay."

On a good day, Cathy was only mildly air-headed, but put a few beers in her and she could be clueless. This being one of the latter, Cathy finally seemed to notice the female couples in various stages of having sex in the corners of the bathroom. Nikki had to chuckle, seeing Cathy's wide eyes.

Arriving back at their table, Nikki switched seats with Cathy. She wanted to be able to see the whole room. Additionally, it gave her a better view of Alex and The Bitch.

✝

Alex sighed. She was tired and this woman, Ann, was grating on her nerves. Why had she agreed to go out with her? Just because she was the assistant D.A. didn't mean she had any class. Alex wished the night were through.

"Alex, that woman two tables away is staring at you and has been doing so for more than thirty minutes," Ann said. "Please go and tell her to stop."

She leaned in close and tried to nuzzle Alex's neck.

It was highly unusual that Alex didn't notice someone watching them. Trying not to be obvious, Alex slowly turned her head in the direction her date had indicated. *I might as well look. I hope it's no one I know. I really don't want anyone to see me with this nut job.*

Alex was stunned. She couldn't move.

No, it can't be her! Shit, she's seen me. What do I do now?

Nikki looked hurt. Alex's guilt took control. She was about to do something she knew she might regret. Alex had to talk to her. As Alex stood to go to her, Nikki and her friends proceeded to leave.

"Ann, please excuse me a minute. I need to talk to someone."

Alex ran to catch up with them. As her feet hit the pavement outside, she called out. "Nikki!"

Continuing to walk, Nikki acted as if she didn't hear.

Catching up to them, Alex took hold of Nikki's arm, stopping her. She gently turned her around. "Nikki, wait, please. I can tell you're upset. Let me explain. It's—"

Nikki put her hand up to stop Alex, cutting her off.

"Please, detective, don't give me the old 'it's not what it looks like' line." Nikki tried to free her arm. Alex's grip was too tight.

"Damn it, Nikki, it *isn't* what it looks like. It's nothing but a blind date my sister roped me into. I'm here just to be nice to her. I've never lied to you. I haven't even been out on a date since my last relationship went bust."

Alex's mind rallied against her. Sure, she had fucked quite a few, but Nikki didn't need to know that.

"Plus, like I told you before, I'm not relationship material."

Nikki's anger was not at Alex, as the others thought. It was at herself.

How could I have believed Alex when she told me she didn't date? It's more as if she would never be interested in someone like me.

Nikki felt like a fool once again. "Please, don't bother."

"Damn it, Nikki! I meant what I said that day. You're a kind, wonderful girl who can do better than someone like me."

Alex let go of her arm and put her hands in her pockets, not knowing what else to say. Why couldn't she just walk away? Alex wondered why she was trying to justify her actions to this woman. She made it clear the last time they met that she wasn't interested. Then the reality hit her like a racecar hitting the wall on the fourth turn. Was it possible she truly was changing?

Alex's mind screamed she should never have let Kirstin talk her into the date. If she were honest with herself, she wouldn't mind going out with Nikki. It wouldn't hurt her or her reputation to date a nice, good girl. But then her libido kicked in …don't forget, cute too.

A silence hung between them.

What could one date hurt? Alex was realizing that quite possibly Nikki could be a little hell raiser though. It could turn out to be fun.

"I'm an adult, you know. Don't you think I can make up my own mind? And why of all the women in Rochester, that bitch?" Nikki spat the final sentence out as if it tasted nasty.

Alex was confused. Cautiously, Alex asked her. "Why? Do you know her?"

Nikki backed up a few steps, running into Mike, who had moved right behind her.

"She's a bitch, who uses people then throws them away like they're garbage." Nikki looked at her feet, not wanting to look Alex in the eye. "She's my ex."

Nikki spoke so low Alex could barely hear her.

"Oh." Alex paused, feeling twice as bad. "I'm sorry."

The one date was sounding better and better. Something told her that Nikki would be a real animal in bed. Alex shook her head. She had no idea how she had gotten from date to bed.

"No, I'm sorry. I should have let you explain, not jumped down your throat. I'm surprised that Ann didn't tell you who I was. Yet I'm not surprised. I don't think she really paid much attention to me, even when we were going out. I was just someone to be used."

Both stood in awkward silence for a few moments. Alex took Nikki's hand in hers and studied the back of it. She couldn't even look Nikki directly in the eye. So much for the fearless detective. Alex figured she might as well bite the bullet that was wedged firmly between her teeth. "Drinks tomorrow?"

Nikki was stunned. It was strange how two words could deflate a person's anger, even toward themselves. She smiled. "Yes, I'd love to."

"I'll, uh, pick…pick you up at seven o'clock." Alex could hear the stammering. She felt foolish. She was supposed to be a tough, butch homicide detective who could handle anything. Here she was though, finding it hard to ask a girl out for a drink.

Alex said her goodbyes and walked away muttering to herself. "Damn, when did I get so fucking pathetic? What does this woman do to me? It's just for a drink. Nothing more, nothing less.

Then how come I feel like a spanked puppy that just piddled on the Persian rug?"

It was then that Alex realized why. This woman was too good for her. She stopped by her truck, before going back inside, and looked up at the moon. "Shit, I'm used to possessing and using women, making them want me. She makes me want to…."

She kicked the truck's tire. "Damn, she makes me want her, need her."

Then she felt it. It started as just an inkling, then she knew.

She made her want to protect her. To lay down her life for her.

Chapter Two

Emotions Make Us Human

Paperwork. It was the bane of Alex's existence.

"Give me a gang banger on crack any day of the week. I hate doing all this shit," she muttered.

It had been bad enough when she was a beat cop. However, since becoming a detective, she seemed to spend half her time writing reports.

"Damn, we spend most of the time trying to cover our asses so we don't get sued, instead of doing our real jobs. Yet the public psyches out on us when we don't catch the asshole who stole the antique letter opener that their great-uncle Warren left them when he bit the big one."

Alex sat at her desk as she grumbled, finishing the final notes on the latest gang drive-by. She mumbled under her breath so no one would hear. Their statistics showed that, since the beginning of December, violence was getting worse. Now, a few days before Christmas, it seemed to have spiraled out of control.

Alex shook her head in frustration. "You've got to love the fucking holidays."

It had been one week since the incident at the bar. Alex sat contemplating her upcoming date that evening with Nikki. Twice they tried to get together during the previous week. Both times Alex's job had interfered.

Alex tried to ignore her frayed nerves. *Shit. I'm a wreck.*

In her gut, Alex knew why. She needed to get her life under control. Additionally, she liked Nikki. This relationship could be a turning point in her life. This one had to work. Loss of her temper coupled with trying to control her previous girlfriends had ended every relationship. The past few had been the worst. One of them ended badly when the other woman told Alex she was leaving and she'd received a crushed nose when Alex's temper broke.

Everyone knew everyone else in the lesbian community. Donna had heard rumors about Alex before she started going out with her. And she took it as gospel. One woman told her Alex had a temper, another that Alex was a control freak. All of them shared stories of rough sex-but the best sex they'd ever had. Hearing this, Donna had to have Alex. She had to find out what it was like to be the focus of the detective's powerful desire.

Women pursued Alex as if she were the last lesbian in town.

Donna, who had been her last girlfriend, had been the kicker. As Alex had held the gun to Donna's head, it took all her inner strength not to pull the trigger. To Alex's sheer amazement, Donna called Alex's sister Kirstin, and told her about it.

Kirstin came to Alex after Donna called her. She begged Alex to change, to seek help from a counselor. Alex had lucked out once again as Donna, just like the others, would never consider pressing charges. Alex was a cop. That meant other cops would cover for her.

†

Since running into Nikki again, Alex spent quite a bit of time thinking. She revisited her past failures and came to a decision. She had to clean up her act, before her luck ran out. Alex could not see herself as an abuser, as her sister had hinted. She had a temper. That's all.

It took Alex a few moments to realize Scott was standing by her desk. "Shit, Scott how long have you been standing there?"

"Earth to Alex, you need to stop worrying. If you want my advice, just concentrate on making a good first date impression."

Alex grunted as she turned to look up at him. His curly red hair was in disarray. His disheveled clothes hung loosely on his tall six foot one frame. He looked like he'd gone ten rounds with Ali. Alex noticed he also had lost more weight.

"You mean, a better impression than I've already made. You look like you've lost a couple more pounds there. Is Tess's cooking really that bad? If anyone were to ask me why you're marrying her, I sure as hell can't tell them it's because you love her cooking."

Alex referring to his girlfriend's cooking made him wince. Scott had moved in with her several weeks before, which meant Tessa was cooking for him every morning and night, much to his dismay.

Tessa was one of only two Italians that Alex knew who could not cook. Not wanting to hurt the poor girl's feelings, Alex never brought it up to her. Tessa's food was actually some of the worst she had tasted. On that subject, Alex considered herself an expert. She had tasted some pretty bad food during her childhood.

Alex's mother was a horrible cook, as well. Her favorite joke through her life had been 'that her mother wouldn't know a spice if it hit her in the face'. Alex felt guilty saying that about her mother, even though every time she said it in her parents' home, their father would whole-heartedly agree with her. Of course, her mother was never in the room to defend herself. They'd made sure of that.

"Yeah, her cooking is that bad and I'm marrying her because I love her mind and soul…just not her food. But don't change the subject. Where are you taking her?"

"We're going for a drink is all, no biggie. Then she'll realize, of course, that I'm not really relationship material and that will be the end of that. 'Cause you know I'll do something stupid like ogle another woman while I'm on a date with her. Or something possibly even worse, who knows. With me anything is possible and you know it."

Scott sat on the corner of her desk. He contemplated what Alex said then what remained unspoken. He was never one to hold back. He usually spoke his mind.

"Okay, I heard what you just said, Alex, but I also heard what you weren't saying. You like her, don't you? Maybe more than that even?" Scott leaned in closer. "Come on, say it ain't so, and I'll drop it."

Alex studied his face. He could read her like a book. Scott heard the growl come from his partner. All he could do was laugh. "Are you seriously trying to intimidate me? Get a grip and chill out. You're not all that bad!" He laughed harder.

"Bite me!" Alex stood to walk away.

Scott grabbed her arm to stop her. "Alex."

He knew Alex had had a few girlfriends during the years. He also knew she had a temper that affected her relationships. He had learned about several of her liaisons as they'd shared late night beers. What he didn't know was to what extent her fury could go. Wanting only happiness for his friend, he had pushed Alex to seek a relationship with Nikki. Something told him that Nikki would be good for her.

Sitting down at her desk, Alex studied the neat, tidy piles. "Okay, fine, I like her. Maybe even you know…." She ran her hand through her hair.

Scott realized long ago that that action meant she was close to losing her temper. He would have to use the cattle prod in order to get her to talk. "And…."

"And yes, I want her. I have to have her. She's a good person. I don't want to have to put her through the shit of trying to have me as a girlfriend."

Lately Alex found herself every day, at one in the morning, sitting outside of Nikki's place. Her body would shake so badly with need that she had to go to the club. Picking up a girl to relieve the urges was better than the alternative of using Nikki just for sex if there was any possibility of building a relationship with her.

Scott shook his head. Alex could be stubborn. "Don't you think she should be able to decide for herself? You can't tell her who she's going to fall for. Just like you can't help who you fall for. It's just karma. How do you know she's not the one for you? I think she might be good for you, might help calm your ass down."

Looking up from the papers on her desk, she asked, "Why should I put myself through that again? Can you give me one good reason why I should?" Her patience was being tested. Why couldn't he leave well enough alone?

Her temper verging on exploding, she picked up the ringing phone. The caller, instead of Scott, received the brunt of her anger. "What!" she barked at the offending device.

Closing her eyes, Alex put her hand over her face. "Yes, sir, I'll bring them right in."

She turned back to Scott. "Billy wanted these reports half an hour ago and he thought he'd let me know it. This is why I keep personal stuff out of here. It always interferes."

She picked up the folders, storming off toward the Captain's office.

✝

Captain William Mahoney was a good cop by all accounts. Every man for the previous four generations in his family had been a cop. He himself had no sons, only daughters. Three wonderful daughters, the youngest of which, Billy had just found out, planned to leave college to attend the police academy.

His daughter had gone behind her parents' backs, and applied to the academy. Rachel being accepted into the academy with no problems threw him. When did his little girl grow up? It further bothered him that she was able to accomplish this on her own with no help from him.

He was very proud of her while at the same time, being terrified for her. Working as a cop was hard and dangerous. Billy wanted none of that for his daughters. Hoping that Alex would agree to talk Rachel out of it, he called Alex into his office. Billy knew it would come across sounding sexist. He didn't care. He just wanted his daughter safe.

Alex knocked twice on the doorframe to the captain's office. Noticing the expression on his face, Alex cringed. She'd seen it once before when his eldest had eloped. Her Captain sat holding the picture of his daughters in his hands. Alex was curious as to what was going on.

Setting the picture on the desk, the captain motioned to one of the old tattered chairs sitting in front of his desk. "Alex, have a seat."

Alex slowly sat in the offered chair. She knew this had nothing to do with the paperwork as he had claimed. "Here's the paperwork you were waitin' for." She set the stack of papers on his desk in front of him, then sat back down.

"Alex, um, what I, uh, ah, hell's bells." He was sweating. It was more difficult to ask for help than he thought it was going to be.

He tried again. "Alex, I, uh, asked you in here 'cause I have a personal favor to ask of you. I've known you since your Dad brought you in here when you were a kid. You're the only one I trust to talk to about this."

Stopping, he looked at the pictures of his daughters again. "I need you to talk to Rachel. She quit college and went and got herself accepted to the police academy. I want you to talk her out of it. Wait…."

He held his hand up to stop what she was about to say. "I know she's old enough to make up her own mind and I know it sounds sexist, but I don't want my girls in this line of work. It's too hard for women."

Alex had to speak up. The sexism blindsided her. This was unlike him. "In case you haven't noticed, I'm not a guy."

"I know, I know, but I don't think of you as a woman. You're just one of the guys. You can defend yourself better than the rest of them here. You're a black belt and all that shit. My little girl is just that, a little girl." He threw his hands up in the air, exasperated.

Alex decided to be straight-up with him. "Captain, do you want to lose her? Because if you try to push her into something she doesn't want to do, that's exactly what's going to happen. She needs to make up her own mind. If it happens that she realizes she made a mistake, it's her mistake to make. If everything works out, then it does. Who knows, maybe she'll be a better cop than both of us. Don't be stupid and push her away. I know that's the last thing you want to do. Let her be herself. Okay?"

Wiping his hand across this face, he tried to control his nerves. "Are you sure? Will I be doing the right thing? What if she gets hurt or worse? I couldn't live with that."

"Captain, you're going to have to. You need to support her, to encourage her to be herself, not what *you* want her to be. It would only lead to resentment in the end."

He sighed, knowing she was right. She always was. "I guess this isn't one I'm going to win, is it?"

"Ah… No. Now, if that's everything, Captain, I have a date tonight."

Alex smiled as she stood up, thinking about the green-eyed brunette that she was meeting in a little bit. Walking out of his office to her desk, she still had an ear-to-ear smile.

†

Nikki couldn't contemplate why someone as good-looking and intelligent as Alex would want to go out with her. She didn't dare ask Millie her opinion. She had yet to come out to her sister, knowing, though, the day was coming soon. To make matters worse, her sister continuously tried to fix her up with guys. Then there were the inevitable questions Millie would ask about any new friends in her life. Not that there had been many. There had only been a couple.

Alex rounded the corner of the condo. Watching Nikki through the window, the sadness on Nikki's face brought her to a halt. Alex wondered what put it there. She knew, suddenly, that she would do anything to make this woman happy.

After watching her for a moment, Alex approached the door. Nikki looked so lost in thought Alex thought it better to knock on the storm door than ring the loud doorbell that might be alarming.

Nikki answered the door. "Come on in. I just need to get my boots on and I'll be ready to go."

Trying to think of something to start the conversation rolling, Alex looked down at the Docs Nikki was putting on. She laughed aloud.

Nikki looked up at her with a questioning look.

"Sorry, you, um, have good taste in Docs." Alex pointed to her own feet.

Nikki chuckled when she looked at Alex's feet. Both wore the same boots. "I'd say we both have good taste. Yours look a little more worn-in."

Alex looked down at her boots. "Yeah, I got this pair last year. I live in them and my cowboy boots. They're the most comfortable footwear I have. I loathe anytime I have to wear the dress uniform and shoes. Those kill my feet."

Finished tying her boots, Nikki stood. "I know what you mean. I bought them right before I lost my job and I just love them. I liked them so much, I went back the next day and bought a second pair. Got a deal on them I couldn't pass up. Now, I'm ready if you are."

After pulling on her fleece jacket, she locked the door behind her.

They walked to Alex's truck, each lost in their own thoughts.

Nikki didn't like nights like this. She looked up. No stars showed that evening, adding to the pitch black of the night. She suddenly felt seven years old again, locked in a closet with only darkness and fright as her companions. She shook off the childhood memory, not wanting to revisit the past.

Nikki stood looking at Alex's truck. She realized how big it truly was. "It's a... uh, quite a large truck. I feel like I need a ladder to get into it. It looks even more imposing in the dark."

Alex opened the door for her. "Here, let me help you. I know you had a time of it last time. It is quite high unless you're as tall as I am."

The saying size does matter popped into Nikki's mind, causing her to chuckle. If only she were six inches taller....

"Is that supposed to be a, I'm short comment? Just how tall are you?" Nikki asked teasingly.

Nikki blushed. She was not usually this bold; it made her feel a little naughty. Maybe being around this woman would be good for her. Alex made her feel special, in the way she looked at her. Just for going out with her.

"No, I'm sorry. That's not the way I meant it." Alex laid her hand on Nikki's arm as if Nikki flustered her. Alex dropped her hand to her side waiting for Nikki to make the next move.

Nikki caressed Alex's arm to reassure her of no hard feelings. She didn't want Alex to think badly of her. All she wanted was Alex to like her, possibly to need her.

"Alex, I was only teasing. I didn't mean it to sound the way it did. I'm the one who should be sorry, not you. So, now that we have that cleared up, how about helping me up into this monster of yours? Oh, my God! I forgot to tell you, I landed a job. It's really no big deal. It's only a couple of small projects but at least it's something."

Alex's hand returned to Nikki's arm. This time it traveled to her waist, lingering there. "Wow, that's great. I'm five eleven, by the way."

Nikki turned slightly. As she did, Alex's other hand slipped around the other side of Nikki's waist. Alex couldn't have stopped if she wanted to. She needed to taste those lips.

Looking up at Alex, Nikki drew herself closer to her tall detective. She watched as Alex lowered her head. Nikki knew what was happening. The thought of Alex kissing her sent warmth through her body.

Alex gently pressed her lips to Nikki's. Nikki's arms encircled her neck. It amazed Alex how good it felt to have Nikki's arms there. It was like the most natural thing in the world. When their lips met, the intensity startled both of them.

The kiss was tender and soft, yet intense and mind-blowing. Breaking apart a moment later, they each tried to catch their breath.

Nikki took a deep breath as she rested her forehead on Alex's chest. Alex's cologne tickled her nose. It was the most incredible smell. She would ask her later what it was. "Wow. I have never been kissed like that before. God, Alex you are a wonderful kisser."

Her hand gently caressed Nikki's face. Alex had to kiss her again. Her mouth and hands took control, seeking what they wanted most.

Alex broke away. She had to end the kiss before she became too aggressive and scared Nikki off. She took a deep breath.

"Only for you, babe. Only for you."

Alex had had her fair share of women, and then some, in her life. Not one of them moved her like this one. It scared her that this one singular woman could do this to her. To make her need to change.

✝

Alex had made a vow that she would never think about having a relationship again. There would be nothing past the one night stands to satisfy her needs. That way, no one would be hurt. One thing she never did was get emotionally involved with the women she spent the few hours with. And everything had been going along fine until now.

Looking into Nikki's moss green eyes, she didn't mind it at all though. Alex could think of only one thing at that moment. She wanted this woman to belong to her… to her and her alone. Nikki was like no one else Alex had ever met before, let alone bedded. Startled, she realized she wanted Nikki forever.

Alex's inner demons showed their ugly side. Why would Nikki want someone like her? Nikki was so sweet and innocent. She had probably had one or two girlfriends in her life. Alex couldn't imagine anyone not falling head over heels for this short spitfire. So, why was she alone?

Alex was sure Nikki's bedroom appetites were sweet and innocent, unlike hers. Alex's inner voice told her to walk away, before she hurt the girl. Something in Nikki's eyes told Alex that she had been hurt many times. She could guess that Nikki was used to disappointment, just by her mannerisms. Alex didn't want to add to that. Her conscience told Alex, don't do this to Nikki. Take her for a drink then take her home.

She needed to walk away.

†

Nikki saw the distressed look on Alex's face. "What's wrong?"

"Nothing, we should get going."

Nikki could feel Alex putting the walls up. Somehow, she needed Alex to feel more comfortable with her. Nikki wanted the stoic detective to be able to confide and trust in her.

Alex helped her into the high truck. As the detective got behind the wheel, Nikki decided to take a chance, hoping Alex would agree. "Have you eaten dinner yet?"

Alex shook her head no while buckling her seatbelt. Her hands were shaking. Alex's behavior was pathetic to her own eyes. Curling her hands into fists Alex tried to control the tremors.

"Okay, how about we get some dinner first, then we'll go for a drink later. How does that sound?" Nikki crossed her fingers.

"Only if you really want to 'cause going for a drink is fine with me if you're not hungry."

Nikki turned in her seat to look at Alex. She set her mind on getting Alex to open up. "Alex, why don't we go to dinner and talk for a while? I'd really like that."

Nikki pressed on when Alex didn't answer. "Alex, please don't retreat from me. I don't judge people. That's not my style. I like you very much and would like to get to know you better. If that's what you would like."

Alex fixed her eyes upon the steering wheel, willing it to come up and knock her unconscious. She could feel Nikki's eyes burning into her, waiting for an answer.

She cleared her throat. Why the hell not? "Yes, I'd like that. Any place in mind? What's your favorite food or place?"

Nikki grinned. "How do you feel about Mexican?"

Alex had taken a big step today. All of Alex's mannerisms told Nikki that just dating was not something Alex did often, if at all.

"Love it." Alex started the engine and they were on their way.

†

As dinner progressed, the two women opened up and shared a little of themselves. Each found it to be an enlightening evening. The hours melted away until almost midnight. Even though she felt completely safe with Alex, Nikki still held part of herself back.

I shouldn't feel guilty, I'm sure Alex has held back quite a bit about herself as well.

There were parts of herself Nikki didn't open to anyone. She would never go through that hurt again. Yet she wanted to tell Alex everything, the good *and* the bad. She found Alex extremely easy to talk to, as if she would not be judged. Nikki knew in her heart she would not be able to though, at least not for a long time.

Nikki was positive Alex would feel nothing but pity for her. That was the last thing she wanted from the woman she now found herself caring for. She wondered briefly why Alex's other girlfriends had left her. They must not have known a good thing when they'd had it, which in turn made Nikki wonder what Alex saw in her.

Then it hit her…she was falling for Alex. The thought scared Nikki. That she could fall in love so fast, so undeniably.

†

At that moment, Alex's mind was doing a somersault. She had the same feelings washing through her, only more intensely.

Maybe it was the tequila talking. Alex couldn't help but realize she had fallen in love with Nikki. If Nikki knew how badly she wanted her right then, she would probably run for the hills. Alex told herself she needed to take Nikki home and be done with it, not draw it out any longer. Then she would go cool her libido somewhere else. Those eyes …they cut right through her. Alex had to get away from her before she did something she would regret.

Alex stood. "It's past midnight. I should get you home."

Nikki looked startled, wondering about the abrupt change. "Okay…."

"Well, I know you wanted to go shopping tomorrow for clothes for the new job on Monday. Oh, and uh, by the way, congrats on that."

"Uh, thanks, I guess it is very late. Guess we lost track of time."

As they drove back to Nikki's, neither knew what to say to bridge the gap. Alex felt guilty about the abruptness. Nikki wondered what she did wrong.

After walking Nikki to the door, Alex waited for her to unlock it. She wanted to say something but could not find the words.

Turning in the doorway, Nikki was almost eye level with Alex who stood on the lower porch. Unable to figure out what she had done to cause such a reaction in Alex, she tried not to cry in bewilderment as she put her hand on Alex's arm.

"Thank you for the wonderful evening." She looked into Alex's eyes. What she saw made her breath catch. Alex's eyes were such a deep blue, they were almost black.

The porch light cast its eerie light across Alex, giving her an aura of complete and utter badness. Her leather jacket only added to the effect. It ran through Nikki's mind that if Alex was wearing black leather pants and riding a motorcycle, the effect would be devastating.

Before either could take another breath, their lips met. This kiss was not gentle as the other had been. It spoke of need and hunger. Nikki was the first to break away. "I'd love to ask you to stay. I don't want you to think I'm a slut though. Maybe stay for a little while?"

"I would never think that of you. Never talk about yourself like that."

Alex kissed her once more. Breathless, she thought before speaking. She didn't want it to come out all wrong. She didn't want to hurt Nikki's feelings. Thinking about another person was new to Alex. She wasn't sure how to act. She needed Nikki to want her as badly as she wanted her.

Standing on Nikki's porch looking into her eyes, Alex knew then that she couldn't walk away. No matter what, she wanted Nikki in her life. That decision made Alex do something she'd never done before. She put someone else's needs before her own. Wanting to make sure she did things right this time, Alex made herself slow down.

"Oh, baby, believe me I want to stay. God, how I want to… But," she paused, kissing Nikki on the cheek. "I find myself caring a lot about you. I want, no, make that need, to take things slower. I've made so many mistakes in my life and I want you to be sure this is what you want also."

Alex put her fingers on Nikki's lips as she was about to speak. "Let me finish. What I'm trying to say is that, I find myself having very strong feelings for you. I wanted us to build a relationship, get to know one another, not just fall into bed together. That's what I think we've been building during the months that we've been dating. I'm hoping that is what you want also."

"Yes, I feel the same way. I must say I've never felt this comfortable with anyone. Now Ms. Big Bad Detective, kiss me good night so I can go take a cold shower."

She kissed her so gently Nikki wasn't sure Alex's lips had touched her. "And I think you need an ice cold shower also. So… good night for now. Call me later. 'Kay?"

Alex could only nod as Nikki closed the door, chuckling. She however thought of only one place to go and it was not home. She needed to relieve the tension between her legs. There was only one place to do that.

Alex drove toward Pleasure's, where a couple of drinks in the right person could get you anything you wanted, including a more than willing partner for the night. She was in the mood for one that would be her sex slave for the evening.

†

Frustration was getting the better of Nikki. The cold shower she took each time they went out did nothing to cool down her desire for Alex. Either they had to have sex soon or she didn't know what she was going to do. Her right hand was cramping up because it was being used much too often.

Alex never once made an inappropriate move toward Nikki. She took her out to dinner then would return her home, with only a kiss on the cheek. The same held true for after the times they'd gone to the movies or when they went to a play, even the garden show.

Surprising Nikki, the detective was even a complete gentleman when she dropped Alex off at her apartment after Scott and Tess's wedding.

The night of Scott's wedding, Alex's intoxicated mind told her to pull Nikki into her place and ravage her, but something else inside her won out. Alex found it ironic what being in love and wanting to do the right thing could do to a person. It made them noble, something she wanted to be. Alex found it shocking, because noble was the last thing anyone would ever say about her.

†

Nikki was beginning to think Alex had changed her mind, not wanting a relationship, only friendship. But that couldn't be it.

They'd been seeing one another for four months. If that were the case, Alex would have taken her out once or twice then dumped her. Plus, if she only wanted sex, Alex would have had her on that first night and never called again.

"Are you okay over there?" Mike asked her.

Mike and Cathy had come for dinner and Nikki had made her to-die-for lasagna. Now the two of them were having coffee along with their usual heart-to-heart conversation. It was just the two of them. Cathy, true to form, had long since passed out from over indulging.

"God, Mike, I tell you, if she doesn't sleep with me soon, I'm going to explode. We've been going out for four months now and every night I either have to take a cold shower or take care of myself." Nikki turned back to the dining room table in time to see a wolfish look on his face.

She threw the dishtowel at him. "I know what is going through that mind of yours."

"What?" His smile grew. "I was just thinking how I could be a good Samaritan and help you."

"Like I said, you're a little piggie." She laughed as she got the coffee cups down from the cupboard.

"Hey, I was just thinking I could buy you some fresh batteries." Mike said, laughing.

Nikki rolled her eyes. "Yeah, sure that's what you meant."

"Sorry, you know me, gutter first. Kinda like you!" Mike snickered. "Does she know how much of a little perv you can be or are you on your best behavior?"

Snagging a cookie from the platter, he crammed the entire thing in his mouth.

She turned just in time to see the huge chocolate chip cookie disappear. She laughed. His stomach seemed to be never-ending.

Nikki sat the coffee carafe and cups on the table.

"I want so badly for her to need me, but she keeps her distance. She drives me home every night and that's it. I just don't want to scare her away by how much I need and want her. I'm afraid she'll think I'm pathetic and clingy. However, soon I'm just not going to be able to hold out any longer. I want her so much."

Nikki stood by the table, looking out into the dark night. She made a mental note that the windows needed washing.

Mike poured their coffee, adding enough sugar to his own to make Nikki cringe. "Yuck, how do you drink it like that?" She shuddered.

"I don't like the taste of coffee, so I just add tons of sugar."

Nikki sat shaking her head. "It's still gross. So, should we wake sleeping beauty or just let her sleep and you can crash on the floor?"

He looked into the other room at his passed out wife. "Let her sleep. I'll just crash later where I happen to land. Nikki, I want you to take to heart what I am about to say, okay?"

Nikki nodded.

"You are a wonderful woman and I consider it an honor to have you as a friend. Alex seems to be a good person too. What I see is that she is just taking things slow, to make sure that both of you are sure of what you want. I know this is going to sound really freakin' corny, but here goes. I think meeting Alex is the best thing that has happened to you. You have had some terrible things happen to you. Take those things and let them make you stronger. Don't let them break you. What I see is that the two of you need one another. She needs someone to protect and you need a protector, even if it is from yourself."

He smiled at himself, thinking he was smart at being able to give such wisdom.

"So, now that I have imparted a lifetime's worth of wisdom in five seconds, when is Millie coming back?"

He watched as she rolled her eyes at him.

She patted him on the shoulder. "You're wise beyond your years. Thanks, for setting me right when I lose my way. As for my nutcase sister, she'll be back next weekend. She was off to California this time. It's kinda nice without her here. I like the peace and quiet. I really feel like I'm going to have to tell her soon why I don't want to go out with guys. She's been hinting again about fixing me up with a friend of a friend of a friend, yada, yada. I was just hoping to be out on my own when I had that conversation with her."

"Nikki, if you don't want to tell her, you don't have to. It's your life. I say if people don't like it that you're gay, fuck 'em! It's your life to live how you want. Now, if you'll excuse me, I have to take a pee."

Nikki laughed. "Oh Mike, you have so much class."

†

Two nights later Alex was dropping Nikki off at home after a wonderful dinner at her favorite Thai restaurant. Nikki stopped on the porch. Alex stood in front of her on the sidewalk. Pulling Alex to her, Nikki liked the feeling of the detective's back pressed into her breasts. "Thank you for a nice night, Alex, I love Thai food."

Alex smiled. "You're welcome, babe."

Putting her arms around Alex's neck, she placed her cold cheek against Alex's warmer one.

"What a beautiful night, you can see all of the stars out tonight." She turned her head just a little so she could whisper in Alex's ear. "Alex, I don't want this night to end."

Alex turned in her arms and kissed her. "Neither do I…."

"Stay."

Alex shivered, feeling the sexual tension between them. "Baby, I want to so much it hurts. But…I want it to be perfect. Please have patience with me."

In reality, it was more than that. It terrified Alex how much she needed Nikki. She was afraid she would scare her away by how she wanted to possess her, to make Nikki hers.

Alex knew one thing for sure. Nikki wanted her. Holding off had only intensified Nikki's feelings for Alex. There was only one flaw to it. Alex, in turn, wanted only Nikki. The other women she seduced and bedded after their dates never appeased the hunger inside her for the woman beside her. After she had been dating Nikki for several weeks, Alex stopped going altogether. Instead, she would go home crash and replay their time together earlier in the day.

"Okay, I understand. I can wait because I want the same things. Tell Scott I said congrats. I'll call Tessa in the morning to discuss throwing her a baby shower."

Alex kissed her once more, leaving only after Nikki locked the door behind her.

✝

At nine the next morning, Alex and Scott could be found sitting in the butt-ass ugly and smelly unmarked car. She had already railed on him twice in the past hour.

Her first outrage had been at Scott not getting a better car for them. She later proceeded to go off on a tangent about how disrespectful the rookies coming in from the latest academy class seemed to be.

Now she was on a tirade about having to go across town to pick-up a gang banger from another district that they'd been looking for on a murder charge. "This is fucking rookie schlep work!" she scolded.

Scott's patience and temper were at an end, finally causing him to snap. Slamming on the brakes, he pulled to the curb in front of their favorite coffee and pastry shop. His knuckles were white on the steering wheel and he had trouble letting go of it. Finally giving up, he left his hands where they were.

Alex looked at where they had stopped, wondering why. "Stopping for coffee? You still have some. There's no need to stop."

She looked back down at the paperwork on their boy they were picking up.

Scott gritted his teeth. "Alex, you obviously had a bad night last night. Well, guess what, you're not the only fucking one that can have a bad night, you know! Did you even wonder why I was more than an hour late this morning? Especially since I've never been late in my life?"

By the end of his sentence, he was almost screaming.

Alex turned to look at Scott. She had never seen his face turn that particular shade of red. Additionally, he sure as hell had never gone off like this before at her. Sure, he would set her straight about something, but he would never lose it on her as he just did.

"Scott," she drawled. "What's wrong? Is Tessa okay?"

"Yes, she's fine. We had a bit of a scare last night though. She started having pains, so we went to the hospital and it turned out to be a false alarm. It was scary though, seeing as she's not anywhere near being due. Now, what in the hell is up with you? You and Nikki have a fight or something?" He loosened his grip on the wheel.

"No, no fight. I'm just frustrated and not sure what to do. I'm admitting to you and you only…I'm in love with her. I think maybe she loves me too. Why would she even like someone like me, let alone love me. I've been around the block too many times."

Scott snorted at that statement. "Hell girl, you've left ruts."

She glared at him, ignoring his remark. "I want to be with her so much, I'm going to explode. It has to be special with her. I need to know she loves me too. I'm not just looking for a good night and be gone in the morning. She needs to be mine for the rest of my life."

"That scares the shit out of you, doesn't it? That you want someone that much? Have you told her how you feel yet?"

Alex was silent.

"Ah. Then don't you think that's the place to start? If you truly feel this way about her, you need to take the chance and plunge in with both feet. Before someone comes along that will."

Alex growled. She felt it come up from her toes with such a force she couldn't stop it. "May God have mercy on anyone's soul who comes near her, after I finish with them! She is mine."

The force of her conviction made Scott a little leery. He knew in his heart that all the relationships she'd had to this point were lust driven. Scott knew when Alex finally fell for someone that she would fall hard. He knew she had never been in love with any of the women she bedded because Scott had never heard such venom in her voice before. He thought maybe Nikki was the perfect woman for her. She would keep Alex grounded.

After the previous girlfriend, Alex told him she would do whatever she could never to be betrayed again. Scott hoped she wouldn't do something stupid. He had been in her life for the good as well as the very bad. The worst had been when he didn't know if she would lose control and hurt someone else. Alex had explained the breaking of one of her previous girlfriend's noses, by telling Scott she caught her cheating and doing drugs.

"Then do something about it. Take that final step. If you're still going to the clubs, you need to stop and commit yourself one hundred percent to being with her. Okay? Oh by the way, we decided to name our daughter Tabitha."

Those words scared Alex even more.

She abruptly accommodated the change of subject. "Cool name, I like it. Okay, let's go get our boy and bring him back home. I want to make his crew squirm some."

✝

Some hours and forty-two stitches in her arm later, Alex dialed Nikki's number to invite her for dinner. The phone rang four times then the voicemail kicked on. Knowing Millie was at a conference, Alex left a quick message. "Nikki, it's a little after four. I was wondering if you'd like to come for dinner. So give me a call. Bye."

When Nikki failed to call her back by six, Alex was tired of waiting around. Extremely irritable, Alex threw on her leather jacket. Grabbing her truck keys, she headed out the door. "What the hell am I doing? It's not as if we're married or attached at the hips. Besides, it'll show her I'm not sitting around waiting for her to call me back. I'll just go grab a bite to eat."

She decided on Mexican, her favorite. She knew that, even though it was six on a Saturday night, it wouldn't be too busy yet. When the guilt set in Alex called Nikki to let her know where she'd be. Alex walked in, going straight to her favorite table. Her friend, the owner of the restaurant, walked to her.

"Hey Rico, how's it goin'?"

"Not bad, Alex, long time no see. Alone tonight?"

"Looks like it." She frowned once again. Now that she had more time to think about the day, she had cooled down. *Ah hell, she's probably out with Mike. Knowing Nikki, they're probably shopping up a storm. I'm just being an ass thinking she should be sitting at home, waiting for me to call.*

"The usual, chica? Maybe you want something a little different tonight?"

Alex waved off the menu, knowing it by heart, and removed her jacket. "Actually today I think I'll have two chicken enchiladas, one cheese enchilada and a side of rice and beans. Make all of that with extra cheese on it. A bowl of chili too."

"How can one woman eat so much?"

Alex called after him before he got too far. "'Cause I love food. Also, could you grab me a bigger dish of salsa while you're back there? Put some extra jalapeño in it too."

Alex was lost in thought about how she had ended up with stitches in her arm when Rico brought her a beer. He looked down at her arm. "Damn Alex, what happened to your arm? That's a mighty big bandage."

"Ah well, the short of it is, we went to pick up a banger of ours from Jake's precinct and well… they forgot to check his boots for weapons. He had a razor in his boot and it went downhill after that. I ended up with forty-two stitches, end of story."

"That sucks. You're back to work tomorrow though, right?" Alex nodded her head to confirm. He knew her well, after years of dining in his establishment at least four nights a week. Plus, at least once a month, several tables were pushed together with Alex and fellow officers sharing pitchers of beer late into the night.

"Well, I'll be right out with your dinner and another beer. It's on the house tonight by the way."

Alex just shook her head and smiled. She knew he was trying to make her feel better. What she needed right then though was a certain green-eyed woman sitting across from her, not empty space.

Rico returned with her dinner and a fresh beer. He turned to the door when he heard it open. What walked through was a vision for sure and just as dangerous. She had not been into the restaurant for a while and she had not been missed. She was hell on wheels and he didn't like her one bit.

"Shit!" he muttered and walked away from Alex's table.

Walking toward her, he picked up a menu on the way. "Do you want a table tonight or would you rather sit at the bar?" He wanted to keep her away from Alex, knowing sparks were sure to fly.

She looked around the room, her eyes falling on Alex. "Actually Rico, I see an old friend is here. I'll have the same as her." Casually she walked to Alex's table and sat down across from her.

"Hello Alex, nice to see you again." Alex looked up. Dropping her fork to her plate, her appetite suddenly vanished.

"Hello Ann. I didn't see you come in. I also don't remember asking you to sit down."

Nikki was such a wonderful loving woman. She deserved to be treated like a princess. Alex wondered what she had done to Nikki.

Those thoughts brought another to Alex's mind. Surely, she would be even worse for her. Alex's heart told her she did not have much more to offer Nikki. *Then what in the hell am I doing falling in love with her?*

All the doubts surfaced once more. After looking at the woman sitting across from her, for a moment, Alex knew she would be better for Nikki than anyone else ever would.

Coming to a crossroads in her life, Alex made the only choice she could. Nikki would be the center of her world. There would be nothing she wouldn't do for Nikki; nothing she wouldn't give her.

"Oh, Alex please, I knew you'd ask me to join you since we both seem to be alone." An evil grin etched across Ann's face. "And pray tell why are you dining alone?"

"Ann, I really don't see that it's any of your fucking business. Now, if you'll excuse me, I'd really like to eat my dinner in peace."

Rico sat Ann's drink on the table then quickly departed not wanting to get in between the two tigers facing off against one another.

"Don't be such a bitchy butch. I was only looking for some polite chit-chat during dinner."

Ann picked up her drink and downed half of it in one gulp.

Alex was so engrossed in trying to get rid of Ann that she never saw Nikki enter the restaurant.

✝

Nikki had arrived home from shopping with Mike to find two messages on her machine. Both were from Alex, the first being the dinner invitation, the second saying she would be at Rico's. Nikki thought she would surprise Alex by just showing up.

She couldn't believe the scene before her eyes. The woman she loved sitting at the same table as the woman who had used her and thrown her away like yesterday's garbage. Nikki's anger flared.

It had to be some kind of cosmic joke. *A wide awake nightmare is what it is!* she thought.

Nikki couldn't stop her feet. She wanted nothing more than to run from the restaurant. The feet however, seemed to have a mind of their own. She walked toward where the two were sitting.

Alex looked up as Nikki approached the table. She felt her heart stop.

"Fuck!" The word left her mouth before she could stop it.

Nikki stood beside the table and looked down at the two. Anger was evident on her reddened face.

Ann looked up at her like a petulant child with her hand caught in the cookie jar. "Hello Nikki, care to join us for dinner?"

She could feel her blood starting to boil and Nikki knew she'd better get control of her temper before she spoke. She breathed deeply but still no words came out.

"Nikki, Ann and I are not having dinner together. She just saw me here and made herself at home," Alex said gently.

Nikki's body language, thinly drawn eyes and clenched teeth clearly showed her anger.

Alex silently pleaded with Nikki to believe her, to trust her.

It took only a second. Nikki smiled. Her heart made the choice for her. She believed Alex.

At that moment, Alex knew. Nikki was hers.

Nikki turned to Ann. "I don't believe you. What do I have to do to get you out of my life for good? What will it take?"

Nikki's control was slipping. She clenched her fists tight, losing feeling in her fingers.

Nikki leaned down so they were face-to-face. She was so close that Ann could see the gold flecks in her ex's eyes. Nikki clenched her teeth.

"Ann, I suggest you move, or I'll move you. Got it? Or do I need to spell it out for you?" Nikki, for the first time in her life, was standing up and protecting what was hers.

Ann couldn't believe her ears. Nikki had never raised her voice before. When their relationship went sour, Nikki just cowered and shrank into a corner. She took all the shit Ann could throw at her, never batting her eyes. Now she stood here going off on her. It made her a little excited. Then Ann made a stupid move.

"Oh, come on, Nikki, it's not like the two of you are married or anything. We were just having some dinner together."

Ann never saw it coming. Nikki grabbed her roughly by the arm, yanking her out of the chair. "I don't think you understood me correctly. I asked you to remove yourself from this table. You are sitting in my seat, with my girlfriend, and I'm starving. So, I'd advise you to move, now!"

Looking at Ann, Alex laughed. The vile woman finally caught on. Alex couldn't believe what she'd just heard. Nikki had used the word *girlfriend.* It stunned her, yet warmed her inside to hear the words.

Alex sat back, and drank her beer pondering the scene playing out in front of her. Nikki believed Ann was up to no good. Alex found the whole situation a little amusing.

Nikki had been working on her low self-esteem a little at a time. When cornered, Nikki would fight for what was hers, and Alex was hers. Before meeting Alex, she would never have had the courage to stand up to Ann.

"Well, I guess I know when I'm not wanted. So I'll just leave now."

Rico stood by the door, holding it open for Ann as she huffed through it. Walking back into the kitchen, he roared with laughter. "Finally someone set that puta in her place," he roared.

Nikki plopped down in the chair, took the beer from Alex's hand and finished it off. She couldn't believe she'd had the nerve to do that.

Alex sat smiling at her. She closed her eyes for a moment. When she opened them, they were a deep blue. Nikki had come to know what that look meant.

What her eyes conveyed was not lust. It was pure, raw desire. Alex suddenly lost her appetite, for food that is. Replacing it was a deeper, different kind of hunger. Leaning across the table, Alex covered Nikki's hands with hers. "Are you truly hungry?"

"Starving," Nikki licked her lips slowly.

Standing, Alex pulled Nikki up with her. "Good. Let's go, I'll drive."

The ride to her apartment was silent and short. Alex let them into the second floor apartment, turning on a table lamp with a switch just inside the door. She threw her truck keys on the table next to the lamp, her jacket landing on the black leather couch. Reaching for Nikki, Alex helped her out of her jacket.

Alex's fingertips casually grazed Nikki's neck. She threw Nikki's jacket on top of her own. With her hands on Nikki's waist, she slowly turned the shorter woman around. Alex looked down into the most beautiful eyes she had ever seen. They held nothing but love and desire in them.

Nikki looked up what seemed like a mile. What she saw sent a shiver down her spine straight to her center. She wanted this woman as she had wanted no other. Nikki prayed the feeling was mutual.

All Nikki wanted was someone who would love her a little. The rest would be icing on the cake. Most thought she was a strong person. If they'd really looked inside, they would see a small, scared child.

Even if Alex wasn't perfect, Nikki would take her. She knew she herself was far from perfection. Nikki wished she knew if Alex loved her or if she would be just another notch on the detective's belt.

Nikki felt one of Alex's hands leave her waist and touch her cheek.

With her other hand still on Nikki's waist, Alex drew them closer, their bodies almost touching. It was then that Nikki placed such a gentle kiss to Alex's lips that she wasn't even sure Nikki had touched her.

The cologne she wore tonight was Nikki's favorite. It made her want to melt into Alex. She only wore a few select colognes, all of them men's. Alex found women's perfume to be too flowery for her tastes. Anytime Nikki smelled this particular cologne, she would look around for Alex.

If Alex would love her, she would gladly give the detective her soul. With that thought in mind, Nikki pressed her body to Alex's, feeling the hard muscles beneath the fabric.

Alex bent her head, their lips touching once more. It was as if it was the first time either of them had ever been kissed. It was loving and timid. Yet it was with a familiarity as if they had been together for years. Alex drew away.

"I want to make love to you. No more waiting. No more cold showers. Right here, right now."

Kissing her again, Alex's hand left Nikki's face, landing on her chest. She wanted to touch her. The aching was so bad, she hurt. The contact through the fabric only eased the hunger slightly.

Alex laid her hand on Nikki's breast. She wanted to make love to Nikki slowly, gently. Alex could feel the wetness gathering in her jeans. She had to slow herself down or her libido would take control.

Nikki was having issues of her own. She had waited so long for someone to want her this much, she didn't know if she could go slowly. She could feel Alex holding back as if she were going to break her. She felt herself leaning into the caress, her aching nipples hardening. "I won't break, Alex, please."

Alex's hand pressed harder. Nikki involuntarily moaned.

"You like that, huh?" She pressed harder. Then, much to Nikki's delight, she squeezed the nipple through the shirt and bra.

It was then that Nikki felt it. It was the point of no return. She gave herself willingly to Alex, no matter the cost. It seemed Alex knew exactly what pushed her buttons. She squeezed the nipple a little more.

Nikki's breathing became ragged. "Harder, please."

That was all Alex needed to hear. She ripped Nikki's clothes from her body, going directly to Nikki's left nipple, sucking it while she squeezed the other one with her fingertips. The harder she sucked the louder Nikki moaned.

Nikki could feel the wetness running down her thighs. The more Alex sucked, the further gone she was. She was hesitant, if Alex only knew what that did to her. What would Alex think of her if she told her that sometimes she liked it hard and rough? Would Alex hate her if she knew? Did Alex prefer a nice little femme, the kind that likes it sweet and gentle?

She was driving Nikki crazy.

Alex switched to her other nipple when she had a better idea. She took both of Nikki's breasts in her hands, squeezed them together bringing both of them into her mouth at once.

This got an immediate response from Nikki. She felt her knees give out. "God, yes! Bite them, hard."

Hearing this sent Alex to the edge. She knew Nikki's appetite would match her own. Alex shed her clothes while pushing the two of them toward the bedroom. Alex wanted to claim Nikki's body as hers. She was going to show Nikki how badly she wanted her. Her bed was higher than most so she lifted Nikki up onto the bed. She lay on top of her, once more lavishing attention to her lover's breasts.

Nikki knew they'd hurt tomorrow but she didn't care. She urged Alex to suck and bite them even harder.

Alex opened her eyes and lifted her head from where she had it buried. What she found was a vision laying spread out under her. "God, you are so precious. I want to taste you so badly."

"What are you waiting for? I'm all yours. Do with me what you want. Anything at all, my body's yours."

She spread her legs wider.

"Soon, baby, soon. Thought I'd let my fingers do the walking first." Alex wiggled her eyebrows. Nikki could see Alex even as dusk fell and darkened the room.

The suggestion sent a new flood of wetness to Nikki's center. She was throbbing, her clit so swollen she thought it would burst. Alex sucked her left nipple squeezing her breast at the same time. Alex was quickly rewarded for her actions.

"Yes, like that. Oh, just like that. I love that so much."

Alex's own wetness ran onto Nikki's thigh where she laid on top of her. She knew she had to hold out, wanting to concentrate on her lover. She wanted to hear Nikki scream and beg for more. Nikki was so wet and ready. She had to feel her. Alex reached into the drawer of her nightstand. She pulled out the bottle of lube just in case she might need it later.

With her free hand, Alex made her way to the wetness she knew she'd find. *So wet, so ready.* Alex had to take her, to make Nikki hers. "All mine. Forever…."

Nikki was having trouble concentrating. Alex was everywhere at once. She felt Alex's hand travel down her body. Nikki felt the fingers hesitate, then slide into the wetness.

"Yes, oh…Alex."

Alex started rubbing very slowly up and down, gathering speed. She could feel Nikki's body pulsing under hers. Nikki arched up. "Please, take me Alex…take me."

That was all Alex needed to hear. She slid two fingers into her, slowly withdrawing and sliding in again. The slow speed with which Alex took her was agonizing. At that moment, Nikki's body craved fast and hard.

Nikki's body lifted off the bed. She knew it wouldn't be much longer for her. Alex continued to rub herself against Nikki as she went deeper with each thrust. Nikki couldn't take it any longer. She was going mad. She needed more. "Alex, please."

She was begging. She didn't care.

Alex smiled, continuing slowly. "Please what, baby?" Alex was teasing her. She wanted to hear it, to hear Nikki ask for it. Alex fed on the power it gave her to hear women beg. "Please what, Nik?" she asked again.

She felt Nikki squirm under her trying to get her hand in deeper.

"Oh God, Alex, please." Nikki was begging, as she never had before.

"Uh, uh, uh. You've got to tell me, baby." Alex slipped in slowly.

Nikki broke, all rational thought leaving her. She screamed. "Fuck me. Fuck me harder." As if a dam had broken loose, the wetness ran down Alex's hand.

"Faster! Please, Alex. Need more of you…."

Alex couldn't control her actions. She wanted to put her whole fist in Nikki. Unsure of how Nikki would react or if she would even like it, she instead opted for just a third finger. The feelings of control and domination spurred Alex on. That is all sex had ever been about to Alex, a way to control her lovers. Knowing she should have gone with her first instinct, she heard Nikki scream 'more' when she put the third finger in.

"God, yes!" Pulling out, Alex quickly pumped lube onto her fingers from the bottle beside her bed. "Please, Alex, more."

Nikki's brain melted; her insides ready to explode. She could feel it building. She needed more of Alex inside of her. She needed all of her.

Alex could tell it would be any second now. On the next thrust in, she moved her thumb to her palm sliding her whole hand into Nikki. She had never met anyone as responsive. Alex moved her own body frantically up and down Nikki's thigh. Close to coming herself, Alex tried to hold off because Nikki was almost there. She could feel Nikki's walls closing around her hand as she moved inside of her.

Nikki couldn't hold out any longer. "Please, I need your mouth on me."

Alex obeyed.

"Yes, suck it. Harder. Oh…yes…" Nikki felt like she'd gone out of her body. She could feel herself shaking while Alex's hand took her harder and faster. Then it hit. Nikki came so hard she was sure the neighbors must have heard her.

Alex had to come, her center was screaming to be touched. She reached down with her free hand, sliding her fingers through her own wetness, then back up across her clit and back into herself. She repeated the movement each time faster and harder. She came, her scream muffled against her lover's center.

A flow of wetness bathed the hand that was still inside of Nikki. Alex collapsed, her head lying on Nikki's thigh. She started slowly removing her hand when Nikki gasped.

"No, please, leave it there just a moment longer. It feels so good." Alex moved her hand ever so slightly. Then she started to move her fingers upward.

All Nikki could manage was to moan, asking for more. Several moments later found them coming once more as Alex moved her hand inside Nikki and rubbed herself against the bed.

She kissed Nikki's throbbing center. Removing her hand from its warm place, Alex moved up so she could kiss her mouth.

"Mmm, you taste like me," Nikki smiled.

Alex licked her lips, not wanting to miss a drop. "Delicious."

She pulled back a little to be able to look into Nikki's eyes. "I love you, Nik. I have from the first moment I saw you. I've wanted you so badly ever since."

She saw tears in Nikki's eyes. "What's wrong, babe?"

Nikki ran her fingers through Alex's silky blonde hair. "I just never thought I'd find someone as wonderful as you...someone to love me. I thought I'd be alone the rest of my life."

Alex pulled Nikki into her arms, holding her tightly. She wished she could wash away all of her fears.

"Babe, I'll always love you and you'll never be alone again. I'll always be with you. Always..."

They fell asleep curled in one another's arms.

Chapter Three

Ramifications of War

As with all new lovers, they spent every free moment they could together. Not wanting to chance Millie answering, Alex bought Nikki a cell phone. Most weeks they were able to spend several nights together.

A few weeks after their first night together, Alex found she couldn't handle the nights she spent alone any longer. Not being able to see Nikki for a full week because of her caseload sent Alex into overload.

Alex asked Nikki if she felt it possible they could share a home in the future.

Overjoyed at the idea, both knew this was the only way they could be together and Nikki not having to live in fear of Millie. Even though Alex had been talking about the future, Nikki began searching the weekly homebuyers section. She didn't see any reason not to start looking early. While on the web searching for a new design program she wished to buy, Nikki came across several articles on the current real estate market. Realizing the market was not at its best, the couple decided an apartment might be better, at least for the time being.

†

Nikki arrived home exhausted from working fourteen hours a day for twelve days in a row. She was enjoying the current freelancing project she was working on. It was the first one she had actually enjoyed. The job was a marketing campaign for the new BMW dealership in town.

For the past few hours though, all Nikki had wanted to do was go home and crash. She even called off her date with Alex because she was so tired. It upset Nikki to cancel, but she felt it unfair to Alex not to have her undivided attention.

Yeah, I'd probably fall asleep in the theatre. Then I'd probably snore, causing her further embarrassment.

Walking in the door, Nikki found her sister and a young man sitting in the living room. She recognized him immediately as the type Millie would try to fix her up with. This was a very young one she noted.

Nikki stood in the doorway muttering, just loud enough so she was sure he would hear. "Oh no.… No. Not today, I am so not in the mood."

"Nikki, I don't think you've ever met John before? You know Marcy, who I work with? This is her son, John." Millie turned to John. "John, this is my sister Nikki. I think you both are the same age and probably share most of the same interests. Nikki, why don't you sit down, relax and I'll get you a soda."

Millie, as usual, was completely oblivious to her sister's distress.

Millie went into the kitchen, thinking if she left them alone they might hit it off. Millie really couldn't understand why Nikki hadn't taken an interest in any of the young men she tried to set her up with.

Nikki was in no mood for any of this. She was exhausted on many different levels. She was beat from work, mentally toasted from trying to fend off the losers Millie was always setting her up with and last, but most importantly, bone tired of being someone she wasn't. Nikki wanted to be who she was and be respected for it.

Sitting on the couch, she looked at this latest schmuck. Feeling this was a fix up, Nikki was trying to keep from finally losing it. When he smiled at her, Nikki felt her blood pressure rising. Clenching her fists on her lap, she could feel it coming.

Millie walked back into the living room, setting the glass of soda next to her. Picking it up, Nikki downed the entire thing in one long gulp. She could feel her throat drying even after the liquid.

Standing in the middle of the room, Millie turned to Nikki. "I'm going to go get ready for my date for the theatre tonight. It's one of those dinner theatre things, so I won't be eating home tonight. I thought it might be a nice idea for the two of you to go out to dinner together."

She turned toward the door.

Before Nikki realized it, the word left her mouth. "No!"

Millie froze midstride. Clearing her throat, she turned to Nikki. "Excuse me?"

"You heard me. I said no." For the first time she stood her ground.

Nikki turned to the young man. "John, I'm sure you're a very nice guy. I'm not interested now nor will I ever be. Sorry." She felt sorry for him.

Millie looked like someone had hit her with a two by four. "Nikki, there is no reason to be rude. I think a night out would be good for you."

John watched them eagerly, like he was watching a war start.

"I feel you should apologize to John and then the two of you go to dinner."

Crossing her arms, Millie looked smug, thinking she would win, just as she always did.

Seeing the smugness, Nikki's temper blew. "Damn it, Millie, would you get a clue? I don't want to go out with him. I don't want to go out with any of the guys you try to fix me up with. Maybe if you tried to fix me up with their *sisters*, I'd consider it."

Millie's jaw hit the floor. The reality of what Nikki was saying finally hit home.

John laughed so hard he almost fell out of his chair. "Oh, this is too rich. You didn't know this whole time that she was gay? Hello, I could have told you that the minute she walked through the door."

Millie spun around, glaring at him. "I really don't think this is any of your business, young man. In fact, why don't you just be on your way? This is a family matter."

She pulled him up from the chair and practically threw him out the door. Turning toward Nikki, she started her tirade on the evils of being a lesbian.

"Nikki, I know you are not one of those sick people. It was not a very nice thing to do. If you didn't like him, all you had to do was say so. I know you are not one of those things. You were raised properly. There is no way you are one of those perverts. You wouldn't dare be."

Nikki could take no more of her sister's bigotry. "Millie, I'm a lesbian. Get over it! When I was twelve, I knew I was interested in girls. Did you really think I was just playing house with the girl next door? I was also playing doctor with her. I am who I am. I'm not going to change, for you or for anyone. I'm very happy with who I am."

She could see Millie was getting more distraught as the conversation went on.

"Nikki, I'll make an appointment with a psychiatrist I know. He'll be able to help you. He'll fix this mess. I'll also make an appointment with Dr. Williams to make sure you're physically okay. Maybe you have a brain tumor or something. Between the two of them they will fix you."

"Enough!" Nikki slammed her fists on the coffee table and sent the coasters to the floor.

"There is nothing, I repeat, nothing wrong with me. My body and mind are fine. Every damn thing in my life is fine, except you. Actually, I've never been happier in my life than I am now. I enjoy the work I'm doing and I have a great woman in my life."

Millie looked like she was going to suffer a stroke. She dropped onto the couch, looking ill.

Nikki couldn't stop herself though. Now that the gates had opened, it was all flooding through the breach.

"Yes, I said a great woman. Her name is Alex. She's a cop and a damn good one."

Recognition clicked on in Millie's brain. "She's that woman you've been spending all your time with lately, isn't she?"

Nikki nodded. She didn't want to bring Alex into this mess but there was no choice.

"Well, you are not allowed see her anymore. I don't want her here ever again. Do you understand? She's done this to you, turned you evil; made you perverted. Mother would be so disappointed in you. She's probably having a seizure in her grave right now. You wouldn't want that, would you? You wouldn't want Mom to think you're a pervert?"

"Mother would have loved me no matter what! Don't you dare speak of Mom that way. I know she would have never hated me. It's your bigotry that she wouldn't tolerate."

Nikki stood, clenching her fists by her sides.

"What I understand, Millie, is that you're a bigot, a control freak and sometimes just plain fucking nuts. I have my own life to live and I plan to do just that. I've tried my best to put up with you meddling in my life, but I can't do it anymore. I was born gay. I'm not sick in any way. I am who I am. If you can't accept that, well, so be it."

Nikki dropped exhausted into the chair. Her head pounded so badly she saw black specks before her eyes. She knew a migraine was setting in.

Millie stood from the couch and headed toward the kitchen. "I want you to find a place of your own immediately. I won't have any of that perverted behavior under my roof. I won't allow it."

Nikki stood, fleeing for her room. "Fine, I was looking for an apartment anyway."

Nikki tossed and turned all night. The confrontation replayed through her mind. She knew she shouldn't have lost her temper but Millie had pushed too far this time. She had just snapped and that was that. There was no going back now. She would talk to Alex in the morning to see if she could help her find them an apartment. It seemed she was going to be moving sooner than expected.

Alex called her sister the next morning to have breakfast with her. It was better that she talk things through with her sister than to go and scream at Nikki's sister, Millie.

Kirstin knew something was up when Alex called her at seven in the morning wanting to have breakfast with her, just the two of them. Knowing Alex was not one for relationships, Kirstin was furious, thinking Alex was going to stop seeing Nikki. She fumed the whole way, running a stop sign. Luckily, there were no cops around. If there had been and she'd received a ticket, she would have strangled Alex.

She knew all about her one night stands and that she'd never been able to commit to just one woman. Kirstin spent the entire drive to the restaurant yelling at the imaginary Alex sitting next to her in the car.

Pounding on the steering wheel, Kirstin thought of ways to torture Alex. "If that's what this is about, I am going to give her hell. She'll never find anyone better than Nikki, especially someone who would put up with her shit. She had damn well better not blow this one."

Kirstin walked into the small diner, not letting go of the foul mood. She found Alex sitting in a booth in the back. Motioning to their favorite server for coffee, she sat down opposite Alex. Kirstin noticed her sister looked disheveled, which was highly unusual.

"Okay, sis, what's up? I get a strange call from you to meet you for breakfast, just the two of us, plus you look like something the cat threw up. What's going on?"

The waitress set coffee in front of her and took their orders. Alex looked anywhere but at her sister.

"Right to the point, huh? I, um, I called you 'cause I wanted to talk to you about Nikki. I like her a lot. Well, I mean," Alex fiddled with her silverware. She finally looked at Kirstin. Her sister had a smirk on her face.

"Ah shit, all right, I love her. Okay? There, happy? I love her. God, I'm so afraid I'll blow it though. You know I'm not good at this shit. I'm much better at the three f's. Find them, fuck 'em and forget them. But, God help me, I love her and I can't imagine life without her."

"Does she feel the same way? Have you talked to her about this?" Kirstin already knew the answer. She hadn't.

"Ah well, kinda. She knows I love her." Alex stopped as the waitress set their food in front of them. She didn't want her to overhear their conversation. Kirstin picked up the ball before Alex could speak again.

"So you told her you love her. Did you tell her you wanted a relationship? Or did you beat around the bush about it? 'Cause let me tell you bluntly, if you don't, well, let's just say this, she's a great woman and I'm sure that there are more than a couple of women in the world who would scoop her up in a heartbeat."

Kirstin laughed as Alex growled. She knew that would get Alex's goat. She hated to prod her like this but sometimes it was the only way to get her sister to wake up.

"What was that, Alex? I didn't quite hear that. Were you trying to say something or were you just clearing your throat?" Knowing she really shouldn't egg Alex on any longer, she just couldn't help herself.

Alex spoke so low Kirstin almost missed it. "She's mine, she belongs to me."

"Sorry, what was that?" Kirstin smiled, having heard every word. Alex's words and action confirmed to Kirstin that Alex *had* finally fallen in love.

Alex gritted her teeth. "You heard me. I am not going to repeat myself. So… to continue, there's a little complication now. Nikki called me this morning. She and her sister Millie had a big blow up last night. Her sister tried to fix her up with another guy and she lost it on her. The result is they aren't speaking. Her sister is a bigot, she wants her out and I'm not permitted anywhere near the house. Which suits me just fine, 'cause I'm liable to kill the bitch just for the fun of it!"

Alex's tightly wound control on her emotions was unraveling causing the end of her tirade to come out in a bellow that the surrounding people could hear.

Kirstin looked around them. She noticed a few people staring at them. She had to get her sister calmed down. Alex could have a nasty temper. Kirstin didn't want her sister doing anything foolish.

Alex clenched her fists. "Mine."

"Alex, calm down. You need to look at this rationally. Okay? You need to take a step back and look at everything. You love her, you want to have a relationship with her, and now the issue with her sister has come up. You have to think about how to resolve the issue with her sister first if you want to continue seeing her."

Alex nodded. "I know. I was thinking about it on the way here this morning. Nikki already knows I want us to share a home. I was just hoping I'd have my promotion first. You know, less hours, yada yada. It doesn't look like it's going to work out that way. I want for us to find a place to live together now rather than later."

"Wow… wait a second. She knows you want to share a home? See…she obviously does know you love her and want a relationship. However, don't you think that it's too soon for that type of move? Don't get me wrong. I'm very happy to see you make such a commitment, yet I'm a little nervous."

Alex got a faraway look on her face. "No, I don't think it is. I love her, she loves me and I want us to be together. This thing with Millie came at the perfect time actually."

Kirstin thought for a moment. These past few months had been the happiest she had ever seen Alex. It was about time she settled down, in her opinion.

"No, Alex, you know what, maybe you are right. She's good for you. Settling down very well might be the best thing that's ever happened to you. Hey, who knows, maybe the two of you will start a family."

Alex dropped her fork onto the table, staring at Kirstin.

Kirstin couldn't help but laugh at the look of horror on her sister's face.

"Kids, uh? I'm not too sure about that. Shit, Kir, don't even go there. You know I'm not the mothering type." Alex's face went white. "Damn, do you think she's going to want kids? Crap, I didn't even think about it. What am I going to do?"

Kirstin covered Alex's hand with hers. "Alex, please don't jump the gun. She might not want kids either. I think the two of you need to sit down and talk everything out and I mean *everything* before you get any more ideas. Okay?"

Alex pushed her plate away. She'd lost her appetite altogether.

She thought of something else. "Oh, fuck me! Nikki said Millie told her she was sick and needed to see a doctor. What if Nikki falls for that line of crap? Millie has always manipulated her. Shit! I need to get her out of there."

Alex threw her napkin on the table, standing to leave.

"Alex, stop. You're not thinking clearly. Nikki is very intelligent. She would never fall for a crock of shit like that. She knows the difference between right and wrong. She would know that doing anything like that would be crazy."

Kirstin paused, "And I don't take her as the crazy type person. Alex, she loves you, right? Go with that. Go see her, talk to her and tell her how you feel. Things will work out. Okay?"

Alex sat back down. The server had long since cleared the dishes, leaving the check. "Alex, it's my turn, I'll get this. Now, I want you to call her and go see her."

"I can't. Millie doesn't want me near the place, and Nikki left her cell phone at my place two days ago. If I call there and Millie answers, I'm sure the bitch won't let me talk to her."

Kirstin just shook her head. Sometimes Alex could be a little pig-headed and sometimes a little dense. "Since when did you ever let anything stop you? Did you lose your balls or something? The Alex I know, that is my sister, would just show up there and demand to see her girlfriend. She would then help her girlfriend pack her belongings and get her the hell out of there."

Alex grinned at Kirstin. "Woman, did you just verbally bitch-slap me?"

Kirstin laughed and puffed out her chest. "Yes, I did,' she said, standing. "Now, get your ass moving and go get your woman."

She threw her napkin at Alex and went to pay the check.

✝

Nikki made it her mission to search weekly for a nice apartment. She discarded immediately any that didn't have an extra bedroom that could double as a den for Alex. The room would also need a large closet to hold Alex's gun safe.

Finally, towards the end of the summer, they found one. The moment they walked through the door they knew it was what they had been looking for.

Their new home was not far from Alex's precinct, which made it perfect. If Nikki needed her, she could be home in a heartbeat.

†

Across town, two sisters stood in the living room facing off against one another, neither willing to budge an inch. Millie tried day and night to get through to Nikki, to make her see the evil error of her ways. Eventually Nikki refused even to be in the same room with her. The only reason she was now was that Millie had cornered her, starting in on her in a last ditch effort to save her.

"I'm sorry, Millie. This is not open for discussion. Alex and I are moving in together. I know you don't like her. You think both of us are evil, etc… etc. I really don't give a shit any longer what you think of me. It's my life. I love her and that's all there is to it. She'll be here in a few minutes to help move my stuff. If you don't want to see her then I suggest you leave."

Millie tried everything she could think of to make her see reason; that she was wasting her life. "I told you I don't want that *thing* in my house!"

Nikki spun around like a woman possessed. "Fine, I'll have her stand on the sidewalk and bring the boxes out to her there. It would get us out of your face faster though if she could come in and help me."

She and Millie had been sparring all morning and Nikki was exhausted. She looked out the window, feeling the sun warm her face.

Millie slammed her fist on the kitchen counter. "Fine, then I'm leaving. Be gone by the time I come back."

"Fine, you better leave now then because she's coming up the street."

Nikki turned from the window to see her sister slamming the door behind her. The pictures on the wall shook and the door bounced back open.

"Well, that could have gone better. Hell, this whole situation could've gone better. I didn't expect her to accept it, but I sure didn't think she would be this volatile. Damn."

Nikki's migraine was going strong, causing her to feel nauseous. Standing in the kitchen, she took her medication when it suddenly occurred to her. The final living member of her family had just walked out of her life. Nikki didn't want Alex to see her so upset. So, as usual, she bottled it up.

Leaning against the counter, she tried to steady herself as another wave of nausea rolled through her. "Everyone thinks I don't let anything get to me. Well, I do what I have to do." She sighed. "Why couldn't my family be like the Cleavers?

Everyone loved one another on the show, no matter what."

Alex was almost to Nikki's when she saw Millie backing out. Alex had to pull way to the side and Millie still almost plowed into her truck. "Damn bitch better watch where she's driving."

Millie's car window was down. Alex could hear the woman swearing like a sailor as she drove by. She was always prim and proper, according to Nikki. Pulling her truck in next to Nikki's car, she sat for a moment collecting her thoughts. She was a nervous wreck and didn't want Nikki to see it.

She gripped the steering wheel tightly. "Good God, you'd think I was a virgin again, going on my first date. We know and love one another. We're building a life with one another. Shit, what about what Kirstin said though? What if she wants kids? I'm a cop and not exactly mother material. Okay now, Alex, no second thoughts here, get your ass moving, and get in there."

After berating herself enough, Alex slowly got out of the truck and made her way to the door. She found it standing open and went in.

Walking through the living room into the kitchen, what she saw was a vision of beauty. There was the love of her life leaning her hip against the counter, so deep in thought she never heard Alex come in. Alex watched her for a moment afraid to disturb her, knowing she would probably scare her half to death. The longer she stood watching her, the more she fell in love with her, as if that were possible. Alex loved Nikki so much she knew she would be lost without her in her life. Alex gently cleared her throat.

Nikki jumped. Turning, she found Alex staring at her.

"Jesus, you scared the snot out of me." She walked to Alex, wrapped her arms around her waist pulling Alex close. "And I think I deserve a kiss for it."

Alex ran her fingers through Nikki's hair, noting how soft it always was. "I'm sorry baby. I didn't mean to scare you. I just couldn't help but stand and look at you for a few moments. You are so beautiful."

She put her hand around Nikki's upper arm as her other hand slipped behind Nikki's neck, tilting her head up. "I love you, Nik."

Alex's lips met Nikki's gently. She ran her tongue across Nikki's bottom lip. Gently, Alex parted Nikki's lips with her tongue, seeking entry.

Nikki pulled away, needing to breath. She had never felt anything as intense as when Alex kissed her. Looking up into Alex's eyes, she saw love and something else. She saw power. Nikki knew she was defenseless to Alex's charms. She would do anything for her because Alex loved her and only her. Knowing there had been others didn't matter now. Now it was just the two of them.

"Darling, as much as I want to continue this, I think we need to get my stuff and get out of here. Millie left in a huff and said she didn't want us here when she got back, which is fine by me, of course."

✝

It took them almost an hour to load the remaining boxes of Nikki's possessions into Alex's truck. They had left Nikki's vehicle at their new home on the first trip. Nikki thought of leaving the key behind but couldn't do it. She needed some connection to her sister, even if Millie wanted nothing to do with her.

Nikki left a note on the kitchen counter with their phone number and address on it. She left it even knowing Millie would throw it out. Nikki could walk away and not look back, but she couldn't be that cold. Even though her sister could have a black heart, Nikki wouldn't stoop to her sister's level and hate her back. Nikki hated when there were bad feelings between anyone she knew, so she would at least try.

Both were lost in their own thoughts on the final trip across town to their new apartment. Nikki was thinking of how she was closing one door in her life and opening another chapter. Alex on the other hand was terrified she was going to screw up this relationship as she had all the others. Alex pulled up in front of the apartment building and shut off the truck. She turned in the seat to face Nikki.

"Alex, are you sure?" Nikki looked worried.

"Babe, what's wrong? Are you having second thoughts?" Alex was afraid Nikki was regretting their relationship. Possibly the pressure from Millie had finally gotten to her.

"Nikki, we've talked about everything and this is what we both want, right?" Alex was willing her with her thoughts to say yes. If Nikki hesitated, Alex didn't know what she would do.

"No. No second thoughts at all. I was just wondering how you knew you loved me." Nikki looked away sheepishly. She felt foolish for asking.

"Nikki, I just know I love you. I can't picture my life without you in it. I need you so much that if I could keep you with me twenty-four seven, I would. I've been thinking about something for some time. If you wouldn't mind…I don't want you to work any longer. With my schedule, I feel we don't get enough time together, so if you didn't work we could be with one another more."

Alex slid her arm across the seat, running her fingers through Nikki's hair.

"Thanks, honey, and I'll think about the work issue. Mind you, I'm not going to guarantee anything, but we'll talk about it later. Let's get these boxes in then I'll start dinner." Nikki opened the truck door and jumped down.

Alex was already in the bed of the truck with the gate down by the time Nikki got there. "Geez, you're fast." Nikki said, laughing.

Alex returned the laugh as she handed Nikki a box of her clothes. "Long legs are the key. What do you say you take that box in and start dinner while I get the rest into the apartment? Okay?"

Nikki nodded and was on her way.

Nikki could never say no to Alex. Whatever the detective asked of her, she would gladly do. She was unsure how she had fallen so hard or so fast but it didn't matter.

Just as Nikki would give her soul for her lover, the same held true for Alex. She would not only give her life for Nikki, she would destroy any living being that touched or hurt her lover.

Later that evening, while relaxing, they watched old reruns of The Dick Van Dyke Show on cable. Alex propped her feet in Nikki's lap. She pampered Alex by rubbing them.

"Hon, with Mike and Cathy and Scott and Tess coming for dinner tomorrow night, what would you like me to make? I have no jobs lined up for tomorrow so I can make anything you want. I was also thinking about cheesecake for dessert. So, have any ideas?"

Alex pretended to contemplate what she would like. Nikki was a fantastic cook. She could cook anything from Italian to Chinese to Mexican.

"I'm thinking Garlic Chicken and maybe some Kung Pao Shrimp. I love the garlic sauce and vegetables you use, plus you're not stingy on the garlic."

Alex's mouth watered.

"Your Kung Pao Shrimp… mmm… I don't know how you do it. The peanuts never get soft, the sauce is always so spicy and the shrimp. What do you do to the shrimp? They are always perfect. I've tried both of them at the best restaurants and they're never as good as yours. Can you make those for us?" She looked up at Nikki, giving her the smile that always melted her.

Nikki looked down, seeing the Cheshire smile and twinkling eyes. "You already had this all planned out, didn't you? Do I dare ask if the others were involved?"

Nikki chuckled. Alex and Scott probably had the whole menu planned out a week ago. Scott ate at Alex's place any chance he got.

Alex grinned.

"I thought so. Are there any other spontaneous requests? Perhaps some jasmine rice too. How about some very spicy hot and sour soup? Also maybe you would like me to make you the fresh spring rolls that you like so much?" Nikki swatted Alex's stomach as she teased her.

"Yep, that should about do it. However, feel free to make any other items that tickle your fancy. If you make something really special, let's say…mango mousse, you'll be rewarded after everyone leaves." Alex wiggled her eyebrows lecherously.

Nikki swatted her again and left her hand lingering on Alex's thigh. "You are a perv, my love."

Alex covered Nikki's hand with her own. "Ah yes, but I'm your perv. How 'bout I give you a little demonstration of my talents?"

☦

Things had gotten worse between Nikki and her sister since she came out to her. As a direct result of that day, Nikki had not spoken to her sister in a little over four months. Millie wouldn't even permit Alex near her home.

Millie's parting words the day Alex showed up to help Nikki move her belongings were anything but pleasant. It was one of the worst days of Nikki's life. That day she realized she had truly lost the last member of her family.

†

A week before Thanksgiving Nikki unpacked the last of the boxes that she had finally brought up from the storage unit. Looking around, seeing her personal little knick-knacks placed around the room, she finally felt settled into their new home. Alex had left early that morning for work, making it easier for her. This way she didn't have to work around her. Sitting down, Nikki put her feet on the coffee table.

Yay, that's it. I need a shower so I can hit the road to go shopping. Nikki thought of something else. It had been almost a year since she first met Alex.

They were happy even with what Nikki had had to endure from Millie during the past few weeks of living under the same roof as her sister. Going through the turmoil had only bonded their love further.

With only days until Thanksgiving, Nikki ran from one end of town to the other trying to get the things she needed before Alex came home. It made it so much easier to get things done during the day now that she was not working.

However, sometimes she became bored. Nikki liked to work, liked the daily grind of it all. Alex insisted though that she not work. She wanted her to take it easy, not having to worry about anything but their life together.

Alex had rationalized her brainstorm to Nikki. She told her there was no need for her to work because Alex's grandmother had left her a tidy sum of money in her will. She told Nikki that it was more than a million dollars.

Speechless, Nikki tried to argue that if she let Alex support her, Alex's family might think she was only after her money. Alex told Nikki that her family loved her and that they would think no such thing. Even with that in mind, it was still hard for Nikki not to earn her own way.

For two weeks, Nikki stressed about her employment situation before finally coming to a decision. Being honest with herself, she realized she wasn't completely happy with her job. In fact, when it got right down to it, she really didn't like it at all. She found no satisfaction in freelancing as she had in working for one company alone.

When offered the freelancing, Nikki had been desperate. Now that she didn't have to worry about money, she could look for something that really appealed to her. However, first she would take some time off to get their house and lives in order.

Nikki gladly volunteered their home for Thanksgiving dinner. She planned to show Alex's family that she was worthy of Alex's love. She didn't realize how much work it was though. "God, how do the stay at home moms and dads do it? Without going completely insane that is."

Having finished loading her car with the last box from the liquor store, it hit her that this would be her first Thanksgiving without a family member present. Closing the rear door on the car she leaned against it, too stunned to move. Had it been only a few short months since she walked out of her sister's house for the final time? It was like a sucker punch to her system. She thought about how Alex was her family now and her mood picked back up.

†

Nothing in life went the way Nikki had thought it would. She was happy though. She had the woman of her dreams and she was preparing Thanksgiving dinner for her new family, a dinner that was almost ready and still no Alex or Scott.

The house smelled of turkey and hot pumpkin pie. The aroma from the sage in the stuffing and the turkey permeated the senses. It was earthy and wonderful. All the different tantalizing scents made her mouth water, knowing what was in store for dinner. Nikki loved Thanksgiving dinner.

When Nikki took the pie from the oven, everyone salivated. Alex's father, Tony suggested they start with dessert, saving the turkey for later, for which he received a slap on the back of his head from his wife, Alice. "Behave, or you won't get any at all."

Nikki had spent all day cooking. Their guests, having arrived hours before, were enjoying the appetizers she'd made earlier. When Alex had to leave in the wee hours of the morning, she promised Nikki that she would be back in time for dinner.

Alex had been called out to a multiple homicide. The holidays always seemed to bring out the worst in people. It was just human nature, pure and simple.

A man distraught because his family left him sought them out at his in-laws home, shooting them all and killing them. He then turned the gun on himself. He seemed to have forgotten, in his anger, that she was leaving him because she had come home and found him with another woman.

"Ah yes, the holidays, they bring out the best in all of us." Nikki muttered as she retrieved more shrimp and cocktail sauce from the refrigerator. As an afterthought, she grabbed another lime for the margaritas while she was there.

Millie had not returned one of Nikki's phone calls. Nikki hoped that by now she would have calmed down and would be willing to put emotions aside in order to spend Thanksgiving together. No such luck was to be on Nikki's side this holiday. She truly believed that your family is what you make it. Hers was now Alex.

✝

Nikki waited as long as she could to serve dinner. Tessa had fed Tabitha earlier and put her down for a nap. As they were sitting down to eat, Alex walked through the door. Nikki wasn't upset with her, only worried. Alex hadn't called her as she said she would.

With Alex's inconsistent hours, Nikki never started dinner until the detective would call her to say she was on her way home. This however, was a holiday and they had company, so there was no getting around eating on time, not at midnight as they sometimes did.

"Sorry that I'm late everyone. Let me go get cleaned up and I'll be right back." Alex yelled as she entered the bedroom, walking straight through to the bathroom. She stripped out of her clothes, throwing them into the tub, knowing they were going from there right into a trash bag to be disposed of.

Alex had not wanted them to see that she was a wreck. She, Scott and Dom had all ended up covered in blood. When they'd walked into the house, they'd found blood everywhere. Alex and Scott however, became doused with it by different means than the others.

Trying to clean up the best she could at the station, Alex finally gave up and went home. Scott decided to go home to take a shower before continuing to their place. Closing her eyes, memories of earlier that day flooded in.

†

Alex and Scott responded as fast as they could, after the call came in. What they didn't know was that the husband was standing in the kitchen waiting for the police to walk through the house. He stood, biding his time, listening to the officers.

The first responding officer to the domestic disturbance call walked through the open front door when no one answered him. Taking a step through the doorway, he saw the bodies in the dining room and blood everywhere. Quickly, the officer backed out the same way he came in. He called dispatch. After speaking with the sergeant, he waited for back up to arrive.

Sergeant Carson called the two detectives who were on-call for the holiday. "It's a mess, Alex. Scott will meet you there. He's about two minutes out."

"Thanks, Carson. I'm on my way." Alex put on old jeans and a sweatshirt. She kissed Nikki good-bye and was on her way in a few minutes.

When she arrived, she found Scott talking with one of the three officers standing on the front porch. She only personally knew one of the officers. One of the other two was a rookie and the other a transfer from Jake's precinct. She had heard nothing good about the transfer. Alex had heard rumors that he was demoted and transferred as a direct result of a botched investigation.

"Hey Mitchell, it's good to see you. Who's your new partner?"

Mitchell pointed to the young man standing beside him. "This is Officer Tandy, fresh from the academy two weeks ago. That officer there is Officer McBride. He was the first on the scene."

Alex shook her head. Just what she didn't need was a rookie on a holiday murder scene. "So, what have we got?"

Behind her, she heard Dom's van pull up.

Officer Tandy pulled out his notebook. "Detective Canton, we have four bodies and a real mess. It's very bloody in there. Officer McBride checked the rest of the house while I checked the bodies in the dining room. They were all dead upon arrival."

"McBride, give me your blow-by-blow from the moment you arrived until Mitchell got here." Alex didn't trust him.

"I arrived at four thirty-two, found the door open. I called out who I was and why I was here. I received no response so I pushed the door the rest of the way open. I took two steps in and saw the bodies. I quickly checked for a pulse on them. Finding none, I immediately stepped back out and called Sergeant Carson."

Something felt off to Alex. She just couldn't put her finger on it. This man gave her the creeps since the first time she'd met him when she was a rookie.

Dom stepped up behind Alex. "Alex, shall we? I have the missus and a turkey waiting at home."

"Nice to see your priorities are all lined up, Dom. Scott, you ready?" Scott nodded.

"Officer Tandy, McBride, you both stay here and secure the perimeter."

Dom was already snapping pictures as she talked.

McBride could not keep his dislike of the detective quiet after she walked away. "Let the fucking dyke do it. She wants to work in a man's world let her do the fucking disgusting work, not me. All she needs is to be fucked by the right man." He leered at her. "I could help her with that too."

Going off to do the job assigned to him, Officer Tandy ignored the ignorance of the older cop.

"Dom, can you start with the body over there?" Alex pointed to the right side of the room. "I'll get a first look at the ones here."

"Scott, I only see three bodies here. I got a feeling if you follow that you'll find the remaining one." She pointed to the blood on the floor.

Alex stayed in the dining room to look at the bodies there. Thinking McBride had thoroughly checked out the house, Scott followed a bloody trail into the kitchen expecting to find another body.

Swinging open the door, he stood face to face with a man covered in blood holding a gun in one hand and a large knife in the other. Scott backed up two steps into the dining room in the direction he had come from.

"Ah, Alex...."

Looking up as the husband followed Scott into the room, Alex's heart stopped. "Fuck."

Alex slowly stood from a crouching position. She stood motionless. She realized McBride had lied. He didn't check the rest of the house. If he did, he did a piss poor job and it was going to cost them their lives.

Under her breath, Alex muttered, "If we get out of here alive, I'll kill him."

Oh well, I guess today is as good as any to die.

She quickly motioned with her hand for Dom to stay put.

"Listen… let's talk about this, okay? You really don't want to do this."

The man looked at her, then Scott.

Dom pressed himself into the corner behind the sofa. He sent a silent prayer to whatever God would listen, to let them all get out alive.

The man's eyes held a wild animal look, bouncing back and forth between the two detectives, never resting on Dom in the corner of the room.

Alex's eyes were on the gun and the man's finger. One thought whispered from her lips as she watched his finger move. *Nikki, I'm sorry, baby.*

Alex held her breath, not knowing who the man was going to take with him. As he pulled the trigger, Alex and Scott both instinctively dived for the ground. Neither of them cared that they were landing in pools of cold, sticky blood.

Luck smiled upon the two detectives and Dom. The husband had turned the gun on himself.

†

As Alex finished dressing, she looked at the sweet, innocent child sleeping on their bed.

This was the reason they did what they did for a living. Somehow, they had to make a difference. Make it a safer place for the Tabithas of the world to grow up in.

Wow, she's getting so big, she thought. *She's going to be as tall as Scott. Of course, she already has the attitude. Poor Scott and Tess, they have a handful.*

Alex laughed as she realized she took every opportunity to tell them her observation. Tess kept saying she would grow out of it. Alex knew it would be tough going for that to be true. Dom spoiled the little girl rotten, letting her get away with everything. Of course, Aunt Alex was just as bad.

Alex walked into the dining room to join the others. "Hey, everyone, sorry I was gone all day."

She walked around the table and kissed her parents on the cheek. "Mom… Dad...sorry I haven't talked to either of you in a couple of weeks."

Continuing around the table, she hugged Nikki and kissed her on the top of her head. "Hi babe, sorry I was gone so long."

Alex noted the concerned look on Nikki's face. "I'm okay, don't worry," she whispered.

Tess filled the lull in the conversation. "So, I take it Scott will be here shortly?"

Alex sat next to Nikki, with Kirstin on the other side of her.

"Yeah, he should be here in a few. He stopped home to change. I see that little fart in there gets bigger every day. What's in those bottles, Miracle Grow?"

Alex's mother saw her opening to jump into the conversation. "She is just so precious. I'm hoping someday I'll be a grandmother."

Alice looked at Alex. "Oh Alex, get that look off your face. I was hinting at your sister. A grandchild would be great now that your father has decided to take early retirement. With the heart attack last year, we decided he needed to enjoy life more."

Tess provided a diversion from the subject of children. "So Mr. Canton, do you plan on doing any gardening in the spring?"

He passed the potatoes to Alex, who was thankful to Tess for changing the subject. "Please call me Tony. Actually, I have several bags of bulbs to plant before it snows anymore. I haven't had a chance to get to them. I was thinking that in the spring I'll plant a vegetable garden in the back corner."

The door buzzer saved him from Alice's nudging foot.

Tony quietly scolded Alice. "Stop kicking me. I'm not mentioning grandkids again just so you can brag to your friends."

Tony stood. "I'm closest, I'll get it."

Alex was shoving a mouthful of potatoes in. "Thanks, Dad."

This got her swatted on the arm by Nikki. "Don't talk with your mouth full. It's very unladylike."

That earned a snort from across the room. Everyone turned to see Scott walking in the door. "Please, ladylike is one thing she ain't."

Walking around the table, he hugged Nikki, then turned, kissed his wife and sat down to eat.

Over dessert, everyone discussed plans for Christmas. Even though Kirstin's husband Tom was a firefighter and his shift would start after everyone arrived, the decision was made that everyone would get together at Kirstin and Tom's on Christmas Eve. Halfway through dessert, Mike and Cathy finally arrived after visiting Cathy's parents first. They rehashed where Christmas was going to be while enjoying coffee and pastries.

Later that night as they lay in bed, Nikki thought about what Alice said. She remembered the subsequent look on Alex's face. They hadn't talked about children, but it was obvious what Alex thought. Others' were fine as long as she could send them home with their parents at the end of the day.

Nikki, on the other hand, wanted children. She was just unsure how to bring up the subject. Did she drop subtle hints or just jump in with both feet? Nikki knew it was going to be a difficult conversation.

"Alex, I've been thinking about what your mother said about grandchildren. How opposed are you to children, really?"

Alex didn't think the subject would come up so soon. She felt nauseous even thinking about having kids. Somehow, she had to talk Nikki out of the idea without her knowing it. Maybe she could try stalling, for the time being. "Nikki, why don't we talk about this later when we're a little less tired? I'm exhausted."

Nikki laughed. "Well if you hadn't woken Tabitha up, then proceeded to play so rough with her, she wouldn't have puked on you."

Alex winced at the reminder of the vile-smelling goo she had been covered with. It was just one more reason not to have kids. Alex was sure she wasn't going to die at the hands of one of her suspects. Instead, if they had kids, it would be one of them.

"Alex, seriously though, I could tell by the look on your face what you thought of having kids when your mother brought the subject up. Please, for me, don't totally dismiss the idea. I would love to have kids. First, because I love them, second because I would love to give you children and third because I'm the last of my line. I know Millie is never going to have children. So who will carry on the family line? Plus," Nikki snuggled closer. "It would make your mother so happy."

Alex was going to be sick. How could she tell Nikki that no way in hell did she want kids, without breaking her heart?

Her inner voice screamed at Alex to steer Nikki in another direction. What was she going to do? Kids were not on her agenda. They interfered with everything. She would have to tell Nikki what Kirstin called her about the day before. That might make Nikki drop it for the moment.

"Kirstin's pregnant. They found out yesterday." It was out of her mouth before she thought twice about it. Her sister was going to kill her for spilling the beans early.

Nikki sat up, looking down at Alex. "What? Why didn't they say something today?" Alex gently rubbed Nikki's back, slowly, in small circles. "Why didn't you tell me yesterday when she called?"

"She didn't want anyone else to know yet, in case something went wrong and she miscarried again. By Christmas, she should be far enough along to tell Mom and Dad. I'm sorry, baby, I wanted to tell you but you know things got a little crazy last night and this morning."

Nikki laid back down in Alex's arms, enjoying the body heat. "I know, I found the present in the bathroom. Since they were some of your older clothes, I just put them in a garbage bag and put them in the back of your truck for you. Want to talk about it?"

"Maybe tomorrow, babe, I don't want to go into it tonight. I'm not really tired anymore, how about you?" Alex slowly slid her hand up Nikki's thigh, under her nightshirt and felt she was wearing no panties. "Oh, going commando, huh?"

Nikki's own hand strayed. It found its way to Alex's left breast, pinching the already hardened nipple through her t-shirt. "You must have been reading my mind, love."

Hours later Alex still lay awake. Today was too close. She played the talk she was going to have with her captain in her head many times. Her gut instincts told her McBride had lied. Alex knew though that she couldn't prove it. She was not about to sit by while he got someone killed because of his ignorance. Alex planned to talk to Captain Billy in the morning, telling him in detail everything that went down the previous day. She also was going to request he have someone keep a watch on the officer. The captain trusted her instincts and would do as she asked.

†

"My God, woman, are you nuts? You did all of this shopping in one day? Sweet Jesus! There have to be at least thirty bags here. Did the two of you buy out the mall? How did you carry all of this? Did you have to hire a lackey for the day?" Alex was laughing so hard, tears were running down her cheeks.

"Very funny, Alex! We do the mall in sections, moving Mike's truck as we go. I warned you that Mike and I go on a one-day marathon-shopping trip every year. That way we don't have to deal with all those shoppers. I even got something for you, so keep your hands out of those bags."

Nikki smiled, thinking about Alex's presents.

Nikki knew Alex had been looking at the leather bomber jacket for a couple of months. Alex just couldn't bring herself to replace her old worn out one that she'd had since high school. Nikki also thought of the other little surprise she had for Alex in one of the bags.

The two shoppers had great fun when they stopped at the adult store before going to lunch. Nikki found exactly what she was looking for. One was a cool shade of blue and waterproof to boot and the other supple black leather. *Oh yeah, they'll both make great gifts.* Nikki smiled slyly.

"I thought we'd decorate the tree tonight since Mike and Cathy are coming for dinner tomorrow night. I'll make shrimp scampi with fettuccini and a nice salad with all the fixings in it. Oh, I stopped at the grocery store after shopping. We were out of your beloved sunflower seeds and I picked up a few other things while I was there. What do you think about some nice fresh bread to go with dinner tomorrow night?"

Alex unpacked the groceries as Nikki put the wine in the refrigerator. Even though it was still a week before Christmas, it was a matter of storage space in the kitchen. "I hope I got enough wine."

Just as Alex went to ask, Nikki was already a step ahead of her. "Yes, I got your beer. It's in the trunk of the car. Can you get it for me? It's a little heavy."

Alex could tell Nikki was a nervous wreck about their first Christmas together. Nikki had a habit of rambling when she was nervous. She would flit from one subject to the next and not give anyone the chance to answer. Alex knew Nikki wanted everything to be perfect so she wrapped her hands around Nikki's hips, and pulled her tight against her body.

"Baby, relax, everything will be fine. The tree is already up. All we have to do is decorate it. The apartment looks great, all the shopping's done and I love you more every day. Everything is perfect. Our first Christmas will be wonderful. Now, tell me sweetie, what did you buy me for Christmas?"

Nikki swatted her bicep. "You can ask another ten times. I still won't tell you. Go bring in your beer and get over it."

Nikki was still laughing at Alex's antics when she came back through the door with two cases of beer in her arms.

"Okay how 'bout a hint then?"

Nikki picked up the cloth napkin from the counter and threw it at her. "You are incorrigible! Let's bring up the decorations from the storage locker in the basement."

"Sure, just give me a sec. I want to put some of this in the fridge, then I'll be right down to help you."

†

Finally crawling into bed a little after three in the morning, they were exhausted. The apartment was beautiful and Nikki was very proud of what they'd done with the place. She couldn't wait to have company visit so she could show it all off.

When Alex got up at nine-thirty to make coffee Nikki rolled and fell back asleep. "Just let me sleep another hour babe, okay?"

Alex turned from pulling on her boxer shorts and t-shirt to see Nikki already asleep again. Alex always wished she could fall asleep at the drop of a hat. Sometimes she would lay awake for hours. She guessed it came as part of the job or because of it.

Alex's pager went off. "Ah, come on! I'm supposed to be off today. It's Sunday for God's sakes! It's football day." She picked up the pager, looking at the number.

Nikki was semi-awake now. "What's wrong?"

Alex continued looking at the pager. On it was a code that she and Scott used when they needed to relay that something bad and personal was going down. She cleared out the message as fast as she could.

"It's just work, babe, let me give them a call and see what they want." Setting the pager on the dresser, Alex went to the living room to call Scott.

When she hung up the receiver, she had to pry her fingers off it. She looked down at her hand to find her knuckles as white as flour. She hadn't realized she had been grasping it that tightly.

Alex went to the kitchen to be as far away from the bedroom as possible. "Oh God! Oh, shit! How am I going to tell her? She so does not need this right now. She is just now starting to get past the hurt her sister has caused her. I'll just go handle this and think of how to tell her while I'm gone. Shit! This is going to break her heart."

Alex walked into the bedroom as quietly as she could. She hoped that Nikki had fallen back to sleep. Looking at the bed, she saw green eyes staring back at her. She quickly pulled a pair of jeans out of the closet. She could feel Nikki waiting for an explanation.

"That was Scott, there's been a really bad accident involving a drunk driver and they're calling us in since we're the senior detectives. I'll be back as soon as I can, all right?" She leaned, giving Nikki a kiss on the cheek. "Sorry, babe."

Nikki felt there was more to it than she was saying. She could feel the sadness rolling off her. She knew not to push Alex to talk about it though. She would tell Nikki about it when she was ready.

"Please be careful, okay? I don't want to have to throw any more clothes out." Nikki tried to joke to lighten the mood. It remained unheard, as Alex was already halfway to the door.

"Please come home safe," Nikki whispered.

✝

Nikki spent the afternoon preparing everything for dinner that night. Before she knew it,

140

seven hours had passed with still no word from Alex. She could text her but she would only do that if there were an emergency.

When another two hours went by and still nothing, she grew concerned. Nikki was anxious because Mike and Cathy were more than an hour late. After no one answered at their apartment, she called Mike's cell phone. It remained unanswered as well.

Just as Nikki picked up the phone to try Mike again, Alex opened the apartment door. She stepped inside, slowly closing the door behind her, stalling for an extra few seconds. She turned to look at Nikki. When she did, Nikki gasped. Alex looked like she had gone ten rounds in the ring and lost.

Nikki sobbed as she checked Alex carefully head to toe.

Alex looked and felt physically exhausted. She leaned against the doorway so that she wouldn't fall, while Nikki visually examined her. Alex told Nikki to stop fussing, that she was okay, but that she needed a few moments to regroup.

She was pale with dark circles under her eyes, which were extremely red as if she had been crying for hours. Nikki found a goose egg on her forehead. What worried her even more was Alex's bandaged right hand.

Nikki felt nauseous at the thought of Alex being hurt. Nikki loved Alex more than anything in the universe. There wasn't a thing she wouldn't do for her lover. When she had first started going out with Alex, Nikki was so unsure of everything.

The only person she confessed her doubts to was Mike. He, of course, understood fully. He didn't start out loving Cathy but had only wanted friendship. It had eventually grown into more, just as her relationship with Alex had done. She knew she would never find anyone else that would treat her like Alex did.

Alex was wonderful to her. She treated Nikki like a princess, making sure she never wanted for anything. One of the things she loved most was Alex's strength. Not just in a physical sense, but in every aspect of life. There was not a thing that Alex couldn't handle and knowing that, Nikki became extremely worried.

"Hon, sit down. You don't look very good. What's going on? What happened to your forehead and hand?" She knelt beside Alex holding her good hand between hers.

Alex looked at the floor. "Head connected with a wall and fist with someone's face." Alex couldn't look at Nikki.

She didn't want to tell her. She never had these problems telling total strangers bad news. This was different. It was something she was going to have to force herself to do.

"Babe, why don't you sit up here next to me? We need to talk about something." Alex ran her good hand through her hair. She started picking at the bandage on her hand.

"Alex, what's going on? You're scaring me here." Nikki held onto Alex like a lifeline.

"Baby, just remember that I love you more than anything and I'm always here for you when things get bad. I, um, I have some bad news."

The words caught in her throat. Alex was thankful when there was a knock on the door. She hoped it was Scott. She could not do it on her own. Having left the front security door ajar for him, he was only a minute or two behind her.

Nikki stood to answer the door. "You sit still and relax. I'll get it. It's probably just Mike and Cathy running late as usual. I wonder how they got in though." Nikki opened the door to find a haggard looking Scott standing at the threshold. "Oh my God, Scott, what happened to your face? Who hit you?"

Nikki looked at Alex, who looked away from her. She started to the kitchen. "Ah, I see. Why don't you sit down and I'll get you a beer. Do you want to stay for dinner? As soon as Mike and Cathy get here, I'll start dinner. It won't take very long at all to cook, just long enough for the pasta to cook."

Carrying the beers, Nikki walked back into the living room. She stopped in her tracks when she heard the conversation. "Who's dead? What's going on?"

She looked back and forth between the two. "What aren't you telling me?"

"Nikki, come sit down, please." Alex patted the couch cushion next to her. Nikki handed Scott his beer then sat next to Alex. "Nik, there's no good way to tell you this. Mike and Cathy won't be coming tonight. They were involved in a car accident."

Nikki clasped Alex's hand tighter as the tears threatened. She felt what was coming next. Her stomach flipped.

Alex sighed. "Cathy was driving drunk, ran a red light, hitting another car head on. Both had massive internal injuries and died on the way to the hospital. I'm sorry, baby, nothing could be done. Their injuries were too severe. The driver of the other car died instantly. I'm so sorry."

Something inside of Nikki snapped. "No!"

She let go of Alex's hand. "I won't believe this. This is one of his sick jokes that he likes to pull on me. He wouldn't leave me behind."

In complete denial, Nikki turned to Scott. "I'm going to start dinner, will you be staying?" She stood waiting for his reply.

"Ah… Sure. I'll just call Tess to let her know where I am." He went into Alex's den, to use the phone.

Upon his return, he found Alex resting her head in her hands. Sitting back down, he polished off his beer.

Alex looked at him. "This is so fucked up. I knew she would take it hard, but not this badly. They were closer than twins. Nikki's going to be even more upset when she finds out I'm on suspension. How am I going to help her through this if I can't control my temper?" Alex looked at Scott, hoping he had some answers.

"First thing you're going to do is not lose that temper of yours again. I don't think my face can take it or the wall in the captain's office. Plus, I don't think your hand is doing too well either."

Alex grimaced at Scott. "Well, I didn't ask your face to get in the way. Such a stupid loss! By the way, thanks for coming by and for staying for dinner. When it hits her, it's going to be bad."

Scott would support both of them through anything. "She's strong Alex, stronger than most people give her credit for."

Nikki yelled from the kitchen that dinner was ready and to come get what they wanted to drink.

Dinner was very quiet. Most of the conversation revolved around Tabitha and what all of them were getting for Christmas. Nikki was getting dessert from the kitchen when Alex told her she was going to call Millie to let her know what happened. She knew Nikki was in rough shape, so she made the call. Alex came back into the dining room swearing up a storm.

Scott gave her a puzzled look. "What's going on?"

"Her sister is such a bitch! God, if they gave a name to the witch that got the house dropped on her, they would call her Millie. I don't think I've ever met a nastier person in my life."

Nikki came in from the kitchen. "What did she do now? She just doesn't know when to keep her mouth shut!" Nikki threw the apple pie down and slammed the coffee carafe on the dining room table.

Alex didn't want to upset her further. They'd agreed though from the beginning never to lie to one another, no matter how hard it was on the other to hear the truth. "I told her what happened and her response was, well, less than polite. Nikki, you really don't need to hear this right now. We'll talk about it later."

Nikki shook her head. "No, I want to know. " She sighed, resigning herself to the fact that her sister was the cruelest person she had ever had the displeasure of knowing.

Alex cringed. She sat down, taking a long drink of her beer. "She, uh, said that she won't be going anywhere near the funeral. She feels they deserved what they got for having anything to do with us."

Nikki calmly sat her coffee cup back on the dining room table. "Oh I see. I, um, I forgot the creamer for the coffee, I'll be right back." She abruptly fled to the kitchen. First, they heard the refrigerator door slam, then they heard one crash after another. Alex and Scott both ran to the kitchen, almost knocking one another off their feet in the process. Alex was through the door first, then Scott. What they found was Nikki throwing everything that was not too heavy to lift across the kitchen.

Alex saw in her eyes a mixture of anger and something else she knew all too well, a sense of aloneness. She knew Nikki would snap but didn't think it would be so soon. Scott stayed in the doorway as Alex slowly made her way to her lover. She didn't want to approach her too fast. She knew Nikki had a little bit of a temper but never knew she was capable of losing control like this. A coffee cup flew by Alex's head, crashing against the wall behind her.

Nikki picked up another cup. In her rage, she wasn't aiming at anyone or thing in particular, only what happened to be in her way. "Damn bitch. Why can't she just for once be a decent human being?"

She launched the cup across the room, immediately picking up a salad plate. This time Alex unfortunately didn't duck in time. The cup hit her in the shoulder, the plate in the chest. Both crashed to the floor.

Alex thought she would have run out of steam by now. Nikki however was just getting started as she picked up more dishes. "The bitch killed him. How could she do that? How could he let her do it? How could he do this to me?"

Flying across the room next was a bowl, which Alex swiftly caught with both hands as it sailed by her. Slowly she had been making her way to where Nikki stood by the counter. Standing by her side, Alex calmly put her hand on Nikki's arm. It was then that Alex realized her lover had not even acknowledged her presence in the room.

When Alex touched her, it startled Nikki back to reality. She looked around the room at the war zone of broken dishes.

"What the hell?" She looked at Alex.

"Baby, why don't we go back into the living room and sit. Okay? She is not worth destroying everything we own. Come on, let's go sit down." Alex put her arm around Nikki's waist, pulling her toward the living room.

After quickly cleaning up the broken dishes, Scott took their cups and the carafe into the living room. He sat sipping his coffee as Alex coaxed Nikki back to the couch. Nikki laid her head upon Alex's shoulder. She let herself be held as tears fell onto Alex's shirt, leaving a growing wet spot.

They stayed that way for what seemed like hours when actually only ten minutes had passed. Alex pulled several tissues from the box and wiped Nikki's face.

"Thanks, love." Nikki looked at the wet spot on Alex's shirt. "I'm sorry, hon. I made your shirt soggy."

Alex looked down, noticing the spot. "Don't worry, it'll dry. Are you feeling a little better now? Please don't take to heart what she says. She's a miserable, lonely woman. I don't think she can stand to see anyone else happy. Mike's mother said she would call us tomorrow with the details of the funeral. We should just relax, think about happier things and enjoy Scott's company. I love you, babe."

Alex caressed the side of Nikki's face. She leaned in, placing a gentle kiss on her lips. "Babe, why don't you take one of those pills that knocks you out? You'll feel better if you sleep for a while."

†

Nikki fell asleep with her head on Alex's lap. Scott had discarded the coffee. Now they both sat drinking beer, their favorite beverage of choice, while they talked. "I tell you, Scott, I feel like going there and pounding some sense into Millie. I really don't give a damn how she treats me, but she has no right to treat Nikki like this. She's done everything for that bitch and none of it has mattered. It makes my blood boil to think how she's treated her these past five months."

Scott gulped down the remaining half of his beer. "You want another one?"

Alex nodded.

Scott went to retrieve two fresh beers from the fridge.

Alex looked down at Nikki who remained sound asleep. She gently brushed the hair that had fallen across Nikki's face back behind her ear. She ran her knuckles down the side of her face and let her fingertips linger on her lover's face.

Alex didn't hear, but felt Scott come back into the room. She continued to study Nikki's facial features, already knowing them by heart. She took the beer from him. She quickly downed three-quarters of the bottle.

"She's so innocent and naive really. Everyone sees this tough exterior, but she doesn't let anyone inside. She's been hurt so much already in her life. Sometimes when she's sleeping, I can see the hurt and the fear. She doesn't know it shows and I won't ever tell her. I just wish there was something I could do to take away all the pain and heartache she's feeling right now."

After putting down the now empty bottle, she slowly stood with her lover in her arms. Quietly, she motioned to Scott where she was going. Making sure Nikki didn't awaken, Alex tucked her in bed. Retrieving two fresh beers from the kitchen, she returned to the couch in the living room. Alex leaned her head on the back of the couch, looking at Scott.

"Got any ideas, my old friend?"

Scott stretched out in the black leather recliner with his beer resting on his thigh. "Support her, that's the number one key to this mess. 'Cause she's going to need it, even though she may not show it. You got yourself a fine woman there."

Scott contemplated what he was going to say next. He didn't want to piss her off, but it had to be said.

"Alex, you and I are best friends, right?" Alex nodded. "Okay, we've always been straight with one another. That's why I have to say this. Don't mess up this relationship. Ah, not a word 'til I'm finished. I think that woman of yours loves you more than anything in the world." He paused putting the rest of his thoughts together, the beer slowing the process a little.

"So anyway…don't hurt her is what I'm trying to say. I say that because I saw the way you looked at that blonde the other day. You looked at her like she was your next meal."

Alex had an outraged look on her face.

"Don't give me that look, Alex. I've known you for years now. I feel I have a bond with you that I don't even have with my own wife and child. If you're completely honest with yourself, you contemplated what it would have been like to sleep with her. Am I right?"

He sat waiting for her response. He finished his beer in the minutes that passed.

Alex seemed lost in thought until she looked at him, shaking her head. "Fine… You're right. I was thinking along those lines. She was a hell of a good looking woman." Alex smiled, thinking of the petite blonde.

Scott could feel it in his bones that Alex was having an internal war.

"Alex, don't… If you're not completely happy with Nikki, walk away now. If you want this to work, then don't even let thoughts about screwing another woman into your mind. Because if you do cheat on her and hurt her… I really feel you'll do irreparable damage. I think her heart has been broken several times before. Can you truly give up playing the field in order to be with her? What if she wants you two to get married? What about children? Have you two discussed those items? I'm just being the little devil inside your head."

"I'd marry her someday. However, kids I don't know about. I don't even want to think about any of that right now. I just want to help her get through the next few days and Christmas. I'm going to focus on that and only that. God, I hope she likes what I got her. Thanks again for helping me pick it out."

Alex's eyes twinkled when she thought of the jewelry box sitting next to her gun in the safe.

"Alex, my friend, you can never go wrong with jewelry, always remember that. It'll come in handy during the next, say oh, forty years. Especially, every time you get yourself in trouble." Scott laughed so hard, he almost dropped the fresh beer he had just picked up.

"I hope she likes it. I'm glad I went with the sapphires set in platinum instead of emeralds, even though they would have gone with her eyes. I think she'll like the blue better."

Scott thought about her choice. "I think you made the perfect choice buying the sapphire bracelet. Tess is going to be jealous though, 'cause all she's getting is a new washer and dryer."

Alex cringed. "Ouch. Did you at least get her something little?"

He shook his head. "We can't afford it with having to buy Tabitha stuff, including all new winter clothes. She's growing way too fast."

"Scott, if you need money to buy Tess something I'll loan it to you. Just let me know how much."

Alex polished off another beer and set the bottle on the end table, next to the other three empties. Knowing it was going to be a long night,

Alex ran to the kitchen, grabbed two fresh beers and was back before Scott barely knew she was gone.

Scott couldn't stop the shiver that went through his body. Looking at Alex, he laughed when she had the same reaction. "No, I can't do that. She knows things are tight right now. She would kill me if I suddenly bought her something. Then she'd come after your ass for giving me the money. No, we don't want to open that can of worms, thanks anyway though."

"No, Scott, we definitely don't want that. You ended up spending two weeks on my couch because of borrowing that money for her engagement ring. That was on top of her not talking to me for another two weeks after that. I think this time it would be worse though. 'Cause you know Nikki would side with Tess and we'd both be in trouble. And, we're going to try to avoid bringing down the wrath of both of them at the same time as much as possible."

They both sat laughing well into the night, reminiscing about all the bad scrapes they'd gotten one another out of during the years.

Chapter Four

The Gifts of Love and Trust

Cathy's funeral was two days before Mike's. Nikki couldn't bring herself to attend, blaming her for taking away her best friend. Mike had helped her through so much. She didn't know how she was going to cope without him. She had Alex, but it wasn't the same.

Mike's funeral was the typical long Italian variety. It was complete with a two-hour mass, including the traditional incense. Alex's anxiety grew when she saw the priest putting the incense into the cauldron. She hated the stuff with a passion with good reason. The doctors called it a severe allergic reaction. She called it hell. Alex had lived through it twice before and she didn't care to repeat it.

Incense caused such a reaction she couldn't breathe. Reaching into her jacket pocket, she came up empty. "Shit."

Alex rapidly checked all her pockets. She remembered setting it on the console between the two front seats. Knowing how rude it would be to stand and leave, she waited. The second the service was finished, she would have to get to her truck for the inhaler.

All stood as the casket was wheeled slowly down the aisle. Alex whispered to Nikki that she needed her inhaler.

"I thought you had it with you."

"So did I." Within mere seconds, she was wheezing.

The casket, with the priest next to it, stopped for a moment at the aisle in front of Alex. She gasped for breath. Alex knew she had to get out of there, but the large woman on the other side of her wouldn't move.

When the woman finally moved it was too late. Alex doubled from lack of oxygen. Everyone around them was aware that something was wrong. Alex dropped to the pew, putting her head in her hands, trying to get her chest under control. Scott had been sitting farther back. Pushing his way through to them, he couldn't understand why Alex wasn't using her inhaler. *Why hasn't she gotten out of the church*?

When Scott reached them, Nikki thrust Alex's keys into his hands. "Her inhaler is in the truck. Hurry, Scott, she can't breathe." Nikki was frantic with worry. "Alex, we need to get you out into the fresh air. Can you stand up?"

When Alex shook her head no, two men from the pew ahead of them helped her to her feet. One of them told everyone to move out of the way. The two men, one on either side of her, helped her down the aisle toward the door, where Scott met them with the inhaler.

A few moments later, Alex started to breathe better, feeling like a fool. She thanked the two men. Handing them her business card, she told them to call if they ever needed anything. If they were shocked to find out she was a cop, they didn't show it.

"It's no big deal, detective. It's an everyday occurrence for me. I'm a doctor and glad I could be of help."

"Well, thanks anyway. Like I said if you ever need anything, call me."

The other attendees were getting into their cars to head to the cemetery. Scott, Alex and Nikki headed toward their car.

"Damn, that's the worst reaction I've ever had. I don't think it's something I care to have ever happen again. For a moment there, I thought I was a goner."

Nikki squeezed Alex's hand. "Darling, don't even joke about that. I don't plan on giving you up for a very long time."

Alex frowned, knowing they needed to have that talk soon. *I live a dangerous life. Being a cop, the next bullet could easily be mine. I tried to bring it up before but she didn't want to discuss it. Very soon, baby you're going to have to understand. That coffin they were putting in the ground very easily could be mine. I'm a target for all the crazies out there.*

†

With the passing of Mike and Cathy, Christmas Eve festivities changed to everyone gathering on Christmas Day at Alice and Tony's home. Alex agreed with her father that Nikki would need one on one time with her on Christmas Eve. Besides, it was their first Christmas as a couple. It was supposed to be a happy and special time. Alex did everything in her power to make it a wonderful day for Nikki.

Half past eleven the night before Christmas found the lovers snuggled together on the leather sofa facing the tree. Looking through the window, one would think they were looking at the perfect Norman Rockwell picture. It was a picture of a loving couple sitting, noticing only one another, enjoying the lighted tree on Christmas Eve.

Nikki hadn't been herself the two weeks since Mike's funeral. Alex tried to draw her out, to comfort her. Nikki just withdrew even more, especially the night Alex came home with a bruise on her cheek and a small limp.

Nikki hadn't even asked Alex what had happened. Normally, she would've been fretting about her the second she walked in the door. That was two days ago.

Enjoying the evening in front of the tree, they shared a bottle of Nikki's favorite wine. Alex stroked Nikki's hair, pushing a loose strand behind her ear. "I love this hair cut on you. It's so adorable. It makes it easier to run my fingers through it."

Nikki turned in Alex's arms, looking up at her. Alex saw the smile on her face, the first one in two weeks. "Thanks. I was hoping you would like it. I needed a change."

"That's why you asked me the other day if I liked that girl's haircut. The brunette at the gas station, right?" Alex smiled, remembering how hot looking the girl was.

"Yeah, I liked her hairstyle and tried to have my hairdresser copy it. You don't think it's too short, do you? I mean, if it is, I'll grow it back out."

She fingered the edge of her hairline by her ear, hoping that Alex really did like it.

"Babe, don't worry, I like it." Alex caught Nikki's fingers with her own. "I like it a lot. Now, do you want to open gifts tonight or in the morning?"

Nikki laid her head on Alex's chest, snuggling back into her arms.

"It doesn't matter to me, darling. It might be a little crazy tomorrow, with going to your parent's house and everything. If you want, you can start with the big blue one with the white snowflakes on it."

Nikki's eyes twinkled when she thought of the fun she had picking out the gifts for Alex. Then she remembered who she had spent the day shopping with. Reality hit home once more when she realized Mike would no longer be there for her to call.

Alex got up, walked to the tree and picked up two boxes. One box she handed to Nikki, the other with her name on it, she opened. Alex was shocked when found inside the box the leather jacket she had been looking at a few months before.

Nikki opened hers to find the lithograph that she had been eyeing in the gallery. Alex hugged and kissed her for the jacket. She tried it on. It was a perfect fit, as if it had been tailor made just for her.

"Oh Alex, it fits perfectly. Do you really like it?" She ran her hand down Alex's arm.

"I love it, thanks so much. This gives me a reason to get rid of the old nasty one I have."

Nikki smiled, thinking about what was in the final box. "Thank you for the print, it's wonderful. Why don't you grab the silver box?"

Alex pulled the top off the box. She couldn't believe her eyes. "Oh. My. God. Nikki! Leather pants." Alex pulled them out of the box only to find a couple more surprises.

"Nik!" Alex pulled out a black leather harness, a flesh colored dildo and a blue vibrator from the bottom of the box. Alex sat admiring her gifts as Nikki opened her other gift.

"I uh, know you have a toy chest but I wanted things that were ours only."

She couldn't believe Nikki would buy something like this. Sure Nikki was a little wild and a little loud, but Alex was unsure if her lover would be into this kind of thing. Alex had hoped she was but she wasn't going to suggest it until they'd been together a little longer.

Alex handed Nikki a small oblong box. Opening it, she found the most beautiful bracelet she'd ever seen. With her hands shaking badly, Nikki couldn't get the clasp open.

"Oh Alex, it's beautiful, I love it. It seems I'm having a little problem with the clasp. Will you help me on with it?"

Alex grasped her wrist gently. She draped the bracelet around Nikki's wrist, locking the clasp in place. Moving her wrist around, Nikki watched the lights from the tree twinkle on the sapphires.

"Oh Alex, thank you so much." Nikki noticed Alex had been a little quiet since opening her gift. "So, ah, Alex, how do you like the pants? Care to model them for me?"

A lecherous look crossed Alex's face. "Oh yeah, I am. I'm going to model them for you all right." Then she would thank Nikki properly for the gifts. Alex silently wondered if she bought any of the stuff to go with it.

Alex smiled at her. "Why don't you get our stockings, babe?"

Nikki retrieved their stockings from the doorknobs. She handed Alex hers then looked in her own. For a moment, Alex watched her pull out all of the little items she had picked up at her favorite bath and body shop.

Alex reached into her stocking. What she pulled out made her pulse race. She pulled several packages of non-latex condoms and trial sizes of flavored lube. The condoms were to keep the toys clean. "This is going to be fun!"

"Oh babe, perfect. You got an assortment of everything. We'll just have to experiment to find out what you like best."

Nikki reached out, touching the side of Alex's face. "What *we* like best." Nikki smiled, warmth starting in her stomach spreading downward.

"I think I'll go try these on now. I'll be back out in a few."

Alex stood, walking through the bedroom into the bathroom, taking the box with her. She stopped only a second to pull a t-shirt from the drawer. Closing the bathroom door behind her, she pulled the leather pants from the box, laying them on the toilet lid. She set the remaining items on the counter.

She stepped out of her Docs and pants. Pulling her boxers and socks off, she threw them on the floor with her pants. After straightening the harness, she stepped into it. She adjusted the straps and stepped into the leather pants, only pulling them up three quarters of the way.

Alex inserted the dildo into the harness.

God, I'm so wet already, just thinking about using this on Nikki. I can't believe she bought this. It looks a little large. I wonder if we should start out with a smaller one. Then we could work up to the really large one in my drawer. I can't wait to use that one on her. I'm actually dripping.

Alex reached down to adjust the harness and dildo. She brushed her fingers along her outer lips close to her clit. Having no willpower, she touched herself again. She ran her fingers across her swollen clit into the wetness.

"Jesus! I'm like a river. Another stroke or two and I'll come. Ah, that feels so good. I have to wait. I want to be inside her when I come."

Taking her fingers away, she pulled the pants the rest of the way up. Carefully tucking the dildo in, she zipped them. It was a bit of a tight fit with the harness and dildo, but she knew they wouldn't be on for very long.

Pulling on a black muscle tee shirt, she looked at herself in the mirror.

"Damn, I look good!"

Opening the door, she stepped into the bedroom, took two steps and stopped.

Alex was in awe. The room smelled of oranges and apples. Placed around the room were lit candles, the room's only light. It was enough to see the woman standing at the foot of the bed.

Alex appraised Nikki, starting at her legs. They were covered in white fishnet stockings. Letting her gaze travel farther up, she saw a white lacy garter belt. Under the garter belt was a white lacy thong panty. Her eyes continued up to find a beautiful white lace bodice. Nikki was completely dressed in white. The only color on her body, the sapphire bracelet around her wrist. Alex looked her up and down one more time. She stood planted in place.

"Sweet Jesus, you're hot!"

"All for you, only you. Forever. I belong to you." Nikki strode slowly to Alex, standing just out of arms reach. "Dance with me, my love."

Alex noticed the low classical music playing. They stepped into one another's arms. Nikki laid her head on Alex's chest as they swayed to the music. Alex looked in the dresser mirror at the two of them together.

It was like a sight out of medieval times. The tall warrior dressed all in black and the virgin maiden all in white. "You planned this, didn't you?"

Nikki smiled.

"You've taken my breath away tonight. I don't know how you do it, but I love you more every day. You're the light and I'm the darkness. You brought me back my life. For that alone I will love you forever."

Alex pressed her hips against Nikki. That was when Nikki felt it. "Ooh, what do we have here? Hmm?" She caressed down the zipper to between Alex's legs. "So tell me, what do you plan on doing with this? I kinda like it under the leather pants. God... how I love leather."

Alex grabbed Nikki's wandering hand, moving it back up to her waist. "Babe, please don't do that. It's more than I can take right this second. I want this night to last and if you continue doing that, I'll come right here and now. I just want to dance with you and hold you for a while."

"Okay, I'll be good, for now."

Nikki had the most wonderfully wicked look on her face. It did nothing but turn Alex on all the more. She had figured out what Alex liked, rough sex and her woman submissive. Nikki's heart told her Alex was the only one who had ever truly loved her. She would do whatever was necessary to keep her happy.

Alex shook her head. "Babe, you're trying to kill me here!"

As they danced, Alex nibbled on her neck, caressing her backside in a circular motion. Each nibble was a little harder, causing Nikki's moans to be a little louder. She could sense the desire building within Nikki.

Unfortunately, Alex was beyond excited, almost to the brink of breaking. She wanted to make love to Nikki slowly and tenderly. However, she didn't know if she could hold back her own desire just to take her, to make her scream repeatedly.

A ribbon held the bodice of Nikki's outfit together. Alex bowed her head, taking one of the ends of the bow between her teeth and pulling. The bow slowly loosened, coming untied. Moving her hand up, Alex freed the ribbon, lips following her fingers.

She kissed the valley between Nikki's breasts. Alex slowly pulled the lace down Nikki's left breast to reveal a nipple so erect it had to ache. Alex kissed around it, but did not touch it. She drove Nikki mad.

Nikki tilted her head back as she pushed her breast up farther. Just as Alex took her nipple between her lips, Nikki pressed her body hard against Alex.

Alex gently bit down as she simultaneously sucked on it. Nikki gasped. "Yes! Please!"

Releasing the nipple, Alex licked it. "Please what, baby?"

"Please." Nikki pleaded needing the contact, needing the pleasure. Alex licked it again only slower this time.

"Oh God, Alex. Harder."

She gladly obliged.

Nikki knew she wouldn't be able to stand much longer. Nor could she hold out much longer before she would scream for Alex to take her. Alex bit harder, alternating between licking and biting. She had both hands on Alex's head, holding her in place. Her need was beyond control. "Suck it baby, hard."

Alex squeezed Nikki's right butt cheek hard as she sucked her nipple into her mouth. She was afraid she was going to hurt her.

Nikki urged her on. "Oh. Yes!"

Alex could take it no longer. She wanted Nikki under her now. "The hell with slow! I've got to fuck you now."

The words finally sunk in when Nikki heard Alex growl as she picked her up and threw her onto the bed. Nikki automatically spread her legs as she looked up at Alex.

Nikki pulled the thong panties to the side, exposing her dripping center. "I need you Alex, I need you inside now!"

Alex pulled the zipper down, slipping out of her pants as fast as she could. She took the last step to the edge of the bed. Reaching to the bedside table, Alex ripped open a condom, quickly slipping it onto the dildo. She didn't add any lube. Nikki was dripping wet. She looked down at her beautiful lover, lying on the bed waiting. Waiting and begging to be taken.

"I know what you want and need. I can see it in your eyes, in your mouth and especially here." With that, Alex pushed into her in one fluid motion.

"Yes. Oh, Alex!"

She slowly pulled out, just leaving the tip touching her opening. She looked down, finding Nikki staring down to where their bodies met. She looked up at Alex. "Please, Alex, more."

"More of what, my love?" Alex loved to tease Nikki, prolonging the fun.

She slowly slid in then back out again. Hovering, barely touching her.

"Take me please. Do it!"

Alex matched Nikki's thrusts with her hips, going faster with every plunge. Nikki's body was on fire. She needed to come. She couldn't hold it back much longer. She wanted it hard and fast tonight. Nice and slow could come later. The words harder and faster was all she could get out with what little breath she had.

Any shred of control Alex had was now gone as she pushed hard into her lover. "Harder and faster what? Tell me!"

Being in control made her feel powerful, made her push boundaries. Alex pushed Nikki's legs open so wide that they lay almost flat on the bed.

Alex pulled out then thrust in harder. "Tell me. Or I stop!"

The words ripped from Nikki's lungs. "Fuck me harder!" That was when she heard it, the growl that started deep inside Alex. Nikki had never heard anything like it.

"You want it harder, baby? I'll give you harder!"

With a motion so swift Nikki never knew what was happening until it was done, Alex pulled out of her then flipped her on her stomach. She pulled Nikki up onto all fours with her ass sticking up high in the air. She quickly spread Nikki's legs apart and rammed into her.

"I'll fuck you like you've never had it before! When you scream, the world will hear you baby."

Alex rammed into her so hard and fast that all the air was pushed from her lungs. It was an unreal feeling for both of them. Nikki had never been taken this way before. She had never had a dildo used on her. It was unbelievable. She had never felt anything so wonderful in her life.

It was a first for Alex, also. She had never wanted to possess any woman so completely before. She had never wanted to give anyone all of herself.

"Oh God, Alex, oh God! Yes…yes—"

Alex could feel her coming, which set off her own orgasm. As it ripped through her, she thought she saw stars.

She could hear Nikki crying out. She was like a wild animal set free. "Can you feel it, Alex? Don't stop!" She couldn't stop yelling. She wanted more. Nikki could feel another even bigger orgasm coming.

Alex could feel everything. It was as if the world was spinning. "You belong to me. You're mine to do with what I want. Anything I want."

"Yes, yours… all yours... Yes!" The orgasm tore through her causing Nikki to collapse onto the bed. Alex fell spent on top of her, unable to move.

Nikki had been reborn. Never in her life had she felt so loved.

It was some time before either could talk, let alone move. Both were overwhelmed with what had just happened. Alex slowly rolled off her and pulled Nikki's head onto her chest. Alex couldn't even find the words to describe how she was feeling.

Nikki's hand started drawing lazy circles around Alex's right nipple. It immediately sprang to life. She pinched it and Alex groaned. "Hmm, seems my detective is still a little excited. Let me see what I can do about that."

Nikki released the harness, sliding it down Alex's legs.

The sudden loss of pressure against her throbbing clit was painful. Nikki threw the harness onto the floor, holding up the dildo for Alex to see. She ran it down across Alex's stomach just to the edge of her hairline. She teased her further by brushing the dildo lightly down her inner thigh, then back up, positioning it just above her opening.

Alex opened her legs as wide as she could. Leaning over her, Nikki smelled Alex's excitement.

"God, you smell good." Her eyes locked with Alex's. "Yes?" Nikki asked.

"Do it!"

Unable to deny her any longer, Nikki thrust it into her, burying it completely. Alex's body thrashed and arched high above the bed.

Nikki hesitated, thinking she was going to hurt her.

"Harder. You won't hurt me."

Nikki continued taking Alex harder with every thrust. Alex's body stiffened as she felt the waves roll through her. Her body collapsed back onto the bed.

Wanting to give Alex the same kind of pleasure she had given her, Nikki whispered, "Hold that thought, honey. I'll be right with you."

Nikki slid off the bed, retrieved the harness from the floor. She adjusted it then inserted the dildo into place.

Alex knew what Nikki was going to do. She wanted it as bad as Nikki wanted to give it to her. She wanted something else however. Did she dare ask for it? Would it freak Nikki out hearing what else she wanted? Alex thought that maybe she could get Nikki to think of it on her own. She rolled onto her stomach then onto all fours. She could see that Nikki was ready and something else, a little scared. "You'll do fine, babe. Why don't you put some lube on it okay?"

Nikki did as Alex suggested. She stepped up behind Alex. Alex moved her ass up and down so the dildo was rubbing against her back opening.

"Oh, that feels good." Alex hoped this would tell her what she wanted.

Nikki noticed where it was touching Alex. She was a little afraid. She remembered seeing a smaller one in the drawer beside the bed. Retrieving the smaller dildo, she inserted it in place of the bigger. Putting a condom on it, she applied lube generously.

Back behind Alex, she applied a little more pressure. Alex immediately responded. "Oh yeah."

"Do you like what I'm doing, love? Do you want me to continue?" She pressed a little harder.

"Yes, oh yes. Pour some of the lube on me and enter slowly." Alex felt the liquid trickle down between her cheeks.

Alex felt the exquisite pressure of being entered slowly. "Oh yes, baby. That's it, a little more."

Nikki pushed a little farther in, having no problem because of all the lube. Alex knew she would have to walk her through the first time.

Alex couldn't help but wiggle her ass a little to get it farther in. "Oh yeah, that's it. Farther, you won't hurt me. Don't be afraid. Okay, pull it out then push it back in a little farther than it was. Oh, yes. That feels good. Keep that up, go a little farther each time. You're doing great. Oh, yes, just like that! A little faster."

Alex could feel it building fast. She knew this one was going to blow her away. Soon Nikki was thrusting in and out much faster. She could feel the orgasm start. "Oh God, baby, fuck me, yes!"

It did indeed blow her away, she came the closest she ever had to passing out from the ecstasy.

Alex lay spent on the bed, watching Nikki take off the condom and dispose of it. She took off the harness and dildo, setting it on the bedside table. Nikki crawled into bed beside her.

She lay in amazement. Nikki had never felt anything so incredible in her life. It wasn't just the mind-blowing orgasms, but also the trust that Alex had in her. Nikki realized she could've done anything to her and Alex would have loved it. That, she knew was real commitment, real trust. Real love. She wanted to ask Alex what it had felt like to be taken like that but she was too shy.

Nikki curled up in Alex's arms. Tilting her head slightly, she brushed her lips against Alex's. "Oh Alex, I didn't think it could get much better, but wow, I feel so completely loved."

Kissing the top of Nikki's head Alex tightened her hold on her. She rested her head on top of Nikki's. "Oh babe, I can guarantee it's going to keep getting better. I'm so glad that you bought this when the two of you went shopping."

Alex could feel Nikki's body tense. "It's okay, babe, I miss him too. It'll get better in time."

Nikki curled her fingers around Alex's. "I miss him so much. We used to do everything together and we knew everything about one another.

We could talk about anything. It took me so long to trust him, but he managed to drag every little thing out of me. When I first met him, I was depressed and didn't like life that much. We talked forever, then, when I thought he'd just drop the subject, he'd get in my face about it again and not let up."

Nikki's body shook a little, feeling the grief settling in once more.

"Nik, I'm here. I always will be. Anytime anything bothers you, I'm always here for you. I know we haven't talked much about your youth but I want to know everything about you. I want the good right along with the bad. Nothing you could ever tell me would make me love you any less."

"Oh Alex, what did I ever do to deserve you? I do trust your love, but please understand there are some things that I've never shared with anyone ever, except Mike. He was the only one and even that took a lot of prying and booze. I would never wish my childhood on anyone. Not even my worst enemy."

Alex propped herself up against the headboard, plopping a pillow behind her. Motioning for Nikki to join her, Alex pulled the sheet up onto their laps. She put her arm around Nikki's shoulder and held her tight. With her other hand she intertwined their fingers.

"Tell me something about your mother. Oh, and babe, we'll discuss that tattoo on your butt that wasn't there yesterday later. Okay?"

Nikki made herself comfortable, resting her head on Alex's chest. "So you like it, huh? I thought it was kinda cool. It is really quite the perfect symbol for us, the yin/yang symbol. So, my mother, hmm…Grace Mildred Christian, what can I say, she was a saint. I loved my mother. Picture a five-four, green-eyed German, no shit kinda woman. I tell you, she suffered no fools, but she would never really say anything bad about anyone. She took after grandpa in that respect. He also was a kind, gentle and loving man. I was his favorite out of everyone.

"Mom passed away when I was fourteen. When she was alive, I never wanted for anything. She always got me the cutest little things for Christmas and my birthday. For every holiday, she would always make me a new, frilly dress. Of course, that dress would only stay clean for about two hours. It was usually filthy and tattered by the end of the night.

"She used to get so flustered with me. Mom would always buy me dolls and things like that, but I always wanted to play with my cousin's dump trucks and fire engines."

She paused reflectively.

"She was the pillar of the family. Everyone loved her. Don't get me wrong. I had my rebel stage at about the age of eleven but it lasted all of about five minutes.

"You've got to understand, I hated my step-father so much that I never wanted to be around the house if he was there. All I wanted to do was go hang out on the streets with my friends. Yes, I learned to be a bit of a hellion at an early age. It wasn't that I hated him because he was my stepfather. I hated the man because he was pure evil. But, I don't want to go there right now."

Nikki sat up and looked Alex directly in the eye.

"My first and only defiance against my mother was extremely short lived. Dad, yes, believe it or not, I actually called that man Dad, was home and it was the day before Mom and I were going to visit relatives in New York, like we did every summer, just the two of us. So anyway, I was already in a bad mood because of him and because I wouldn't be able to see my two best friends until Thanksgiving. When I was scheduled to return, they would be leaving to go back to their dad's in Denver. Mom had asked me to switch the load from the washer to the dryer and bring the clothes upstairs that were in the dryer and fold them.

"Well, of course I didn't want to because I wanted to go up the street to my friend's house. So, I was pissy and, oh, did I mention my mother's hormones were raging? Well, they were because she was pregnant."

Alex went to ask the question, but Nikki put her fingers on her lips to stop her.

"I'll tell you later about it. So, I was being pouty and pissy in the living room when I heard her calling from the basement. I ignored her. Then I heard her coming up the steps and thought I should at least make an effort. So I headed to the kitchen. She met me halfway and asked me why I didn't do what she asked."

Memory filled Nikki's mind.

"Nikkoletta McLoud, didn't I ask you to take care of the laundry for me?"

"I know, Mom, but I want to go see Sara and Missy, 'cause they'll be gone when we get back. Come on, Mom, please?"

Nikki's whining grated on her mother's final nerve. "Nikki, you got to spend the whole summer with them. You'll see them again in a couple of months. Now, I need your help so we can leave first thing in the morning."

Nikki shifted her feet but still didn't budge. "Mom, I want to go visit my friends now, not in a couple of months."

Her mother's patience snapped. "Nikki, go to your room, I'm tired of this. I'm not going to argue with you."

She pointed to the steps and picked up the laundry basket.

"No! I'm going and you can go to hell!"

✝

Alex looked horrified, then amused.

"Oh yes, you guessed it. Within a split second, I was across the room the hard way. Damn, I never knew my mother could move so fast. Plus who knew she had that temper in there. In that respect I'm just like my mother, so I hold my temper in check.

"So anyway, the second the word 'hell' got out of my mouth, she put the laundry basket down and proceeded to backhand me so hard that I flew across the room. Of course, it helped that she caught me completely off guard. That was the first and only time my mother ever hit me. So that was my rebellious stage. Pretty pathetic, huh?"

Alex couldn't hold it in any longer. She let loose the roar of laughter that was dying to get out. "I'm sorry, babe. I just can't picture you telling your mother to go to hell. That's too priceless. Wait 'til I tell Kirstin, she thinks you're this angel. Oh, this is too funny."

Nikki swatted Alex across the stomach. "Stop! It was very traumatic. That was the first time I had ever seen Mom go off like a rocket. Even with the shit Dad pulled, she had never lost it before that, well, not on me at least. I did hear them get into it once in a while. But never on me, it creeped me out."

Nikki's face grew serious once more. "Unfortunately, things got even, shall I say wackier, a couple of months after that. Two months later, she lost the baby. After that she was sick off and on pretty much until she died a little more than two years later."

Alex was rubbing small circles on Nikki's bare back. She could see the tears in Nikki's eyes. "Mom got sicker and Dad got meaner." She looked up again at Alex. "Shit, how did we get on this topic?"

"Nik, we don't have to talk about it anymore tonight, if you don't want to. I know it's hard, baby. Sometimes it helps to just talk it out and get it over with." Kissing the top of Nikki's head, Alex tightened her hold on her.

"I know, hon, I know, but I've lived my whole life hating him more than words can say. The only person I ever told any of it to was Mike. Even Millie has never known what went on in that house. Mom married him when I was six. He was my father's best friend and deacon in the church, so he thought it was his duty to marry Mom. That's just the way it was done in that generation. Millie wasn't around because she stayed with grandma in New York to finish high school when we moved to Pittsburgh. She never knew what he was capable of until Mom died and he kicked me out."

"If you don't want to talk about this you don't have to. It's been a long day and night and it's not as if I'm going anywhere. We can talk about these things anytime."

Nikki shook her head. She wanted to get it out while she could. Maybe it was the wine talking or maybe she felt it was time to let go of the anger. She hoped Alex would accept the bad right along with the good.

"No, it's okay. I'd rather just go with it. You know what I mean? Kinda just, keep going while I can. As I said, my mother was a saint. Not long after they were married and we moved, his true self started to show little by little. I could never do anything right in his eyes. He criticized everything I did. I was never smart enough or pretty enough to meet his standards. The little things started to set him off early on. Things like, the silverware wasn't placed the proper distance from the plate or the knife was facing the wrong way."

"My mother's sister was visiting once with her two sons and one of them got into the fridge. Well, have you ever seen what chocolate sauce looks like spread everywhere in the kitchen? Oh yeah, they did. Well anyway, they got it out, took the top off and proceeded to drizzle it in the kitchen. He walked in, saw it and came after me, blaming it on me, not them."

Nikki could feel Alex tense up. "That's fucking nuts! They're the ones who made the mess, not you!"

"I know, babe, but he knew he couldn't very well beat the snot out of someone else's kids. Well, at least at that point he didn't, that came a few years later. One of my friends Sara didn't like the way he was ordering her around, as if he owned her, and well she kinda talked back to him and he flipped. The closest thing at hand was an iron. He picked it up, ripped the cord out of it. I really think he would have done it if Mom hadn't come in and saw him. Of course, he lied his way out of it. He said she was talking filthy to him. What shit.

"Beatings became a common thing during the years. As that got worse so did the verbal and mental abuse. Most of it he did so subtly that it didn't sink in until later. Other times he would just come right out and call me an evil child who needed to have it beat out of me. I'll tell you who was evil. It was him."

Nikki truly believed her stepfather and the old man next door were two of the most evil people she had ever met.

Can I tell her about the neighbor who had touched me inappropriately as a child or being raped in college? No, I can talk about everything but that.

She was afraid Alex would think she was soiled. Sometimes she still felt like it, even after all these years.

Nikki picked up the bottle of water from the nightstand. She took a nice long drink. "Hell, while I'm on a roll I might as well keep going, huh?"

She handed the bottle to Alex.

"Only if you want babe, if it's too much we can stop."

"Thanks. hon. I have to get this out now, while I have the guts. Like you said, maybe getting it out will help me deal with it."

She reached up and pulled Alex's head down for a kiss. Their lips met and Nikki knew it would all be okay.

"We'll get through it together, okay? I will always support you through anything. Always believe that."

"I do, Alex. A year or so later we moved across town. I was twelve at the time. I thought things couldn't get worse. I was wrong. You know how I told you I found out all about girls at the age of twelve, right? Well, there was this girl next door. God was she talented." Nikki smiled.

"It was about a week after we moved in that I met Jackie and about a week after that I, uh, how do I put this? Found out about sex. I was blown away. Actually, it happened at the perfect time in my life. Mom was getting sicker. It was wonderful to have someone to call my own. I know it sounds weird, but she must have known I was having a tough time. She took me under her wing. She was my age and had three siblings. Her parents were wonderful. They instantly became like real parents to me. I think they knew how nasty Dad was.

"We lived there about a little more than a year when Mom got really bad. She was in the hospital most of the time. Jackie's parents took good care of me. Then my mother didn't come home from one of the hospital trips. Dad didn't tell me she died. Mr. Robertson told me. About two months went by after the funeral and during that time it was actually peaceful. He was too busy, I guess, soaking up all the sympathy from everyone, including the bitch that he had been sleeping with for more than a year, that he married six months after Mom died. But that's for another day."

✝

Samuel Robert Christian was an overbearing, sadistic bastard to his stepdaughter. God had told him she was evil and it needed to be beaten out of her. He was a deacon in his church and his faith was all that mattered.

He truly believed his behavior towards all children was because God talked to him, telling him to do every horrible thing, whether it was mental, verbal or physical abuse. That was what prompted him to go to Nikki's room that night. She and her little friend were making noise and obviously not going to sleep as they had been told. He didn't like Jackie or her parents. The Robertson's had tried to tell him that there was no reason to beat a child. Well, she was his responsibility. He would do what was necessary.

Walking through the bedroom door, what he saw appalled him. The small nightlight gave enough light to see everything. The two young girls lay naked together in bed with the covers thrown off. There was no doubt what they were doing. He always made sure the doors opened without a sound. They never heard him until he was bellowing at them.

"I knew you were evil! Both of you! You…you little whore, get out of my house. I will be informing your parents in the morning. Get! Out! And you, you disgusting evil little pervert, I'm going to beat some sense into you. Tomorrow I'm calling a doctor and I'm going to have that evil taken out of your mind."

Midnight found Nikki unconscious on the floor beside her bed. Samuel made sure not to hit her where others would see it. He hit her so hard and for so long, she finally passed out.

Early the next morning, Samuel found Nikki had crawled into bed. He came in to her room, picking up the mattress and dumping her out of bed. This was his favorite way to wake her up on the mornings he found her still asleep.

"Get your lazy ass out of bed. You need to get the house cleaned and do the laundry. I want it all done by the time I come home. Do you understand, you evil disgusting little whore, huh, do you?"

Nikki pulled herself up from the floor. She put on her bathrobe. "Yes daddy, I'll have it done. I promise."

Samuel kept to his word, taking her to see a psychiatrist. Nikki blamed it all on Jackie. Eventually the doctor concluded she was going through depression due to losing her mother.

His behavior didn't improve though. He knew she was evil. Samuel was going to break her one way or another. The final straw came two weeks before she turned fourteen. He had already remarried by then, now he had help trying to beat it out of her.

One evening his new wife's daughter had spilled milk and blamed it on Nikki. His new wife held Nikki down on the bed as he beat her with the belt.

This time he beat Nikki a little too hard, leaving scars that would stay for many years. That however, was only the catalyst for what happened next.

She was still very sore and couldn't move very fast the next evening. Nikki cleared the table and started washing the dishes. All of the cleaning, including laundry and dishes, were her responsibility. Pamela, his new wife, didn't life a finger. She sat watching television all night & weekend, while Nikki was treated as a slave.

Nikki was washing the dishes, thankful for the alone time. She had her hands in the soapy water when he came into the kitchen.

"You left this on the table! I swear you are so damn lazy. I'm always cleaning up after you. I don't want this to happen again." With that, he stabbed the steak knife down into the water. She watched in slow motion as the blade disappeared below the water into her hand. Nikki knew she didn't dare scream; that would result in a beating also. She watched as the soap suds turned red.

"That's your own fault that happened. Now empty out that water and start over. I don't want to hear any whining that it hurts."

†

It hurt to remember her childhood. Yet at the same time, it helped Nikki to heal.

"I never whined or told anyone. A few weeks after that happened he called my Aunt Peggy and told her to come pick me up or I was going to be out on the street in the snow. She showed up the next day and I went to live with her."

Alex gently rubbed her thumb across Nikki's knuckles. "I wondered about this scar. I'm so sorry babe that these things happened to you. I think they've made you stronger though. They've made you the wonderful person you are today. You know how not to treat people. You know what I'm trying to say, right? I just want to know where the hell Millie was. Why didn't she know what was going on?"

"She was too busy with her own life and with college. She was the first person in our family that ever made it to college. Plus, you didn't think she became so self-centered overnight, did you? If it wasn't about her, then it didn't matter. She would blow into town on Thanksgiving and Christmas and try to be this big shot. I thought she was so cool. It wasn't until years later that I realized what a bitch she was. In some ways, she is as bad as he was.

"I know I'm a good person. I am who I am, but that will never be good enough for her. I highly doubt that if I was suddenly straight and married with two point five kids that I would be good enough in her opinion. She'll always find fault."

"Baby, I don't give a fuck what Millie thinks. You shouldn't either. I know she's your sister, but don't ever let her make you feel like that. Do you understand me?"

Nikki couldn't hold back the tears any longer. She laid her head on Alex's chest and sobbed. "God, Alex, I love you. I didn't think I'd ever find someone to love me, all of me. The good and all the crazy in me. I'd given up, especially after the last one."

With her head on Alex's chest, she was lulled into a restless sleep.

†

Because of the retail industry, holidays became more commercialized every year. There was only one holiday that Nikki especially enjoyed. That was Valentine's Day. She loved the holiday, even when she had no one to call her own Valentine. Celebrating happiness and love got her a little giddy.

Nikki had a wonderful dinner planned for Alex. She was making Alex's favorite, shrimp scampi with angel hair pasta. She even made Alex's favorite dessert, turtle pecan cheesecake.

The table was set and she was just waiting on Alex. She put out two of the china settings from the gift that Alex's parents gave them for Christmas. She still was in shock that they had given them something so extravagant.

The pattern was a black background with small red roses around the edge and one rose in the middle of the plate. They gave them twelve full place settings including all the extra serving pieces. They even went as far as buying the soup tureen, glassware and butter dishes that went with the set.

Nikki had bought a special wine that was chilling in the refrigerator. All the items were lined up on the counter, except the shrimp, to start dinner as soon as Alex got home.

Alex had been having a tough week. Nikki wanted to do something special for her, to show Alex how much she loved her. That's what Valentine's Day was all about, after all…love.

Nikki, thanks to Alex, knew that some people never saw the fourteenth of February as a good day. Alex told her that during her years as an officer, she had watched as some spouses went completely off their rockers. There were some out there that just couldn't handle all the 'love'.

This past week Alex had been cleaning up after spouses gone wild, as she called them. Three husbands in as many days had killed their ex-wives, or soon to be ex-wife like the one that she had worked on the day before.

Nikki really hoped Alex's day had gone better than the previous ones. Hopefully, the gifts she had picked up for Alex would help her mood lighten. She especially loved the boxer shorts that glowed in the dark. They were so cute she couldn't pass them up. They had little dogs kissing, which she thought was very funny. Of course, she really knew Alex would like the other gifts she bought her. Nikki thought the edible chocolate body paint would be especially fun.

†

"Dinner was wonderful, babe. Let's take the rest of the wine into the living room and relax."

Alex picked up the half-full bottle and their glasses. She got settled in while Nikki finished loading the dishwasher. Alex had just enough time before Nikki walked through the doorway to retrieve gifts from her coat pocket.

Nikki pulled two gift bags from under the end table beside the couch. She handed them to Alex. "These are for you love. I hope you like them."

Alex opened the first bag to find boxer shorts. "Ooh, I love them. Let me try them on right now." Alex stood, pulling her jeans and underwear off. Putting on the new boxers, she modeled them.

"I love them, babe, thanks."

She bent, kissing Nikki quickly on the lips. Alex dug into the second gift bag. She pulled out the body oils and the chocolate body paint.

"Oh yeah, this could be fun, lots of fun."

Nikki watched as Alex licked her lips.

Alex thought of all the different uses for such items. Putting the items on the coffee table, she moved to sit beside Nikki. Alex turned so their knees touched. She was so nervous, she didn't know if she could do this without making a fool of herself.

She had to give herself a mental kick. Alex muttered to herself as she fumbled in her pocket.

Stop being such a big wuss.

She pulled the small black velvet box from her pocket. Alex looked up at Nikki, who looked at the box then back to her.

Nikki felt her heart skip.

"Nikki, I love you more than anything in the world. I think of you as mine and mine alone. I want the whole world to know you belong to me, that you're spoken for. I couldn't find anything I liked so I had this custom made for you."

Alex opened the box. "It's just a little something to tell you how much I love you."

Nikki was speechless. It was similar to her bracelet. The band was made of platinum. Set into it were a two-carat square cut diamond and two one-carat blue sapphires, one on each side of the diamond. Alex had told Nikki time and again that nothing was too extravagant for her and she would buy her the world if need be. Nikki was still shocked.

It was positively elegant. Nikki held out her hand as Alex slipped the ring from the box. She slowly placed the ring on Nikki's finger, sliding it past the knuckle. She could see the tears in Nikki's eyes.

"Oh darling, it's beautiful. Thank you. I would be honored to wear this and tell the whole world I love you. I love you, Alex, so very much." With a hand on each side of Alex's face Nikki pulled her in for a kiss.

The kiss started out gentle and innocent, however within a few short breaths it turned into kisses filled with hunger for both of them. Alex broke away resting her forehead against Nikki's. "I want you now, woman. Not later, now!"

Nikki gasped as Alex picked her up, carrying her to their bedroom. Alex was ripping Nikki's clothes from her body before she had a chance to protest. There was something animalistic in her mannerisms. She heard Alex growl when she was having a problem with Nikki's zipper. Any time she heard that sound come from her lover it excited her further.

"I'm going to give you a night you'll never forget, baby. I even bought a new toy to try on you." Alex pushed her back so that she was lying with her legs dangling off the edge. Nikki was already dripping wet.

There was to be no foreplay. Alex pushed apart Nikki's legs, going right for what she wanted. She plunged her tongue into Nikki's wetness. She pulled the wetness up and across Nikki's clit with her tongue. She immediately plunged it back in, tracing the path she had previously taken. She did this repeatedly, going faster each time. Soon Nikki's hips could no longer stay on the bed. Her head thrashed side to side.

She needed to feel Alex inside of her. She needed it desperately. As she was ready to beg for it, Alex thrust two fingers inside of her. "Yes…oh, Alex…yes!"

As she took Nikki with one hand, she reached down sliding her free hand into her boxers. She touched herself. Her clit was so engorged, she knew it would only take another stroke or two and she would come. Alex could tell from the stiffening of Nikki's body and legs that her orgasm was starting.

"Oh God, Alex…harder baby, please. Oh…too…soon, harder! Yes…oh…yes.…"

Feeling Nikki coming around her fingers immediately set off her own orgasm. She couldn't move her fingers fast enough on her own clit.

"Oh Alex, that was wonderful."

Alex stood looking down at her. "I'm only getting started, babe."

That night every time Nikki thought she was about to go over, Alex would bring her just to the edge of oblivion then back off and bring her back to the edge again. When they finally drifted off to sleep, Nikki knew she would be very pleasantly sore in the morning.

†

It was so hot on the third day of August that the air conditioner couldn't keep up. It was unbearable, between the stifling heat and the one hundred percent humidity. Alex and Nikki had not had a good night's sleep in more than a week. It, however, was even more unbearable for Kirstin and Tom. Kirstin because she was nine months pregnant and a week overdue, and Tom, well, he was sleepless for the same reason.

It was two in the morning. Alex had not gotten home until after eleven. They had eaten dinner and retired shortly thereafter. Both had just dozed off when the phone rang.

"This had better be damned important." Alex picked up the phone before it could ring a third time. "What!" she yelled.

Alex sat bolt upright in bed. "Okay, I'll wake Nikki and we'll be there as soon as we can. Do you want me to call Mom and Dad or are you? Okay, see you soon."

Alex turned on her side. She hated to wake Nikki. It had been awhile since they'd had a good night's sleep. Their air conditioner had been broken for the past four days. Now that it was finally up and running, the apartment was finally livable again.

She lay watching Nikki for a moment. "God, you are so beautiful and innocent looking when you're sleeping."

"Nikki, honey, wake up, baby. We need to get up and go to the hospital."

The word hospital soaked into Nikki's subconscious. She sat up, startled. "Hospital, who's hurt, what's going on?"

Alex put her hand on Nikki's thigh. "It's okay, babe, no one's hurt. Kirstin's having the baby. She and Tom are on their way to the hospital. I told them we'd meet them there."

Alex rose and began to dress.

Nikki giggled. "Wow. We're going to be aunts. This is so cool. Do we need to pick up Mom and Dad on the way?"

Nikki was already completely dressed by the time Alex was only half dressed.

"Damn it, woman, how do you get dressed so fast?" Alex was astonished.

Nikki smiled. "Years of practice, love. But you still get undressed faster."

Alex chuckled. "Like you said, years of practice. Now, come on let's get a move on and yes, we have to pick them up. Tom's calling them to let them know we were on our way."

Nikki grabbed her purse from the doorknob and they were on their way. A short time later Alex's parents were in her truck and the four where on their way.

The whole way to the hospital Nikki thought about what it would be like to have children of her own. They had briefly talked about it before. Alex however, had made it clear that she didn't want kids.

After pulling into the parking garage, Alex's parents were out of the truck and into the hospital in a flash. She walked around to Nikki's side of the truck and put her arm around her lover. "You okay, hon? I noticed you were really quiet on the ride here."

"Yeah, I'm fine, lack of sleep probably. Let's catch up to your parents." She stepped away from the truck as she felt Alex's hand on her arm.

"Hon?"

"Really Alex, I'm fine, I was just wool gathering was all."

Alex kissed her on the cheek. "We'll talk more about this later, okay?"

"Alex, it's nothing, really. I'm fine."

Four hours and many curse words later, Kirstin gave birth to Alice and Tony's first two grandchildren, Amanda Elizabeth O'Donnell and Anthony Thomas O'Donnell.

Tom was so excited he couldn't wait for them to have several more. As the morning wore on, they each took turns holding the twins and fussing with them. At nine, Tony decided it was time to let Kirstin and the newborns rest for a while. He volunteered to take them out for breakfast. That made them all happy except Alex, who didn't want to leave her niece. She felt they were bonding already.

"Come on, Alex, I'll feed you while they rest for a while, then you can come back and play some more. Okay?"

Alex stood in the doorway trying to figure out a way to sneak Amanda out of the room. Nikki could see the wheels turning.

"No, Alex, you cannot bring her with us. She needs some sleep now." Nikki pulled her from the room.

"Fine, but I call dibbs when we get back. Ya know, I think she looks just like me. Cool. Maybe she'll grow up to be just like me too."

Alice glared at her daughter in horror. "Oh Lord, please save me from that. One of you is enough for any family."

Alex looked at her mother. "Mom, what are you saying, you couldn't handle another one of me?"

Alice stopped. She contemplated it for about one second. "No! Pure and simple, no way in hell!"

They all walked out of the hospital laughing at Alex's expense.

"That's it, people, laugh it up. Go ahead. I'm really not feeling the love here. And I want to feel some love here."

She grabbed Nikki around the waist, kissed her on the neck, then nibbled her ear, tickling her.

"Alex behave, that tickles. Let's go get something to eat, I'm starving."

Alex whispered into her ear. "So am I, babe, except we'd get arrested on the spot for eating what I am hungry for." Nikki swatted her in the stomach, which made Alex only groan louder at the physical contact.

"Behave, my little perv. If you're a good little girl, you can have dessert later. I even think we have a can of whipped cream in the fridge to put on your dessert."

Nikki grinned. She kept walking, chuckling inwardly. She loved when she could tease Alex, getting the final word in, which happened rarely in their conversations.

Chapter Five

Humanity Comes Calling

Alex had not done one thing to get in the doghouse the first year. When she finally did, what a whopper it was. Not only did she forget it was their first anniversary, but Scott had to help her home at two o'clock in the morning.   The disappointment on Nikki's face when she arrived was worse than a slap across the face, which Alex would have preferred.

Now a year later, their second anniversary was around the corner. Alex was not going to make another screw-up. She made plans to take Nikki to her favorite restaurant in a limousine. Unfortunately, Alex wasn't so sure about the other gift. She just hoped Scott didn't ask her what she got Nikki. If he did, she'd have to admit to the ludicrous item.

With the Fourth of July around the corner, her anniversary was only a matter of days away. There were two days left before the holiday weekend and the murders were already double what it had been the previous year. The greatest concentration seemed to be occurring in Alex and Scott's precinct. Neither could remember when they had this many open cases.

The past four months were throwing their conviction stats even further off. Neither of them liked it one bit. Their percentage rating had been in the mid-nineties for more than three years. Alex fumed when she scanned the report in the morning, finding they had only closed eighteen percent of their cases during the past two months. Several hours later, she was still going on about it.

Alex was pissed at the numbers the Captain handed her earlier that morning. "At this rate our fucking year is going to be blown all to hell. I think I'll just shoot the next criminal we arrest for the fun of it."

Scott shook his head, not wanting to tempt fate by commenting on Alex's foul mood. Instead, he silently followed her out the door.

They left the home of a couple in their early twenties in disgust. The mother had come home to find her daughter dead in her toddler bed. The father, who was supposed to be watching the child, was nowhere to be found.

The medical examiner found no immediate reason for the child's death. He didn't want to undress and examine the child with the mother present. Family members had a tendency to hinder the examination for evidence. With children, it was ten-fold.

Each mulled in their own thoughts on the way back to the precinct. It concerned the two detectives that the house was locked up tight, the father's location unknown, and they had a dead child. Alex felt she was missing something. She just couldn't put her finger on it.

While typing her report, Alex mentally walked back through the apartment. She felt driven to find the missing piece of the puzzle.

"I don't like the looks of this one, Scott. I've got a bad feeling about it. Why would a father just leave his child alone, or worse, why leave the child dead in her bed? Why wouldn't he call for help? I'm going to tell Dom to put a push on this one."

Alex finished printing her notes as she voiced her concerns. Scott hung up with the crime scene technicians and finished his as well.

"I agree with you, something stinks about this one. I hate crimes against children the most. They can't defend themselves. That's what we, as the adults, are supposed to do. I don't get any inkling that the mother had anything to do with it though. The sooner we find the father the better. I think he's the key."

Alex nodded. "I do too. Well, I think this about wraps it up for now. Want to go get a beer? I don't feel quite like going home just yet. What do you say?"

Grimacing, Scott put the final papers in the case folder. "I don't know, Alex. I'm still in the dog house from last week."

Alex laughed. "You shouldn't have told Tess you hated that dress she had on. That was your own fault. Dude, don't you think before you open that yap of yours?"

Scott didn't laugh. He still couldn't find the humor in what had happened. Several of them had stopped for a few drinks after leaving the station. Scott was about ten sheets to the wind by the time Alex carried him home.

Alex pictured Tess standing in the living room when she brought him home.

Upon seeing her, Scott promptly had told her what he thought of her new dress. "You shouldn't have told her the dress…how did you put it? 'It looks like my grandmother's couch cover that I wouldn't even use as rags.' Was that how you put it?"

Scott groaned. "Yeah, well maybe if you hadn't bet Jason that I could keep up with him, I wouldn't have gotten in deep shit, you know?"

He felt sick to his stomach just thinking about his wife's reaction. It would be a long while before he had that much to drink again.

Alex stood, grabbed her truck keys, and patted him on the shoulder. "Easiest two hundred bucks I ever made. Thanks."

"Well, I think I had better just get home. Did Dom say he'd have info for us in the morning?"

"Yeah, first thing, he said."

†

Scott sat at his desk across from Alex's staring at the coroner's report. What they read repulsed both of them. Even with all the sick things each of them had witnessed during the years,

198

neither wanted to believe such depravity ran through a human being.

"Jesus Christ, three years old. This is sick, Scott. What he did to her. This is so fucked-up. I want this guy, bad."

Dom handed her back the reports. "Sick bastard… I don't care if we don't clear any other cases on our desks, we need to get him. Isn't there something there about a brother?"

Alex stood. "Yeah, and I think we should check out his brother's crib on Sixth. That looks like the place to start. Let's go. The sooner we bring him in, the sooner we can put this away."

Alex wanted this man and bad. Even more so, she wanted him dead for what he'd done to this baby, to his own child. She was not the only one though. There wasn't an officer in the station that didn't want him dead.

The car was intolerable until the air conditioning kicked on. Scott was a little quieter than usual. Alex glanced at him. "What's up, Tess still pissed?"

"No, she's over it. Just sitting here thinking that this year is sure sucking so far. Let's hope it gets better and soon. It seems the crimes are getting sicker every month. Anyway… don't you have a second anniversary coming up soon? You need start your shopping. Or maybe you haven't stopped trying to make up for last year? So what did you get her?"

"You're so funny, Scott." Alex tapped her fingers on the steering wheel, afraid to admit to him what she got her. It had been what Nikki was hinting for, so she got it. She knew how lame it was going to sound.

"Alex, you didn't forget again did you?"

"Hell no, I'm not that stupid! Oh shit, I might as well tell you. I got her the blender and food processor set she was looking at."

Alex looked at him. Scott grimaced.

Alex pulled the car up in front of the apartment building they were looking for. It was a run-down tenement house that they had been to several times before. In this neighborhood, gang bangers and crack heads were the everyday norm.

"Alex, please tell me you're going to get her something else too. If not, you'd better. I did something similar to Tess. I thought she was going to behead me. Play it safe, get her something femmy that is just for her. What about those teardrop diamond earrings she and Tess saw at the mall? I think she was hinting at those more than a food chopper or a blender."

Getting out of the car, Alex thought about what Scott was saying. Slowly they made their way toward the building, keeping an eye out for trouble. She knew he was right.

"Shit, you're right, as always, I'll go look at the earrings on the way home tonight. If they aren't there, I'll have something made for her. In the meantime, though, let's get this shit done. I hate this place. It's too damn dicey. You know what I mean. It doesn't look too bad today though."

Scott looked around, not seeing the usual shadows. "Yeah, they're all down at the festival picking people's wallets and purses. Let's make this quick and get out of here. We both have wives to get home to."

"Shit. I hate these buildings. Why did they have to build them like a rat experiment gone wild?"

"Well…'cause rats live in them and I'm not talking about just the four legged kind."

They were up the first flight of steps when Alex felt it. The hair on the back of her neck stood up. That was always a bad sign. She warily looked around as they walked down the first hallway.

"Let's make this damn fast, Scott, the hair on my neck is standing at attention. He's in 236D. Let's get a move on it."

He looked at Alex. "Ah shit, that's not good." Scott had been witness before to when Alex got that hinky feeling. Things usually went to hell in a hand basket fast.

They made their way through the dimly lit building as fast as they could, making as little noise as possible. The stench was gut-wrenching. It was a combination of urine, vomit, burnt garlic and stale cigarette smoke.

It took all of Alex's willpower not to toss her cookies right there in the hallway right along with all the other debris. It was a building she would not even want her worst enemy living in.

"What the hell are we doing here? Oh yeah, right…crackhead." Alex mumbled. "Being here pisses me off. I could be home with Nikki instead."

At the end of the hall, they found both light fixtures out, sending the hall into scary darkness.

Alex's foot hit a soda can, then she stepped in something sticky. "Fuck, I don't want to know what I just stepped in. Shit, my favorite pair of Docs too! It should be the next one down on your side."

Scott stopped beside the door. Alex went to the other side. Alex knocked, dropping her voice low. "Hey, we lookin' for Pete. Zack sent us."

Neither heard the door open behind them until it was too late. They both heard the telltale pop of the gun firing.

Alex went down with a thud on the first shot, the second hitting her on the way to the ground. Neither of them had time to react. The third hit Scott. Alex never had a chance even to think of reaching for her gun.

Scott reacted as fast as he could, pulling his gun just as the shooter took aim at him for a final shot. Fortunately, even being wounded he was faster, dropping him in one shot.

Scott slid to the floor beside the crumpled body of his best friend. He reached, pulling Alex to him, feeling for a pulse. Finding a weak one, he breathed a sigh of relief. "Thank God!"

Shit, they'll never find us. The buildings they were in were such a maze any help that would arrive would never find them in time. He tried to wake her up. "Fuck! Alex I'm not leaving you in here while back up tries to find us."

There was no response. "Come on, Alex, stay with me girl."

With the wound to his arm, there was no way he would be able to pick her up. "Sorry Alex, this is going to hurt, but I don't have a choice."

Scott did the best he could at blocking the pain from his mind. Gently he wrapped his good arm around her chest, pulled her up as best he could. "Fuck! That hurts."

Dragging her slowly down the hall, he dialed for back up with his bad arm. "Thank God for speakerphone."

The sergeant picked it up on the first ring. "Scott, what can I do for you?"

"Officers down. Whitmore Complex, south tower…hurry."

"Hang tight we're on our way." Carson rang the captain's office. The cavalry was on its way in seconds.

Taking Alex down the steps was excruciating. Every step not only sent pain shooting through him but also jarred Alex's whole body with the thud of each step as the lower part of her body hit each one. Halfway down the second flight she partially woke, screaming in pain, only to lose consciousness once more.

By the time he got her down to the first floor, he could hear sirens. A cop being down would bring them faster than anything else would, especially to this neighborhood. It was considered one of the forgotten areas that police only went into if they absolutely had to. The residents were left to fend for themselves. The predators usually won out.

"Come on, girl. Hang on, we're almost there. Nikki will kill me if I have to deliver bad news." He looked down at all of the blood.

"Shit, don't you dare bleed-out on me!" Scott knew with this much blood they wouldn't have much time. When he got to the landing, he could go no farther himself. Dropping to his knees, he pulled her up beside him.

Not one person had come out of their apartment to help them. Scott could tell they were there. He could hear the televisions and radios, but not one single person came to their aid. "You're pieces of shit, the whole bunch of you!" he shouted to the empty hall.

Several squad cars with an ambulance hot on their heels pulled up next to Alex's car. "Hey the cavalry's here girl. They even brought a bed for you. What service huh?"

Scott pushed the hair from Alex's face with a blood-covered hand. He pulled her hand up from the dirty floor. He froze. He could no longer feel a pulse. She had bled too much. He looked up the steps, finding a bloody trail down them.

His world spun out of control. It couldn't happen this way. They were supposed to retire together and all live happily ever after. When he still felt no pulse and no breath coming from her, he lifted her eyelid. Only dead, cold eyes stared back at him. He felt a hand on his shoulder and he cried.

✝

Scott watched as they wheeled her into surgery. She had a bullet in her thigh, one in her shoulder. She had lost so much blood that the EMT had started CPR on her within seconds of their arrival on the scene. They continued working on her non-stop all the way to the hospital. He breathed a sigh of relief when they finally got a pulse.

Scott was luckier. The bullet only grazed his upper arm. Twenty-eight stitches and lots of paperwork later he'd looked up to see his captain standing in the doorway. Now the two of them were pacing in the waiting room.

"Um, Captain, we need to call Nikki, Kirstin and Alex's parents. I'll call Kirstin, if you can call her parents. Nikki might already be at Alice and Tony's."

The Captain pulled out his phone. He started to dial Tony's number. Billy had been a detective under Alex's father, so he knew the whole family well.

Scott dialed Kirstin's cell phone. "I'll call Kirstin first. She can go and pick them up. I really don't think they should be driving when they will be so upset, especially Nikki."

✝

Kirstin nervously picked up on the second ring. Scott never called her unless there was an emergency. "Hi Scott, what's wrong?" She had just been getting the kids ready to go to her parent's house to watch the fireworks.

"Hi Kirstin, I'm at Memorial. Alex has been hurt. The Captain is calling Tony right now. I think you should go pick them up. Do you know if Nikki is there yet?"

It took a moment for Scott's words to sink in. "Um, I think…I think she's there already. How bad, Scott?" Kirstin's hand was shaking. She could hardly hold the phone.

"They're rushing her into surgery right now. We'll see you in a few then."

Kirstin put her phone in her pocket. She stood, letting the news settle in. Kirstin was the strongest in the family, the one that everyone always turned to in a crisis. She knew she couldn't fall apart now. She was needed. She walked to the bottom of the steps and yelled up for the kids.

"You kids get your asses down here. We have to go now!" Kirstin never swore at the kids and she had a feeling it would get Tom's attention.

†

Tony slowly put the phone back on the cradle. Time folded in on itself. Never in his life had he felt so helpless. His daughter, the apple of his eye, the one who always had him wrapped around her finger, was being wheeled into surgery with bullets in her.

As a father, he was supposed to protect her, to take the bullets for her. How could he though when it was her job to take them for him, for humanity? He knew it was more than a job for Alex. It was what she was born to do, just as it had been for him.

To serve and protect was the police officer's motto. Alex took it very seriously. Tony saw in his daughter, long ago, that she took the motto to heart in all aspects of life. Just as he knew his daughter's temper, a temper she inherited from her grandfather, would be her undoing one day.

He mused as he thought about several years ago at one late night talk they found themselves having. Alex had showed up on their doorstep drunk and fresh from a fistfight. He laughed at how lucky both of them had been that her mother had been out of town.

He cleaned her up that night the best she would let him. They talked long into the night on how her temper was going to cause her serious trouble if she couldn't control it.

Here he was now, years later worrying about his baby girl once more. Now, however, there was another to worry about as well. Knowing his daughter's sometimes-uncontrollable temper, he worried for Nikki. He wouldn't butt in, unless one of the two of them came to him. Even then, he would only offer fatherly advice.

Even though he knew Alex was an adult capable of taking care of herself, his heart ached for his little one. In his mind's eye when he looked at her he still saw an eight-year-old girl. Her blonde hair in a ponytail under her cap, holding a baseball bat waiting to hit the ball out of the park.

Tony had hoped this day would never come or at least wait until Alex's mother was gone. Alice had never wanted Alex to be a cop. During the years, mother and daughter had fought continuously about it.

Alice walked into the back room. "Tony honey, what's wrong?"

She walked to him, putting her arm around his waist.

Tony wouldn't be able to hide it from her.

"Where's Nikki?"

Alice looked toward the garage. "She's putting the food into the fridge in the garage. Why, what's going on?"

"Why don't you sit down, sweetheart, and I'll tell you." He motioned toward the couch. The day he had feared his whole life was now at hand.

"No! You'll tell me right now." Then it hit her. "Oh God, its Alex, isn't it? Something's happened to her." Just as her knees gave way, Tony helped her to sit.

"She's been shot. They're taking her into surgery right now. Kirstin and Tom are on their way to pick us up to take us to the hospital. I think we should wait until they get here to tell Nikki."

"Yes, I agree, we have to remain strong for her and Alex. Where are the grandkids?"

A few moments later, a car pulled into the driveway. Nikki waved to Kirstin and Tom as they got out.

Kirstin met her parents at the front door. "Mom, I'll go tell her. Why don't all of you go get in the car, okay? We left the kids with a neighbor."

Tom wrapped his arm around Kirstin. "Do you want me to come with you, honey?"

Kirstin patted him on the back. "No, I'd better do this alone."

Nikki put the pie in the refrigerator in the garage as the other three were getting into the car. She thought it weird that they were getting into the car. Walking into the kitchen, Nikki saw Kirstin coming through the living room.

"Hey Kirstin… why's everyone getting in the car and where are the kids?" Nikki knew something was wrong. The haunted look on Kirstin's face said it all.

Kirstin knew the best way was to be direct and honest. "Nikki, um, we need to go to the hospital, Alex has been hurt."

Nikki stopped. "How…I don't…" Nikki couldn't think. This was her worst nightmare, becoming reality. "How bad?"

"They're taking her into surgery. She was shot in the thigh and shoulder."

Kirstin caught Nikki as she collapsed.

"No, no, no…" Nikki let out a sob that broke Kirstin's heart.

The key was to remind her that Alex was strong, that her sister could survive on pure cussedness alone. Kirstin had been dreading this day, not if it came, but when it did. It was just a matter of time. She would hold this family together one way or another.

Just like her father, Kirstin too worried about her sister's temper, knowing that one day it was going to get her in a world of hurt. She had been on the receiving end of that temper more than once. Kirstin however gave it right back to Alex, not ever letting her get away with her temper tantrums. As soon as Alex regained consciousness, she would be in a foul mood and looking for a brawl.

Kirstin would be there as always to defuse things. Their entire lives she, their father, and Scott were the only ones able to calm Alex down. That was, until Nikki came along. She knew she should prepare Nikki for what was to come but just couldn't do it quite yet. Her main concern was Nikki's personal state of mind. In turn, helping Nikki through the next few hours was the best thing she could do for Alex.

Her instinct told her Nikki was starting to panic, second-guessing her own heart's choice of partners. She might possibly even be losing faith in herself at being able to cope with something like this.

"Nikki, we need to go, okay? I know you're hurting and scared but you need to be strong for Alex. I also really don't want to have to deal with Mom's 'I told you so' all on my own. Okay?"

Kirstin was still the most level headed one in the family. She always knew exactly what to do or say, to make the situation better.

Nikki nodded her eyes wide with shock.

Arriving at the hospital they were met by the head nurse Maddie, who they knew from Alex's other scrapes with danger. She informed them that once Alex came out of surgery, she would go to recovery and would be watched there until she could be moved into a private room the next morning.

Doctor Jack, who they also knew very well, told them to go home and get some rest. Knowing how Alex reacted to being hurt, he wanted them well rested to deal with her the next morning.

†

The group made their way back to the hospital at nine the next morning. Not one of them had slept a wink. Nikki had tossed and turned all night in Kirstin's guest bedroom as all the worst scenarios played through her mind. Each of them were beyond exhaustion when they sat down in the waiting room to await Doctor Jack's arrival.

Nikki sat on the couch in the waiting room, her mind a million miles away. Kirstin had worn herself out pacing the floor with Tom and her father. She sat down beside Nikki, putting her arm around her. Nikki was shaking. That was not good. Knowing shock was setting in, Kirstin needed to get her to talk about it.

"Nikki, she's going to be fine. The doctor said everything went well in surgery and she's now in recovery." Kirstin squeezed her shoulder.

"I know what he said, Kirstin, but what about next time? I don't want to lose her. I mean, I always knew she could be hurt, but killed? I guess I never wanted to believe it. I thought if I loved her enough, nothing would ever happen to her. God, Kirstin, I thought that one day in college was the worst day of my life, but that was nothing compared to this hell."

Kirstin looked across the room at her sleeping mother. Her father motioned to her that he and Tom were going for coffee. Scott had left some time ago, to go home and give Tess the news.

She had to get Nikki's mind off Alex being hurt. "Nikki, what happened in college?"

Nikki contemplated those years. Could she tell her? Only one other person ever knew what happened that night. She could trust Kirstin, she knew that much. There was no one else that could overhear them. Sighing, Nikki looked around once more.

"Yeah, you could say I had fun. I mostly drank my way through it. I was finally able to live a little and be myself. I could never do that at home. My family was a little bigoted. Being gay was a big no-no. Once I got to college, everything changed. I changed. I drank like a fish and hopped from bed to bed. It felt so good to finally be able to be me that I guess I went a little overboard."

Kirstin laughed. "Oh please, I couldn't blame you one bit. You were free. You turned out great though. Go on, tell me more about it."

From day one, Kirstin had been working at getting Nikki to open up to her. Kirstin could feel that she always held most of herself back, that possibly she was afraid to let go, showing others the inside parts.

Kirstin herself had a wonderful childhood that had led into a fantastic adult life. Her heart hurt for the pain Nikki held inside herself. Did Nikki think Kirstin would judge her? She judged no one, least of all the woman who would put up with her sister.

"Nikki, know this… I will never, and I mean never, judge you. Understand?"

Nikki nodded. Kirstin smiled. She hoped she was finally getting through to her. "Good, go on."

Nikki's shoulders slumped. "My second year, my bed hopping settled down, I was on the student council. I was also in charge of the first floor students, both female and male. I had a real odd assortment of kids in my group. Maria was lucky—she got all geeks. I got one girl that ended up being a psycho. A couple of months into the school year she was out with one of the local boys, one in a long line of them, and they'd wrecked the snowmobile they were riding. He claimed she had tried to kill him. I wouldn't have doubted it one bit. About a month after that, she was sent home. She was a real nut job.

"Then there was the girl who had a million and one health issues. She had traveled the world with her father so she thought she was better than everyone else. The guys weren't much better. I had one nerd, a playboy, and one that thought Ozzy Osborne was God. He was the one I had problems with. December was great. I had a girlfriend and I was loving life. Things went downhill fast though at the end of January. I didn't think it could get much worse after finding out she already had a girlfriend. What a surprise that one was.

"Well I was wrong. It did get worse. It was Valentine's Day. Mister Ozzy guy was missing his girlfriend. I was by myself after breaking up. We were both bored so we went for pizza. I figured I'd really try to get along with him. He knew I was gay so it was just a friendly meal. Unfortunately, he had a lot to drink. Thankfully, I was completely sober, for once. I only drank soda because I was driving. We got back to the dorm and he said he was still wide-awake, wanting to hang for a while.

"God, if I had known. We were hanging out, talking. Now, mind you, he was more than twice my size. I got cold so went to get a sweatshirt out of my dresser. The next thing I knew I was pinned against the wall. He ripped my tee shirt off. I never stood a chance against him. He hit me across the face. I tried to fight him off, but he was a hell of a lot stronger. He raped me. I was so ashamed. I never said anything to anyone. He was drunk and he never acknowledged anything had ever happened. I'm not sure he even remembered what he had done."

She paused and took a deep breath.

"I haven't told anyone what happened that night, not even Alex. I thought she would see me as damaged goods."

All these years later, she still felt the shame of what had happened. Nikki tried to tell herself it was not her fault but her inner demons told her she should have fought harder. That she deserved it. That she was now soiled and no one would want her.

Kirstin held Nikki's shoulders. "Nikki, you have nothing to be ashamed of. You did nothing wrong. What he did was wrong, so very wrong. Alex would never see you like that. She loves you, all of you. Bad things have happened to all of us. I believe they make us stronger. They make us who we are. As far as bed-hopping goes, Alex wouldn't dare say anything about that. She's done it enough in her life, just as we all have."

Kirstin found herself laughing aloud thinking back to her own wild days. She smiled wickedly, as she thought about some of the things she and Alex had done in their youth.

"Sorry, I was thinking back to my rebel years. I was never as bad as Alex, but I had my moments. Nikki, we all have, so don't ever put yourself down for living life to its fullest. There comes a time in your life when you need to put it all behind you, into the past where it belongs. Do you understand what I'm telling you? Trust in Alex, trust in yourself. Have faith in the Fates that they wouldn't have brought the two of you this far only to lose one another. She's going to make it through this, I know it. When she's recovered, talk to her then. The two of you should never hide anything from one another."

Nikki contemplated what Kirstin said. She knew she was right, but was still terrified that she would lose Alex. Nikki was about to say something when the doctor came into the room. Kirstin walked to the other side of the room to wake her mother.

"Alex is doing well. She's been moved to a room. As I expected, she already had one fit of temper when she woke during the night. I told when I saw her a few moments ago that if she continues, I'll drug her and knock her out for a week. As it is, she'll be asleep on and off for the rest of the day. If you want, you can go see her now, or go grab a bite to eat, then come back later when she might be more awake. I will warn you though, her mood is not good. But of course it never seems to be when I see her."

He chuckled under his breath at his own words. *Bad mood is an understatement*!

Kirstin took control, as always. "How long will her recovery be?"

"A normal person would be here at least two weeks, Alex, that's another story. After one week, let's just take it one day at a time. She'll need physical therapy. The full recovery time will depend on her. Knowing her, probably only about two months. Alex is the type we can't hold down for long. Remember, I've stitched her up before and

I'm sure I'll stitch her up again. She's in room 407. I'll check in on her in a little while."

Kirstin helped her mother up and headed toward the door. "Thanks Doctor, I think we'll go see her now."

✝

Five exhausted people stood outside of Alex's room, afraid of what they would find behind the door. Each of them existed in their own personal version of hell.

Tony blamed himself for her getting hurt. He felt he could have tried harder to talk her out of being a cop. If he had, then she wouldn't be lying there connected to all kinds of machines. Although if Alex hadn't followed her heart she wouldn't have met Nikki, so something good had come out of it.

Alice thought of the terrible scars that the bullets and surgery would leave. The first thing on her agenda was to offer to take care of Alex.

Kirstin's thoughts were of Alex and Nikki. Nikki would need someone there to help her cope with this. Kirstin had seen her sister hurt before like this. Alex was a tough cookie. Kirstin grasped Nikki's hand, squeezing it to reaffirm she was still beside her. Nikki smiled at her gesture.

Tom's pager picked that moment to go off. Even though he had the week off, he was on call. Tom had hoped he wouldn't be called out, wishing for a peaceful week with his family. Being a firefighter sucked sometimes. He leaned, whispering to Kirstin that he had to call in to see what was going on.

Nikki was still in shock. She wanted all of this to go away, for none of it to have ever happened. She thought of all the things she would do for Alex when she got home. Nikki was going to make sure Alex was as comfortable as possible, with all her favorite foods and lots of movies to watch.

The four of them, still lost in their own thoughts, walked through the door to find Alex awake, telling the nurse to stop poking her. The nurse informed them they could stay for a few minutes. "Please do not to get her excited," she whispered as she left the room.

Kirstin and Nikki hung back a moment, knowing that Alice and Tony needed to be with their eldest daughter for a moment by themselves. Both had tears in their eyes as they stepped up to the hospital bed.

"Oh sweetie, how are you feeling? Don't worry, everything will be okay." Alice pulled the sheet up a little higher over Alex's chest. "I think this proves my point that you need to find a different line of work, Alex. Women were not meant to be police officers."

Alex was still a little groggy but her mother's words made their way through the haze. "Mom… not now."

"Well honey, I think you should think about it. Look at you. You were shot twice. You're so pale. All of these tubes and machines, they prove my point."

Tony put a hand on Alice's shoulder.

Kirstin's anger flared. She gritted her teeth. Keeping her voice low, she said, "Mom, stop right now! Alex doesn't need to hear that." Her mother's selfishness always amazed her. Everything was always all about her.

Their mother was so self-centered sometimes that in the past, Kirstin had to walk out of the room for fear she would say something that could never be taken back. This was shaping up to be one of those times. However, one look at Nikki told her she couldn't. She had to put her foot down to bring her mother back to reality.

Alice turned to Kirstin. "Well, it had to be said sometime. Now is as good as any." She turned back to Alex, who was waking up more and growing angrier by the moment.

"Alex, there is no discussion, I want you to quit and find a different job. I don't want to have to go through this worry again. You also are going to come home in order to recuperate. I can take care of you better than anyone else."

Kirstin knew her sister was getting angry and Alex going home to recover was the final straw. Alex was about to blow. Swearing under her breath, Kirstin hoped she could diffuse the situation.

Alex's blood boiled. "That's right, Mom, it's all about you. You don't give a shit that I was shot, only how it affects you. I'm a cop, get over it. As for going to your house, Dad, this isn't meant for you, but you've got be fucking kidding me! There is no fucking way. I'm going home, with Nikki, my girlfriend. She's all I need. I can't even comprehend how disrespectful you've just been to Nikki. God help you when I feel better. Now leave, I'm tired."

Doctor Jack stood in the doorway, waiting for Alex's tirade to end. "Okay, now that we've got that all out of our systems, Alex needs rest. She also needs no more excitement like this for a while." He looked from one person to the next as he spoke. "Why don't you come back later today after she's had some more sleep?"

Nikki stood back and watched the ugly scene unfold in front of her. She knew Alice didn't like what her daughter did for a living, but she hadn't realized to what extent. What was worse though, was the comment about Alex's recovery. It was as if Alice had no respect for either of them or their relationship. She didn't care what Alice thought of her. She did care how Alice treated her own daughter though. Nikki had always thought Alice liked her; now she wasn't so sure.

Afraid for a moment that Alex would agree to return home, Nikki berated herself for not believing in Alex. Yes, Nikki was afraid she wouldn't be able to take care of Alex by herself, but that was for them to decide. That was what relationships were all about.

Alex motioned for Nikki to come to the bed. Nikki took Alex's hand in hers and began to cry. She could no longer hold it back. Bringing Alex's hand to her cheek, she held it there for a moment. She kissed each finger.

Kirstin could tell they needed some time alone. Touching her father's elbow, she nodded toward the door. He got Alice's attention, but she refused to leave. She wanted to remain to care for Alex. "I don't want…" was all she got out. Kirstin cut her off.

She took her mother's arm. "Mom, shut up. Let's go."

At that, the three of them joined Tom in the hallway. He had been waiting to tell Kirstin that he had to leave. He'd only picked up bits and pieces of the conversation. By the look on Alice's face, he could tell that things hadn't gone her way.

Tom's insides did a happy dance at that knowledge. He loved his wife more than life itself and he loved his father-in-law. However, Alice was another story. Tom truly couldn't stand to be in the same room with her. He would never tell Kirstin though, so as usual he bit his tongue, tolerating her presence.

He stepped to his wife, quietly asking if all was okay. She explained in short form what was going on. Tom laughed.

"Oh boy, she's going to be really pissed at you, hon. I know you're going to be upset with me also, because I have to go. Chief called. Johnson was just taken to the hospital. His appendix blew up. There's also a bad fire on West Main. So I've got to go." He kissed Kirstin on her cheek and hugged her.

"It's okay, love, I understand. I'm not upset. Actually, do you think I could come with you?" She looked at him with begging eyes and a grimace.

Tom laughed harder. Kirstin amused him at the predicaments she could get herself into, as well as how she eventually got herself out of them. "Uh-uh, no way, you have to stay here and deal with your mother. Just try to keep her away from Alex for the rest of the day."

Kirstin shook her head, feeling a headache coming on. "Yeah, as if that'll happen. I'll try. Will you call later? Is someone picking you up?"

Tom nodded and left, leaving a very frustrated daughter and husband to deal with Alice. Kirstin made up her mind. She was going to settle a few issues with her mother for the final time. "Mom, let's go to the cafeteria and grab some coffee. The three of us need to talk."

They walked to the elevator in silence. Tony knew this was going to be the first of many tough meals and conversations. It was time to rein in his wife.

Nikki silently thanked Kirstin for shutting up Alice. She didn't want Alex upset any further. Alex looked so pale and vulnerable laying there. Fear ran through her. Fear that she was not strong enough to take care of her lover. That she would falter.

For a moment, she thought maybe Alice was right, that she could care for her daughter better. Alex is the one who took care of her. Her dark brooding lover was the strong one, not Nikki. Alex was going to need someone who could take care of her physically as well as emotionally.

A heart stopping thought reoccurred to her. Nikki laid her head on Alex's chest and sobbed. "By the gods, what if I had lost you?"

Nikki's head upon her chest, Alex put her arm around her the best she could. She comforted Nikki, knowing she'd kept it bottled up inside. She let Nikki release it all, stroking her back softly.

Once the tears stopped, Nikki felt spent. Lifting her head, she looked at Alex once again. It dawned on her that she might be hurting Alex. "Oh darling, I'm sorry. Was I hurting you?" She took Alex's hand back in hers.

"No babe, the pain killers are kicking in again. Sorry, getting tired."

Alex knew Nikki wouldn't take care of herself. "Get something to eat, then go home and get some sleep. Okay?"

Nikki refused to leave Alex's side. "No, I'm staying right here with you. You might need something. Plus, I just want to be with you." She kissed Alex's hand again, putting it to her cheek.

"Oh God, Alex the thought of losing you, I don't know what I would have done. We all need you in our lives. I need you so much. Oh, Alex—"

Nikki gently kissed Alex. She didn't think she'd feel the usual spark coming from Alex, but it was there. Even being hurt didn't diminish it.

Alex felt groggy. "Everything will be okay, baby. Don't you worry that pretty head about a thing. I'm so tired though… the meds."

Nikki pushed Alex's hair away from her face. "Sleep darling, I'll be here when you wake up." She watched Alex drift off. She laid her head on the bed beside Alex's arm. Still holding Alex's hand in hers, she fell asleep not long after Alex.

†

Several hours later Kirstin slowly opened the door to Alex's room. Quietly walking to the bed, she found Nikki sound asleep with Alex looking at her. Alex put her finger to her lips, telling Kirstin to be quiet.

Kirstin went to the opposite side of the bed. "I'm taking Mom and Dad home," she whispered. Kirstin kept the fact their mom wasn't happy about anything at that moment to herself. "The going home issue has been resolved. We'll talk about it later."

Kirstin knew in her heart being home with Nikki would help Alex heal faster than anything else would. Alice tried to argue that she should be the one to take care of *her* daughter. Kirstin lost her temper at that statement. She called her mother out on the fact that it sounded like she had no respect for Nikki or their relationship.

Of course, Kirstin didn't let Alex know about any of that conversation. She didn't think it was her place to tell her sister. It would break Alex's heart to hear such things. They had thought Alice had finally accepted that her oldest daughter was a lesbian. Now Kirstin questioned that. She had the distinct feeling that deep in her mother's mind she still couldn't accept her daughter's lifestyle.

"I'll come back in a while to pick up Nikki. Okay?"

Alex nodded, still trying to fight off the effects of the drugs that were being fed to her through her IV's.

"Get some more sleep, sis, it's best to get as much as you can."

Alex started to nod off again. "Will do… Kir… Thank you."

She was asleep once more.

The next two weeks were a blur for Nikki. Spending most of her time at the hospital, she only went home when Alex insisted. Alex was recovering faster than even the doctor had expected. She had been out of bed and roaming the halls on her second day. She only used the cane because Nikki begged her to.

Alex's temper though was a different story. As her body started healing, her temper unraveled. Three of the four nurses assigned to her side of the floor refused to go back into her room, especially after being subjected to her verbal tirades and frequent throwing of any items she could lay her hands on. One refused after Alex had wrestled the hypodermic from her and threatened her with it.

The only nurse left was a fifty-two year old, four foot ten, stocky, African-American spitfire of a woman. Agatha could take anything Alex would dish out. The behavior never once fazed her. One morning when Alex was at her rarest, she informed 'Mz. Alex' that she 'was not all that' and that she needed to step back and reevaluate her attitude.

Since that morning, Agatha worked double shifts in order to make sure the detective had adequate care. After their butting of heads, the spunky nurse was the only one Alex trusted to be near her.

The physical therapist came to visit with her on her sixth day there. Alex took an instant dislike to the woman. She had seen how the therapist had studied Nikki. Alex swore that the woman had even openly leered at her.

Alex told Kirstin how she felt.

"Alex, I haven't seen any such thing. You need to calm yourself down."

Kirstin not automatically siding with her made Alex even more upset and an argument ensued.

"Alex, don't be such an ass. Even if she looked at Nikki like that, she didn't take any notice of it. You have nothing to worry about. Nikki loves you and you alone."

That only sparked off another of Alex's tirades. "But Kirs, how am I fucking supposed to take care of her? I can't even take care of myself right now! I don't want that woman anywhere near Nikki. God, I can't even protect her now! What if something happens to Nikki before I finish healing? What if I get hurt again?"

Alex's blood pressure monitor was beeping faster. It alerted the nurses' desk.

"Jesus, Alex, would you stop being such a jackass? Nothing is going to happen to her other than that you're going to upset her if she hears you talking like this. She'll feel like you don't trust her. You're treating her like a child. As for getting hurt…look at what you do for a living. Unless you change that, bad things are going to happen. Now…now calm down, your pressure is going through the roof."

Agatha stood in the doorway with her hands on her hips. Alex looked at her and growled. "I know. I know. My fucking pressure is up. I am fine. My sister and I were just having a personal discussion, if you don't mind."

Kirstin rolled her eyes. "Alex, either you calm down and forget the whole matter or I will tell Nikki what has got you up in arms. Okay?"

The nurse looked from the monitors to Alex. "You had better listen to your sister or you are going to give yourself a stroke. It's almost time to change your dressings so I will do it while I'm here."

Alex glared at Agatha. There was not a motherly bone in her body, which made her perfect as Alex's assigned nurse. Kirstin adored Agatha for not taking any of her sister's attitude.

"Damn fuckin' drill sergeant," Alex muttered, just loud enough for them to hear her.

They laughed at Alex. Agatha scolded Alex as if she were a two-year-old child. "You got that right young lady. On the streets, you may be a badass macho tough cookie, but in here, you are all mine. Which means you will do as I say. Got it?"

Kirstin was amused at the sight. Finally, she'd met someone who could get in the final word with her older, pain in the ass sister. Kirstin loved every single laughable minute of Alex's misery.

Kirstin laid her hand on Agatha's arm. "Where have you been all our lives? I could've used you when I was younger to help control this monster and her 'tude."

"You mean to tell me mz. thing here has been like this her whole life? Damn, I feel so sorry for you." She laughed hard as Kirstin joined in.

Alex glared at both of them, hoping to shut them up. "Yeah, yeah… whatever… laugh at the woman laying here with holes in her. Let's get this done."

Wanting to get Kirstin's goat a little and knowing her sister would be grossed out at the sight of the wounds, Alex teased her. "Hey Kirs, want to watch? They look really cool."

Kirstin didn't want to see Alex's wounds. She didn't care that her sister was taunting her; she'd never been able to stomach such things.

"I'm heading out. Nikki will be here in a few minutes, so please calm down." She bent, gave her sister a hug and made her exit before Alex could start again.

The next afternoon Alex walked back into her room from her trip to the vending machine. She stopped in the doorway and took in the sight before her. Fury flowed through her body and out every pore. Before her stood Nikki bent over a table reading, some papers laid out on it.

What angered Alex was that the therapist stood behind Nikki on her left side looking over her shoulder. The woman had her arm wrapped around Nikki's waist and looked like she was whispering in her ear.

"Excuse me, Sheila." She could barely contain her anger. Jealousy reared its ugly head in Alex. It was fueled by the helplessness of not being able to beat the creature in front of her to a bloody pulp if she so desired.

Sheila turned to Alex, not moving her arm from Nikki. Alex couldn't believe the balls of this woman. She was touching Alex's property. "Get your hands off her and get out. Never step foot in my room again, is that understood? I really hope I'm making myself clear."

Sheila tried to explain, but Alex cut her off. "I said, get out!"

Nikki couldn't understand what had gotten into Alex. She hadn't liked Sheila from day one, which puzzled Nikki. She crossed the room to Alex.

"Alex, what's going on? What was that all about?"

She looked up at Alex, looking for understanding. Alex stood there seething.

"Honey, she was showing me the exercises she wants you to do when you get home and how I'm supposed to help you with them."

"No one touches what belongs to me. Understand?" She roughly pulled Nikki to her. Alex kissed her hard to make her point. Jealousy burned its way through the blood in her veins, right into her heart where it found a home.

Alex squeezed her arm hard. "You'd better learn I'm the only one allowed to touch you." Something in Alex had changed. She could no longer keep control of her temper.

"Alex what are you talking about?" Nikki was confused. Did she understand Alex correctly? Was she was accusing Sheila of touching her inappropriately?

"She had her arm around you and was, well, she was just taking advantage of how close she was to you. You belong to me, you're mine and no one touches what's mine." Her hands shook from fury as they held Nikki's face.

"Oh Alex, honey, I never even noticed it. She meant nothing by it. Of course I belong to you love, don't ever question that. Please don't get upset about this, it wasn't like that at all. She and Doctor Jack both said you're doing so well. I love you, Alex, very much." Nikki laid her head on Alex's chest, wrapping her arms around her waist.

Alex couldn't believe it, Nikki had no idea what that woman was up to. Sometimes Nikki was so naive. Alex would hurt anyone who tried to take Nikki away from her.

Scott was standing outside the door listening to bits and pieces of their conversation. He heard enough to understand the gist of it. Alex had blown off steam to him how she felt about the therapist after Kirstin told her to knock it off.

Scott, of course, had previously told her the same thing. Muttering under his breath, "Obviously, she didn't hear a damn word I said. Maybe Nikki can make her see some sense."

He truly hoped so, for all their sakes. Scott knocked on the door as he opened it. "How are two of my favorite ladies doing today?"

Alex turned. She looked at him and laughed. "There's only one lady I see in this room and she's in my arms, or arm should I say. The doc said I could maybe go home early so I feel I'm doing great. As for my lady here, she's also good." Alex kissed her on the cheek to make her point.

Scott chuckled then patted Alex on the shoulder. "You're too much Alex, too much. Anyway, why I stopped by is we hauled in the bastard's brother. He's downtown right now. I tried for a while and now Captain Billy's working on him. We're hoping he'll rat him out. I'm not holding my breath though. We got nothing on him, can't even prove he's seen him. So we'll see."

"If anyone other than me can get someone to crack, it's the Captain. Course, if he can't I'll gladly come in and take a shot at him."

"No you won't. You need to heal and speaking of needing to heal…if I don't get home, Tess is going to come looking for me. I haven't seen her since the day before yesterday morning. As for you half-pint…" He turned to Nikki. "Let me know when you'll be taking her home."

Nikki hugged him. "I will."

What Nikki didn't see was Scott slipping a wrapped box into Alex's robe pocket.

"Well, thanks for everything Scott. We'll talk to you tomorrow." Alex winked at him.

After Scott left, Alex turned back to Nikki. Alex was thankful that the nurse who took care of her the day she was brought in had given her possessions to Kirstin when she got there. She had put them in her purse and forgot about them until Alex asked her where they were two days ago. Alex gave Scott her credit card to go pick up the earrings after she called the jeweler. Jason, the jeweler, was a long-time friend of hers. Jason knew exactly which earrings she was referring to.

Alex asked Jason to change the design a little before wrapping them, as Nikki didn't wear posts, only lever backs. He gladly changed them for her at no charge. Alex requested he charge her for the modifications but he steadfastly refused.

Now the box was in her pocket, ready to be given to Nikki. When he originally told her the price, Alex had almost choked. Who knew blue diamonds could cost so much? Who cared though, Nikki was worth every penny.

"Babe, why don't you sit down for a second?" Alex sat on the bed as Nikki took the chair beside her.

Nikki was confused. "Is everything okay?"

Alex smiled. "Since I couldn't get to the store to pick up your main gift, I had Scott go get it for me. I know it's early, but I want you to know that you mean the world to me." Alex was a little nervous, fiddling with the box in her pocket.

"Love, we can wait until you get home. Beside the other gifts were enough. You didn't need to get me anything more. All I wanted was the food processer and blender."

She couldn't believe Alex would get her anything more. She had gotten Alex season tickets for the following season to her beloved Bills. It was something she knew Alex would not buy for herself. What Alex didn't know was that Tess had gotten the same thing for Scott for his birthday next month, that way the two of them could enjoy the games together and stay out of her and Tessa's hair.

Alex took Nikki's hand in hers. "Baby this is something that is for you and you alone. I really hope you like them." She took the gift from her pocket, handing it to her slowly.

Nikki took great care not to rip the paper. She immediately recognized the name of the jeweler on the front of the box. It was Alex's friend Jason. She had bought Nikki's ring and bracelet there also. Opening the box, she held her breath.

Nikki was floored when she looked into the box. She saw them the last time she had walked by his shop. There was only one difference, the backing on them. They were the most beautiful earrings she had ever seen.

"Oh Alex, they're so beautiful. I saw these in Jason's window and fell in love with them. How did you know? Did Tess tell you? I told her not to say anything." Nikki took her earrings off and put the new ones on.

"Nope, she didn't say a word. So you like them, huh?" Alex was grinning. She knew she'd made the right choice to get them after all.

Nikki stood beside the bed. "Like them? I love them, thank you Alex. Thank you so much. How do they look?" She turned her head from side to side.

"Stunning, baby. Just like you." She pulled Nikki into a searing kiss. "Damn, I can't wait to go home with you, just the two of us."

Nikki pulled away from Alex just a little. "Uh-uh, none of that for a while. Not until that leg and arm heal more." She ran her fingertip down Alex's face.

This was the beautiful face of the woman she loved more than anything in the entire world. The woman she almost lost because of someone else's cruelty. Nikki vowed to Hades himself that she would do anything avoid this agony again. She would give her own life, if necessary, to keep Alex safe.

Alex grabbed Nikki's finger. "Woman, you better stop teasing me or I'm not going to follow Dr. Jack's orders." To make her point she took the digit, licked the tip of it, then sucked the end of it into her mouth.

Nikki moaned. She wondered what she'd started. If only she hadn't run her finger down the side of Alex's face so teasingly. It was unfair of her to do that to Alex. Nikki realized she shouldn't have started something neither of them could finish. Nikki moaned again, pushing her hips into Alex as she sucked her finger harder.

Luckily, Kirstin walked in at that moment. "Good Lord, you two, get a room. Alex I understand, she can do it anywhere, but you Nikki? Geez… Alex must be rubbing off on you. By the way, didn't Dr. Jack say none of that for a while anyway? Hmm?"

Alex knew Kirstin was trying to get a reaction from her. She wasn't going to give her the satisfaction though. She was in a good mood, happy to be living and breathing at that moment. That and she would be going home soon where she belonged. "Jealous?"

Kirstin laughed. "If I was gay, I'd steal her from you. Did he say when you'd be leaving this dump?" Kirstin sat in the chair while the other two continued sitting on the bed.

"He said that if all my tests came back good, he might kick me out of here as early as tomorrow. That, of course, is fine by me. He told me I'm doing way better than he expected."

Nikki scooted closer to Alex, laying a hand on her thigh. "Fine by me, too, I can't wait for you to come home, where you belong. I've missed you terribly."

Alex ran her fingers down Nikki's face. "I've missed you too, baby."

Kirstin made a gagging noise. "Oh, gag me! Anyway, I stopped by to see if Nikki wanted to go to dinner. What do you say? Mexican?"

"Well, I was going to go down to the cafeteria, grab something to bring back here to eat with Alex. Mexican does sound good though." She would not be selfish if Alex wanted her to stay with her.

"Nikki, honey, go with Kirstin. Have an enchilada for me okay? Then come back and we'll have dessert." Alex kissed her on the lips, ensuring her that it was okay.

"Dessert, huh? Like what?" Nikki had a hungry grin on her face.

†

August in Rochester tended to be pleasant and a little cooler at night. Unfortunately, this particular year the month only started out hotter than hell itself but was ending with a bang. With record high temperatures close to ninety, coupled with one hundred percent humidity, there was no relief from the heat.

People who loved the heat and sun flocked to the beaches. Those who had air conditioners chose to do the smart thing— they stayed inside. Those who didn't roamed the malls or contributed to record-breaking numbers at the movie theatres.

It didn't matter to them that all the movies on the big screens were pathetic ventures, sure to win worst movie of the year awards. All that mattered was relief from the mind-melting heat. A few stuck inside their homes were going stir-crazy.

Others were going mad, causing their tempers to flare.

One tall blonde detective in particular was barely containing the beast of anger inside herself from erupting. In the same home, another was pacing, wanting to escape its confines. Fueling Alex's anger at the world were feelings of helplessness. It had been more than several weeks since she'd been confined to their apartment. She could take no more.

Alex had blown through rehab with her new therapist, finally refusing to go anymore. She informed them she could do the rest on her own. To add to her bad mood and much to Alex's dismay, Nikki told her she was going to look for a job. Alex thought they had already decided she didn't need to work.

What Nikki couldn't tell her was that she wanted a job to get away from her. Alex followed her around the apartment, asking her what she was doing every few minutes. Finally not able to take any more, Nikki had to get out from under Alex's constant eyes.

Realization dawned on Alex the next day. It finally hit her - she was driving Nikki crazy with her constantly on her heels.

She lay soaking in the tub after another painful session at the gym. Her entire body hurt. With her head resting on the back of the tub, she wondered if doing the rehab on her own was such a good idea after all. "Damn, I never hurt this much before and I'm lifting the same weight I could before all this shit happened to me."

Alex stood in the tub, sloshing water everywhere. Standing on the bathmat beside the tub, she noticed the mess. "Shit, I'd better clean this up. I've already driven her nuts enough."

Bending down to wipe up the water caused excruciating pain in her shoulder. Changing her mind, she left the mess where it was. Suddenly exhausted, she dropped the towel on the floor by the bed and lay down.

Alex's head hit the pillow just as their apartment door opened. Nikki was returning from an afternoon of shopping, hot and worn out. "God, it's hot out there. It's dangerous to be out there today." She wiped sweat from her forehead with a paper towel.

Her day had started at the mall buying Alex some new boxer shorts and t-shirts. She had to go grocery shopping because their cupboards were empty. She was still afraid to leave Alex alone for too long. Alex tended to push herself too hard. For the past three days, they'd ordered delivery from the pizza place down the street. Nikki couldn't handle another day of pizza.

It took her five trips to bring all the bags into the kitchen from the truck. Nikki was bone tired and sweat covered her head to toe. Setting the final bag on the counter, she put away the perishable items, finally feeling a sense of accomplishment to her day.

In the middle of the living room floor, she found Alex's duffel bag and sneakers. Knowing she was probably soaking in the tub, Nikki headed for the bedroom.

Stepping into the bedroom, she found Alex lying on the bed looking as if she was asleep. Noticing the wet towel and dirty clothes strewn throughout the room, she set about gathering them up, ticked that Alex would leave such a mess. Nikki mumbled as she worked on the mess. "She's well enough to stop rehab and go to the gym every day, yet she can't pick up after herself. She infuriates me sometimes."

Nikki was picking up the towel when Alex touched her arm. She dropped everything in her arms and jumped. "Shit, Alex, you scared me. I thought you were asleep."

Alex couldn't stop the laugh that escaped. "No babe, just resting waiting for you."

Nikki smiled. "Let me take care of these things. I'll be right back."

She went into the bathroom to put the dirty items in the hamper. Nikki stopped in her tracks. The bathroom was a disaster. There was water everywhere. Several soaking wet towels lay on the floor.

It looked to her like Alex had a bubble bath that had exploded overboard. A few bubbles still clung to life on the tile floor and in the tub itself. There also were shampoo and body wash bottles strewn everywhere.

As she cleaned the pigsty, Nikki's anger grew. She knew Alex was getting better every day and could now fend for herself. While wiping up the cold water, feelings of being used settled in, angering her even more.

When she was done cleaning the floor, she stood shakily. Every bone in her legs and feet felt like they had turned to jelly. Nikki held onto the edge of the sink to steady herself while she got her legs under her. Needing to change her soaked clothes, she walked into the bedroom to find Alex sitting up in bed refreshed and totally relaxed.

Nikki opened the top dresser drawer, pulling a clean pair of panties out as she talked. "Bathroom is clean once more. I take it you had trouble getting out of the tub after your long soak, huh?"

Sometimes Alex thought before she opened her mouth, sometimes she didn't. This was one of those times where stupidity reigned.

Alex picked up the water bottle from the bedside table and drank. "Yeah I did, but I knew you'd be home soon to clean it up."

Just as it left her lips, she knew her words were wrong. Nikki whipped around toward her, barely controlled anger and hurt covering her face. Not wanting to say something she might regret, Nikki pulled the red-hot anger she felt back in.

Nikki clenched her teeth. "Excuse me? They did outlaw slavery, you know!"

Alex threw back the covers and stood, causing Nikki to back up a few steps. "I'm sorry, babe. My brain has had a meltdown. I think I overdid it today."

Playing the sympathy card, she put her hands on Nikki's bare waist. "I know this situation has been just as hard on you as on me. I'm sorry, babe. I know you're stressed and I'm not helping."

Nikki lifted her head, looking at her. Tears hung at the corners of her eyes. "Alex, I love you and would do anything for you. It's just that I'm… Well, you're right, I'm tired and stressed out."

Thoughts went back to her conversation with Kirstin. Maybe it was time. Maybe she should finally bare the final pieces to Alex. Maybe she too could heal a little as Alex's body healed.

Nikki quickly threw on one of Alex's t-shirts. It was much too large for her and she looked like a waif in it. "Scoot, let's just sit and talk for a bit."

Over the next hour, Nikki confided in Alex the remainder of her life. Alex's emotions ran the gambit from anger to confusion as to why her lover never told her any of this before, to sorrow that Nikki had been subjected to such things.

Anger though won the battle of emotions. No one touched her property. Her mind twisted with ways she could dispose of those that had hurt what belonged to her. Her mind's eye watched on as she envisioned tearing every strip of flesh from the bones of the one who had touched Nikki as only she was allowed to.

Nikki saw something in Alex's eyes. She saw white-hot anger and hatred. Then a shaking hand cupped her left cheek. Alex ran her thumb along Nikki's bottom lip. "So soft...."

She raised her eyes to meet Nikki's own. "No one will ever hurt you again, in any way. No one touches what belongs to me. You truly are mine…and sure as hell no one ever fucks what is mine."

Alex's body shook with pure rage that she felt in the deepest corners of her being. She couldn't let loose what lay within her, knowing it would terrify Nikki. She rested her forehead against Nikki's, getting the beast inside her under control.

Nikki wasn't sure if she felt better after talking with Alex. It felt good to get it off her chest. She also wanted no secrets between them. Yet, she felt fear course through her when she saw the look in Alex's eyes.

The beautiful eyes looking back at her didn't show anger. It was something else. Something she couldn't quite put her finger on. The closest she could come to it was murder. Nikki knew she never wanted that directed at herself.

Was Alex capable of that? Nikki would never have thought so until now. She seemed so possessive lately. It had to be stress. Nikki was sure that once Alex got back to work, everything would be better.

Knowing she had to defuse what was building within Alex, Nikki relayed the message she had taken that morning.

"Honey, Captain Billy called this morning while you were sleeping. He said to give him a ring on his cell phone when you're up to it. Tess also called. She said they would be here around six tomorrow night for dinner. I thought we would do steaks on the grill."

Alex knew what she was doing. She silently thanked her for it. Nikki was good at defusing the anger within Alex, wrapping her mind around better, more stable things. Lately though, she admitted to herself, it had been happening way too often. Her temper had been getting the best of her. Picking up her phone, she accepted the change of subjects, for the time being.

Nikki dressed as Alex walked into the living room to talk in private. "Sounds good, let me call Billy and see what he wants."

She finished dressing then joined Alex on the sofa. Wondering why the conversation was so brief, she looked up at Alex after slipping on her socks.

Nikki worried about the stunned expression on Alex's face. "Darling…"

The conversation *had* been brief. Alex was shocked. "Babe, you're not going to believe this. I got a big promotion. I mean I knew I was next in line for one but, wow. This is amazing."

"Alex, this is so wonderful. You deserve it so much. I can't believe this. What do you say I make you your favorite meal for dinner?" Nikki put her arms around Alex's waist, hugging her.

It had been a long time since she had seen Alex this happy. The recovery had been hard for her. Nikki couldn't stop herself from giggling with excitement, hugging her even tighter.

Alex put her nose to Nikki's hair, smelling the lavender and jade in her shampoo. It made up the very essence of what she had come to think of as Nikki. Any time she smelled one or the other, it set off something sensual deep inside of her. Her nipples hardened and her center warmed. She laid her head upon Nikki's shoulder trying to reign in her libido. Alex tried to tell herself *no*, yet her body breathed *yes*.

Nikki felt the body against her responding. However, it was feeling Alex's nipples harden against her that made her moan.

Hearing Nikki's moan, Alex kissed her on the neck, moving up to her earlobe. "I have something else in mind, baby."

Nikki reluctantly pulled away from Alex. "Jack said no heavy activity like that for at least another week. As much as I want to, I think we should listen to him and wait."

"Baby, I've been working out at the gym every day."

"Yes and…you're exhausted and in pain every day. I think we should wait. I don't want you hurting yourself."

Alex's frustration showed on her face. "I have an idea. Come with me." Pulling her into the bedroom, Alex started taking Nikki's clothes off.

"Darling, what are you doing? What do you have in mind?"

Alex grinned at her, a wicked little grin. After removing all of Nikki's clothes, she removed her own, leading Nikki to the bed. "Lay with your back against the headboard. Put this pillow behind your back." She sat on the bed in front of her. She pushed Nikki's legs apart and up a bit.

"You're so beautiful. I want you to touch yourself exactly how I tell you. Are you game for it?" When Nikki nodded, Alex continued.

"Rub your palms across your nipples. I know you like to have them touched. Pinch them just a little." Alex felt aroused. "Pinch them harder. Pull on them. Open your eyes and look at me. Never take your eyes off of me." Nikki looked into lust-filled eyes. "I want to taste you. Stick your finger in yourself and let me taste it." Nikki did as she was told, sticking the dripping wet finger into Alex's mouth.

Alex sucked it eagerly. "I want you to pretend it's me doing everything to you."

Nikki was excited at the thought of Alex watching her. Alex reached into the drawer in the nightstand, pulling out a couple of items.

Her heart beat faster. She took a blue eight-inch long dildo from Alex. She licked it while looking into Alex's eyes. She pinched the nipple that she had yet to let go of, a little harder this time. She heard Alex moan. Nikki inserted the tip through the wetness to where she wanted it most. "Do you want me to go slow or fast?"

"Slow and deep...."

She saw Alex's eyes grow a little darker. Alex licked her lips.

"Do you want another taste?" Alex nodded yes. She pushed it into herself to get it nice and wet. Nikki took it out, touching it to Alex's lips.

Alex greedily sucked it into her mouth.

"Hungry, aren't you?" Nikki ran it through Alex's own wetness before offering it back to her. Alex once again sucked it dry.

Alex breathed a little heavier. "Fuck yourself, baby."

As she pulled the dildo out, it made a wonderful sucking sound, a sound that she knew Alex loved. She continued like that until she could no longer go slowly. She wanted it fast and hard. She picked up speed.

Alex felt on the brink. Only a handful of times before had she come without being touched. Just watching Nikki made her so excited. Her hand drifted down to her own clit. "Go harder, baby."

Nikki was on the edge. She wanted to come, but wanted to make it last for Alex. Watching Alex touch herself, she became more excited. She reached and grabbed a vibrator and a larger dildo. Pulling the smaller one out, she inserted the larger to fill herself completely. Touching her clit with the vibrator was almost too much. "Oh God, Alex, it feels so good. Too good…I can't make it last."

"Make it last. Don't come yet." Alex watched her in total amazement. She was ready to come but wanted to hold out until Nikki did. "Let me see you suck your nipple. I'll hold the dildo in you."

Nikki grasped her breast, pulled her nipple into her mouth, sucking on it. She loved to have them sucked on. Sometimes she would come from that alone. She sucked on it harder and harder.

Alex knew she was coming. "Suck it harder, baby. Bite it."

Nikki went over the edge, screaming with her own breast still in her mouth.

Alex went back to rubbing her own clit. When her own orgasm hit, it surprised her by its intensity. She screamed Nikki's name and Alex felt Nikki coming again. "That's it, baby, come again for me. Come on, it feels good doesn't it, you want more, don't you?"

"Yes, more, need more. Please, Alex..."

Alex took the dildo out of her and inserted the vibrator.

"Yes Alex, oh yes. Turn it up higher."

Alex turned it up as high as it would go.

"Sweet Jesus, Alex! *Yes*!" Nikki's whole body lifted off the bed as she screamed. "Yessss..." Just as fast as she had climbed to orgasm, she collapsed back onto the bed, spent.

Her eyes never left Alex's the entire time. It was incredible. Neither had ever felt anything like it.

Alex smiled. "I think we both needed that."

She felt honored that she could give something so special to Alex. Nikki had known from the moment they crossed into the bedroom, which one of them had been in control. There wasn't a thing Nikki could do but to comply with what Alex wanted. She gave herself willingly. Alex had looked into Nikki's eyes and known. Known that Nikki knew she had no control. This knowledge only fueled Alex's fire all the more.

Alex had felt the control and power wash through her. She loved every second of it. Both lay sated and Nikki fell into a heavy, fast sleep.

Alex lay awake a few moments longer. "She'll always belong to me. No one will ever dare touch what is mine. Any that do will be in hell before they can take their next breath."

Another thought occurred to Alex at that moment. Her inner voice screamed at her. *What if?*

Walking to the bathroom, Alex's jealousy took form. "No, Nikki would never dare even look at another woman. She knows she belongs to me. If she ever did though, she'd live to regret it."

Chapter Six

Liars, Cheaters and Life

Alex sat on the edge of their bed, the new shield in her hand. She'd worked long and hard to arrive at the place she was in her professional life. During the years, she'd seen unspeakable acts thrust upon the innocents she had sworn to protect. Alex acknowledged that she herself had done things that she was not proud of, but this promotion was hers and hers alone. It was what she had strived for most of her life. It was who she was.

Turning the badge repeatedly, Alex looked at it from all angles, watching it sparkle as the sunlight hit it. This piece of metal was supposed to be her salvation. It was to make her a better cop, a better person.

Alex assumed that with it, new doors would open. With it also she hoped would come the respect from those who didn't like her or her methods.

She had thought it meant that she would have a little more time to spend with Nikki.

Instead of fewer hours, she and Scott were both putting in even more. They were still looking for the father who murdered his daughter, in addition to all the new cases that either no one else wanted or couldn't be solved in the first twenty-four hours. Her life was more chaotic and out of control than before.

During the years, she had taken anyone's shifts that needed to be covered. She craved the feeling of power it gave her to put handcuffs on someone, to have complete control of their lives. When she had returned to work, Alex continued as she had before, working call outs at all hours of the night.

The dark brooding detective had her fair share of injuries during the years, yet something was different this time. Before her latest injury, she'd never had a problem holding back the true beast living within her. Now, it was as if a switch had been flipped. The scum she pulled from the streets as well as her co-workers caught a glimpse every so often of the darkness as little by little it spread through her.

Alex could do nothing to stop it, nor did she want to. The more she lost control, the more power she felt. It felt like a form of liquid cocaine flowing through her veins, giving her the high of power and invincibility. Accompanying the highs were the crashes of guilt.

She was always the one that drew the line in the dirt. The line that once crossed meant they were hers do with as she pleased. She could go easy on them or tear their lives apart. The hardcore cases were all no-brainers. They never stood a chance. The little petty crimes had depended on her mood. Now though… none were saved from her wrath.

During the couple of months following her return to duty, no one got a second chance. Her mood ranged from foul to downright cruel. She knew Scott's concern grew as each day passed. He knew Alex would never admit to it, but a gut instinct told him that Nikki suffered the brunt of her anger.

✝

It had been another in a string of tiring days for both of the detectives. Alex tried to rein in her temper and Scott tried his best to control her. It started out as a routine day, only to go straight to hell in a hand basket. They were having lunch and Scott was once again trying to make her see reason, when a murder-suicide call came in.

They were met upon arrival by the neighbor, who had called 911. Alex recognized her from calls in the neighborhood during the years. She looked like a typical grandmother, but knew everything that went on around her. All of her neighbors looked up to her, most confiding their darkest secrets to her.

"Well, Miss Rose, what's the scoop today? And don't try to play coy with me, I know that you know every detail of what happened. Especially since your side porch looks right into theirs."

The older, portly woman smiled. "Why Officer Alex, you know I don't try to be nosy. I can't help it if I was sitting here enjoying some iced tea."

Alex sat in the rocker next to her. She picked up the glass of tea that obviously had been poured for her. "Okay Rose, I'm sitting down, having my tea. How did you know I would come?"

"Cause I told that scatter-brained sergeant of yours to call you and Scott. I didn't want to talk to anyone else about what I saw." A tear escaped, which she dabbed with a tissue from her pocket.

Alex sighed. "Rose…what happened?"

Rose looked at the house across from her. "He was working in his workshop, out in the garage. When he works out there, he tries to leave the door open, so he can hear what goes on in the house. You know, just in case one of the kids yells for him. I heard one of the little ones scream… 'Daddy… Daddy, help' I knew right away that something wasn't right. I see him run into the house." She once more pulled the tissue from its hiding place.

She put an arm around the elderly woman. "It's okay, Rose. Take your time."

"Oh, Ms. Alex…I heard terrible screams coming from that house. Daniel was like my own son. When they came home from the honeymoon, I knew there was something not right about her. One minute Sharon would be sweet as apple pie, the next mean as a rattlesnake. When she was having one of her episodes of not getting out of bed for weeks at a time, he and the young ones would come here for dinner. Sometimes it was five or six times a week."

"I know, Rose, you told me once before you thought of their kids as your own grandkids. What happened after he went in the house?" Alex tried to keep her on track.

"After I heard them screaming, it got real quiet and I got worried. He would always sit on the porch after their fights and cool off. He said she had what they call manic-depression and sometimes she would not take her medicine. I thought I should go see if all was okay. Once I finally got there, I looked in the screen door." She looked up at Alex, grief covering her face.

"Oh, Alex…he was standing there crying, looking down the hall. He asked me to call 911. He told me Sharon had drowned the children. He turned to me and told me he beat her when she told him what she did. I came back here to call you. When I opened my door to get the phone, I heard it, a loud bang. I'm old but no fool, I knew what that sound was. I knew he'd shot himself. What's this world come to when parents kill their own children? I don't think it's a world I want to live in anymore, if it's this far off kilter."

"I agree with you, Rose, the world is a crazy place right now. But if you weren't in it to keep an eye on things in this neighborhood, it would be even worse. What I want you to do is sit right here for me and don't talk to anyone, except for the uniformed officer I'm going to have come take your statement. Okay? Unfortunately, you're going to have to repeat all of this again. I'm sorry about that. When the officer comes here, why don't you take him in the house and talk there. It would make me feel better if you were inside."

"Okay, Alex. Thank you for being the one to come."

Alex walked across the lawn to the porch of the house next door. "Mitchell, can you please go and take Rose's full statement? I'm not sure which one of the rookies you have with you today, but take him too. It'll be good experience for him, especially if they're going to be working this neighborhood."

"Sure thing, Alex, this call sure does suck though."

Walking onto the porch behind Scott, she watched a young uniformed officer walking up the driveway, toward Rose's house. It was Rachel, their captain's daughter. Alex noticed what a nice fit her uniform was and before she knew it, the words were out of her mouth. The words meant only for herself, but they were loud enough for Scott to hear.

"Damn, Rachel looks hot in that uniform. What a nice ass. Too bad she's Billy's daughter, 'cause she's damn fine looking." Alex couldn't help it. This was the true Alex coming to the surface.

Scott had thought meeting Nikki and settling down with her would, in turn, settle Alex down. Sure, occasionally it was good to have the old Alex back when dealing with the scum of the earth, but not on a full time basis. Kirstin mentioned it the last time Scott saw her, that she prayed that the old Alex was gone. They both knew she had major commitment issues but thought she had worked through them.

Scott stopped in his tracks and pulled Alex to the side out of earshot of anyone. Scott hoped he had heard her incorrectly. He glared at her while trying to temper the words that were to come from his mouth.

She looked at him and shrugged her shoulders, not understanding what the issue was. "What?"

"What? What do you mean what? Did you hear what just came out of your mouth? What the hell is your deal? I thought you were learning to keep it in your pants, Alex." Scott was pissed off.

"Give me a break. I was just admiring a good-looking woman. Is that a crime? Last time I checked, it wasn't." She moved to take a step toward the house when Scott grabbed her arm.

She looked down at his hand on her arm and then back up at him. He heard a low growl coming from her and winced. The look upon her face could break a diamond in half.

Her voice came out in a deep rumble through clenched teeth, "You better make this worth it, Scott."

"Alex, what the hell is going on? You've been out of control since the hospital. I wish you'd talk to me. If you're having trouble dealing with what happened, talk to me or talk to someone. Don't go taking it out on everyone else and sure as hell don't be taking it out on Nikki. She deserves better than that. It would kill her to find out you were screwing around on her. So don't. Don't even think about doing it. You can look all you want, but

I know you, you want to do more than just look. You're cruisin'. Am I right?"

Thinking about Alex returning to her old ways turned Scott's insides to Jell-O.

Scott clenched his fists at his side, preparing for a fight if Alex became aggressive. He knew in his heart that words had to be said and that he might be the only one to get away with it, other than Kirstin.

Alex stepped so their faces were only an inch apart. She was so close that he knew if he looked, he would be able to see the tiny fine hairs in her nose.

"First of all, what I do in my private life is none of your fucking business. Yes, we're friends, but don't presume to dictate anything to do with Nikki's and my life. And what the hell do you mean, I've been taking it out on Nikki? Has she said something to you? She has nothing to complain about. I take good care of her. She wants for nothing. She doesn't even need to work but for some reason she wants to. She knows she'll never find anyone out there any better than me. I would do anything for her."

Alex had to open and close her jaw several times to make it stop hurting. She had been clenching her teeth together so hard it was painful.

Scott looked at her, hearing what was not said. He also noted her choice of words. That Nikki would never find anyone better than her. Now was not the time to get full-blown into it with her, so he would leave that one for another day. Knowing she might still take her pound of flesh from him, he jumped into the fray once more about her wandering eye.

"I notice you didn't deny you were cruisin' Rachel. Alex if you cheat on Nikki, it will break her. She loves you so much, she'd give her life for you. Man, she wiped your ass for you when you were in the hospital and couldn't, so don't do that to her." Scott turned from her to walk into the house.

He never looked back, fearing what he might see. Quietly, he said, "I won't lie for you if you do." He knew she'd heard him.

†

Their initial findings correlated with what Rose had told them. The mother had drowned their two small children. Her husband came in from his workshop to find his children dead. Alex found a prescription bottle on the counter. It had been filled three weeks previously. However, when she counted the pills and compared the number to what was missing, it told her the mother had only taken four days worth. The husband, in a rage, had beaten her to death. He took his own life out of grief.

As far as Alex was concerned, it was an open and shut case. She would put Dom's reports in the binder the next day and call the case closed. She looked at Scott.

"I am wiped out and going home. Since we missed our day off, I suggest you do the same. We'll finish this up tomorrow, when Dom's done with his reports. Go home to Tessa and take her out to dinner."

"Alex, I'm too beat to argue with you. We however are going for a beer tomorrow night, no matter what." What could it hurt if their talk waited another day? It would give her time to think on what Scott had said.

†

Hours later Alex sat on their bed, contemplating Scott's words. *Would I cheat on Nikki?*

A dozen thoughts raced through her mind, some of them unsavory. "Did I really give Rachel the once over? Sure, I would have before meeting Nikki. Hell, I would have jumped at the chance to bed a hot looking woman, never giving it a second thought."

In the past, Alex always got what she wanted, one way or another. Everything was different now though. She had Nikki in her life and things were going great. Well, they were going great until she was shot.

Shit! What's going on with me? I can't seem to help myself. I keep checking out every woman that crosses my path. I've been treating Nikki like crap, yelling at her for the littlest thing. I keep losing my temper at work, what's happening to me? Things should be going in the opposite direction, especially now that I'm a Lieutenant. I have more responsibility not only at work but in my personal life.

Shaking her head, she tried clearing the jumbled thoughts.

Finally, she admitted some of the truth to herself. "Maybe things got out of control because I couldn't protect her while I was hurt. That's when things seemed to start getting shitty. First with that damn therapist, then a week after I got home from the hospital she burned herself while cooking. Admit it, asshole, her getting burned was your fault. If you hadn't yelled at her when she had that pot of scalding hot soup in her hands, she wouldn't have dropped it. Thank the gods the burn healed so well and only left a small scar."

She sat on the bed trying to be brutally honest. It was something Alex hadn't done in a very long time. Would she cheat on Nikki? Frustrated she pounded her fists on the sides of her head. Would she go out with another woman, even just to have coffee? Could she do that to Nikki and their relationship?

Alex ran her fingers through her hair for the tenth time since she had sat down more than an hour before. Nikki wasn't home yet from the job interview that she had late that afternoon. It was a prime opportunity and Alex was trying to be happy for her.

The evil little voice that lived in her brain reared its ugly head. *Yeah…kind of happy that she'll have something else to put all of her attention into instead of me. She hovers like a mother hen. God, would I cheat on her, really?*

Alex kept coming back to the same question repeatedly.

Alex looked at the picture of the two of them on the wall, the black-white picture that Kirstin had taken of them, sitting naked on a chair that was turned around backwards. Alex sat behind Nikki, resting her chin on her lover's right shoulder. She knew they were nude, yet nothing showed the way they were sitting on the chair. It was quite a beautiful portrait. The best one they had of the two of them. Kirstin had been more than willing to take the picture. It was elegant looking, yet to Alex it oozed power and control.

She set her new shield on top of her gun in the lock box and closed it. In the living room, she was confronted with yet another picture of them. Scott took it the day after their first anniversary. Looking around the apartment, Alex took in their life. "I love her so much, I can't mess that up. No matter what, the answer has to be no. I need to get myself back under control. Maybe Scott is right, talking about it might help."

Her inner voice again took control. *Damn! What goes on behind the doors of our home no one else's business. There has to be an answer.*

Alex heard the key in the door, relieved that Nikki was finally home. She could concentrate on having a good evening and maybe the self-recriminations would stop. It was obvious that Nikki was having trouble with the door.

Alex got to the door just as it swung open. Nikki came through it, her arms packed with bags of groceries. Alex had forgotten, until right that moment, that her family was coming for dinner to celebrate her promotion. She took the bags from Nikki, kissing her hello.

Nikki was a flurry of activity. "Hey, darling, how was your day? Are Scott and Tessa coming for dinner also? I made sure to buy enough of everything just in case." Nikki set the bag she still carried down. Starting to unpack it, she was unaware of Alex slinking out of the room.

Alex quietly ran into the bathroom to call Scott. She explained her error quickly. "Come on Scott you've got help me out here. She'll kill me if she finds out I forgot. Just explain to Tessa, I'm sure she'll understand."

Scott finally gave in and agreed. "You're just having a fucked up day aren't you, girl? And you're trying to make mine just as bad." Alex disconnected, his laughter still ringing in her ears.

Alex quietly re-entered the kitchen. She found all of the items put away and Nikki starting to make the lasagna. Leaning against the doorjamb Alex watched her in fascination. She loved this woman. She would do anything for her. Nikki belonged to her and her alone.

Running around the kitchen, gathering all of the spices needed for her sauce, Nikki was a flurry of motion. Alex continued eyeing her as Nikki pulled the stool close to climb up to get the kettle for the corn down. It was larger so she kept it up on top of the cupboard.

Nikki pulled the two pans down setting them on the counter. She felt rather than heard Alex come up behind her. Alex's hands on Nikki's hips, she turned her around on the stool.

She leaned against the back of it to steady herself. "Alex, darling, what are you up to? I have to get dinner ready. We really don't have time to play, sweetie."

Nikki tried to move Alex's hands off her hips. The next thing she knew Alex was unzipping her jeans, pulling them and her panties down. "Alex, please…we don't have time."

Alex was too fast. She already had her tongue on Nikki, licking as if she were a melting ice cream cone. "Jesus, Alex… not enough time. Oh God…" She couldn't stop her hips from thrusting against Alex's mouth. She felt it building fast. "Alex, please don't—"

Alex began sucking on her. Nikki begged her not to stop. "Yes, harder. Oh yes, please." The doorbell rang.

Growling, Alex pulled away from Nikki. "Fuck."

She stalked off to answer the door, wiping her mouth and face on her sleeve as she went. Yelling back to Nikki, she growled. "We'll finish this later."

It took all Nikki's effort to make herself decent in time. She gulped down two glasses of water while listening to Alex talk to her brother-in-law in the living room. Hearing someone clear her throat behind her, she turned to see Kirstin with a smirk on her face.

"Catch the two of you at a bad time, did we?" Kirstin giggled.

"You're so funny, Kirstin. Sometimes your sister is a little overzealous, you know." Nikki turned back to the stove to start browning the meat. "So, on a different topic, why are you here so early?"

"This is the time Alex told us to be here. Are we too early? What can I help you with?" Kirstin moved to the counter, picking up the knife to cut the veggies for the salad. Since Nikki had none of the dinner started, she knew they were indeed too early.

Kirstin had been hoping to talk to Nikki alone, so it all worked out for the best that Alex had told her the wrong time. She had a feeling Alex was still a little out of control and she wanted to make sure Nikki was doing okay.

"Nikki, is everything going okay? Is Alex getting better?"

"Kirstin, Alex is fine. She's just tired and still healing. Plus she just went back to work. On top of that, she has quite a bit more responsibility with her promotion. I think she just needs some time to try to get a handle on everything. They're still working on finding the man they were after when she was shot. Sure, things sometimes get the best of her, but that is understandable. She just needs some time. Why don't you make the salad and I'll do the lasagna?"

Kirstin knew when a conversation was closed. She only hoped that Nikki would come to her and not try to shoulder it all herself.

Giggling and loud screaming filtered in from the living room, followed by a loud crash. Moments later, Alex sheepishly came into the kitchen with one of Nikki's favorite vases in pieces. "Sorry, babe. I guess I got a little playful."

Nikki turned to see what she had broken. "No one was hurt, were they? That's all that matters."

Alex dumped the glass in the trash. "No, just my pride and your vase. I really am sorry, baby." She walked close and kissed her on the cheek. "I'll buy you a new one tomorrow."

"The vase doesn't matter as long as no one was hurt." She turned back to mix the egg with the ricotta as Alex went back to play with the kids. She stirred the sauce and meat mixture. Not wanting it to get too thick, she turned off the heat. Nikki did anything she could so she wouldn't think about the broken item.

Kirstin asked her quietly, "Wasn't that your mother's vase?" She laid her hand on Nikki's shoulder.

"It's okay, it was only a vase, it's not that important."

Even as Nikki said the words, her heart ached for what could never be replaced.

✝

Later that evening as everyone was saying good night, Scott made sure to steal an extra piece of the cheesecake that was Nikki's specialty. She always made two knowing everyone would take some home with them.

Scott came into the living room with the two containers in his hands. The three women stood staring at him. "What? I got something on my face or something?"

Tessa glared at him. She had attempted to make the same dessert but he ate one piece and didn't touch it again. Yet here he was taking home as much as he'd just eaten.

Alex snickered. "You like it that much, huh?" He looked at the plastic containers then back at Alex.

Without thinking, he said the first thing that popped into his mind. "Nikki is like the best cook I know and her desserts are to die for." As soon as the words left his lips, he knew he was in trouble.

Alex laughed. "Oh man, it's going to suck being you for the next couple of weeks. Start the ass kissing now." She patted him on the back and walked away. He turned looking to Nikki for help.

"No way, Scott, you're on your own now. Good luck." She too walked away.

"Damn, you two are cowards. Yellow-bellies…" Scott did his best imitation of a pouty-puppy as he studied his shoes, but Tess wasn't going to buy into it this time.

Scott heard Alex yell from the kitchen. "Good luck, dude."

He finally looked at Tessa. The look on her face was not good. Not good at all. Little did he know, but he would spend the next two weeks in the spare bedroom on top of cooking all the meals. It would be some time before he would make that mistake again.

Nikki made some fresh peach green tea for herself and grabbed a beer for Alex before she sat down next to her on the leather couch. She had news to tell her but wanted to wait until they were alone. Alex had seemed a little preoccupied all through dinner.

"Alex, is everything okay? You seem a little distracted tonight. Is everything okay at work?"

Alex took a long pull on her beer, contemplating her answer. "Everything's great, babe. I was just thinking about how long we've been together now. Sometimes it seems so much longer than it is. Then sometimes it seems like just yesterday I walked into your office and saw you for the first time."

Nikki snuggled a little closer. "I know what you mean, I feel the same way. This has been the happiest time of my life. I wouldn't trade one second of it for anything. I have some good news that I wanted to wait until tonight to tell you about. I didn't want to take away from your night."

Nikki found herself unsure of how to tell Alex. She picked at the threads on the bottom of Alex's denim shorts.

"What is it, is everything okay? Did the interview not go well today?" Alex pushed a stray lock of hair off Nikki's face and back behind her ear.

Alex wanted her home where she knew she was safe, yet on the other hand, she wanted Nikki to get the position. Alex felt guilty about how she had treated her lately. She hoped being supportive would make up for it and maybe, just maybe, take away some of the guilt.

"Actually he offered me the position right on the spot. It totally shocked me. I said yes without even thinking about it. I hope that's okay. I think I'll really like working for Mark. He's a very nice man. I start next Monday." Once started, the words spilled out one right after another.

Nikki hoped Alex would be supportive in her taking the job without discussing it with her first. It was the perfect opportunity for her. She didn't want to miss out on it by telling him she'd get back to him, so she had accepted immediately.

"That's great, we'll have to go out and celebrate tomorrow night. We'll go to your favorite restaurant. How does that sound?" Alex leaned, capturing Nikki's lips with her own.

Alex caressed the side of Nikki's face with the back of her fingers. "I love you and I'm very happy for you. As long as you're sure this is what you want, I'll stand by your decision. All I've ever wanted for you is your happiness. You understand that, right? I know sometimes that I get bitchy. I don't really mean to. I love you and don't ever want to hurt you."

Her conversation with Scott suddenly was front and center once more. It felt like someone was stabbing her heart with a dagger. "I love you so much that sometimes it hurts. Sometimes I feel I have to keep you with me at all times to protect you, to keep you safe. I know I can't do that and I get frustrated. You are my life." Without realizing, she'd pulled Nikki onto her lap.

Nikki put her arms around Alex's neck, their foreheads touching. "Darling, I love you just as much. You, however, can't protect me twenty-four seven. I, likewise, can't do the same for you. Luckily, with this promotion you won't be out there as much and that makes me very happy."

She kissed Alex, letting her lips linger. "So, you want to go celebrate a little right now?"

Alex pulled back, taking Nikki's face between her hands. She liked when Nikki was sexually aggressive, it made her hot and wet instantly. "I love you, baby, I promise you I will never hurt you in any way. I know I'm not perfect but I'll try. If you'll have me, will you marry me?"

She stood effortlessly with Nikki in her arms and walked toward the bedroom. "I mean, we don't have to run right out tomorrow and do it, but when the time feels right. What do you say?"

Nikki was speechless. She wanted to say yes, but was Alex just asking because things had been strained lately? Or was she asking from her heart? Did she care?

No. There was only one answer. "Yes."

†

As much as Nikki became settled into her new job during the next several months, Alex became unsettled in her own mind. Her inner self tried to convince her that Nikki was cheating on her. Nikki was now the promotions manager which required long hours, working on several projects that were all due at the same time.

Alex, however, didn't see it that way. She thought Nikki was spending time with one of the girls she worked with. Alex went as far as to follow them one day when they went out to lunch. Some would have called it stalking. Alex called it research.

Walking up to the table, Alex looked down at Nikki.

"Hi baby. I called the office and they said you had come here for lunch. I thought I would join you."

Pulling up a chair next to her, Alex turned to the woman sitting across from her lover. "Hi, I'm Alex, Nikki's girlfriend." She unclipped her phone from her belt and set it on the table.

Liz knew who she was. Nikki talked about her all the time. She talked about what a great person and cop she was.

Nikki answered for Liz. "Alex, this is Liz, she is the assistant to the Business Manager for Cyclone Advertising. Liz, this is Alex."

Nikki turned to Alex. "Did you have fun grocery shopping with Aunt Cassie?"

Alex shook her head. "I love her because she's family. However, someday she's going to drive me to use my gun. Know what I mean?"

"Alex! You are so bad. Anyway, how much time do you have? We haven't ordered yet, do you want something?"

Alex's cell phone interrupted them and she answered. "Canton. Fine, I'll be there as soon as I can. I'm about ten minutes out."

Turning it off, she reattached it to her belt. "Sorry, babe, Scott just caught one and needs me there."

Scott was trying to break in the new detective that was assigned as his partner. With Alex being hurt, he should have received a new partner some time ago. Now, with her promotion, there was no choice.

Their captain knew the friends made a good team. Experience also showed him that sometimes Scott was the only one who could keep Alex in line. However, the reassignment was a done deal. Alex agreed to it on a trial basis, truly not liking Scott not having her back.

Alex turned to Liz, extending her hand. "It was nice to meet you, Liz. Maybe you could come for dinner some night this week. Nikki can work out the details."

She bent, kissing Nikki on the lips before leaving. The two watched as Alex walked away. Liz would have sworn Alex was strutting as she left.

The kiss surprised Nikki. Usually Alex didn't like public displays of affection. She was curious as to what precipitated her doing that. Nikki made a mental note to ask Alex about it that night. She looked up to find Liz grinning at her.

Nikki smiled. "She's gorgeous, huh?"

They both laughed.

"Wow. Your description didn't do her justice. She's hot. God, Nikki…she could turn me gay. So, does she show up often when you're at lunch? Or is today an oddity?"

Liz tried not to sound inquisitive but she was curious. She had taken an instant dislike to Alex, finding her overbearing. There was something Liz didn't like nor trust about her. Maybe it was the way she held herself or maybe it was the look in her eyes as Alex had walked up to the table. She thought Alex looked like a predator looking for its next prey to devour. Liz felt the detective was ready to pounce on the innocent at any moment.

"No, she asks beforehand. It was nice though, because you finally got to meet her. When do you want to come for dinner? Any night is good. I was going to make beef soup on Saturday, do you want to come then?" While Liz contemplated, the waiter came to take their orders.

"Saturday sounds good to me. What would you like me to bring? What kind of wine do you like? I'm good at that. That way I don't have to cook, 'cause you know I can't cook."

Over the next half hour, they talked about the project Nikki was currently working on and how things were going in Liz's non-existent love life. When they arrived back at the office, Mark was waiting in Nikki's office. He informed her that the client had moved up the timetable and the project needed to be completed by the next morning.

Luckily, all Nikki had left to do was examine the final draft and approve the last few changes. The new timetable however meant that she would be in the office until at least midnight. She phoned Alex to let her know. As was the norm lately, Alex was a little miffed.

†

Alex closed her phone and turned to Scott. She couldn't believe it. Once again, Nikki was going to be late at the office. She was trying hard not to let her mind play tricks on her.

"I knew I shouldn't have let her take that damn job. Her only job should be to be my girlfriend. Fuck, she has to work late again tonight. If I didn't know better I'd swear she was screwin' around."

Scott stopped, not believing his ears.

"Alex, you know Nikki's faithful to you. She's just trying to prove herself to her new boss. She really loves that job and I think it's good for her. She was bored not having anything to do. Not that making a home for you doesn't count but this job gives her a purpose. Do you understand what I'm trying to say? I hope you do."

He tried his best to warn her subtly. Scott was afraid Alex was going to blow this relationship at the rate she was going.

Alex heard the unspoken words and they pissed her off. What right did he have to come down on her? She didn't need him butting into her life, even though she did consider him her best friend.

"Scott…I can handle things, don't worry. Maybe I'm just feeling a little neglected right now. You want to go for a slice or are you heading home?" Standing next to Alex's truck, they leaned against the tailgate.

"Naw, I better get home. Tessa's making some kind of new dish tonight. You know what that means. I wish I could go for a slice with you."

Alex laughed, thinking about Tessa's cooking.

She slapped him on the back. "Sucks to be you man, good luck with whatever she's brewing up in her cauldron tonight."

Alex was still laughing as she got into her truck and drove away.

✝

Saturday evening came too fast for Alex, yet it couldn't be finished soon enough. It was bad enough Nikki had to go into work that morning, but dealing with their dinner guest was sending her over the edge. Alex had taken an instant dislike to Nikki's co-worker Liz.

Liz arrived early and helped Nikki prepare dinner. Every time Alex looked at the two, it looked as if Liz was draped on Nikki. While they were cooking, Liz kept touching her, while standing too close to her for Alex's tastes.

While they cooked, Alex paced between the kitchen and living room grabbing a fresh beer almost every time. She was on her eleventh bottle by the time dinner was done. Between the beer and her overactive imagination, she had worked her mind into a tizzy.

All through dessert, she wished Liz would disappear from the face of the earth. Nikki knew something was wrong when Alex didn't say goodnight to their guest when she left. She was in the kitchen quietly loading the dishwasher when Alex came in for another beer.

"Alex, is everything okay? I've only ever seen you drink this much when you're upset about something. You don't like Liz, do you?" Nikki closed the dishwasher, turning to face Alex.

With her hands on Alex's hips, she pulled her closer. "Honey, what's wrong? Was there something wrong with dinner? Or is it Liz?"

"I just don't like her. She was all over you and you were letting her." Alex grabbed Nikki's forearm and squeezed hard.

"Alex…" Flinching, Nikki pulled back. Alex released her arm when she realized what she was doing.

"Liz is just a touchy feely type of person. Alex, do you really think I would cheat on you? I hope not. I really hope you trust me more than that." Nikki was hurt. When Nikki walked around her toward the bedroom, Alex roughly grabbed her arm.

"It's not that I don't trust you, I don't trust anyone else. I love you too much and I will not lose you, to anyone."

She pulled Nikki hard against her and kissed her roughly. She wound her fingers through Nikki's hair, tugging on it slightly.

"Alex, please…."

Alex pulled her hair harder forcing her head back.

Nikki felt Alex biting her neck. "Alex, that's too hard. It hurts and you'll leave a mark." Alex pulled back, kissing her more roughly than she ever had before.

"I thought you liked it hard, baby. As far as marks go, I'm only marking what's mine, what is my property." Alex pulled apart Nikki's shirt, sending buttons flying in every direction.

In one fluid motion, she pulled Nikki's bra down, sucking a nipple into her mouth. She bit hard, causing Nikki to flinch. Normally she would be far more excited before Alex became so aggressive.

"Alex, please that hurts, you're biting it too hard. Please, let's slow down. Let's talk, something's bothering you." Alex released her nipple pushing Nikki away from her.

"Yeah, something's wrong all right. I want to fuck you and all you want to do is talk. Maybe you don't want me because you already got some this morning from someone else."

Alex pushed roughly by Nikki causing her to stumble backwards. Losing her balance when she hit the stool behind her, Nikki fell sideways, striking her head on the counter on the way to the tile floor.

Alex regretted her action the second it happened. She couldn't control the anger coursing through her. She realized she'd almost taken Nikki against her will because of her anger. Her only option was to get away from Nikki and calm herself down.

When she heard the chair crashing to the floor and the cry escape Nikki's lips, Alex ran in terror back into the kitchen. What she saw made her heart freeze. Nikki sat on the floor with her back against the cabinet, holding her head in her hand.

"Oh God, baby, I'm so sorry. It's my fault. I got too rough. God, I'm so sorry. Oh babe, I'm sorry."

Alex picked her up in her arms. Taking her into the living room, Alex gently laid her on the sofa. "Let me see, I want to make sure you're okay." Alex pulled Nikki's hand away from her head.

Nikki tried hard not to cry. It hurt so badly that she couldn't stop the tears that ran down her cheeks. She blamed herself for what had happened. Knowing Alex was in a bad mood, she shouldn't have pushed her. She should have just gone along with what Alex wanted. It was so much easier that way. Nikki knew that after Alex released what was built-up inside of her, she would be more rational. After that, she would talk about what was going on.

Alex wiped the tears from Nikki's face. She kissed her gently on the lips. "I'm so sorry babe. I think we should take you to the hospital. I want to make sure you're okay. Oh babe...." She kissed her again.

"Alex, honey, it's not your fault. You had a little too much to drink and were just biting a little too hard. I know you didn't mean to bite that hard and they are still so sensitive from the working you gave them last night. Besides, I'm the one who tripped over the stool. Please, honey, don't blame yourself. Please, look at me, Alex." Nikki touched Alex's chin with her fingertips and tilted her head up.

Their eyes met then Alex's moved up to Nikki's forehead. A new wave of guilt washed across her when she saw the bruise already starting to form.

"Alex, please, it was an accident. It's not your fault. Let's go to bed, love." Alex stood then bent to pick her up. "I can walk on my own. Please, I'll be fine."

Nikki saw the guilt on her lovers face, as Alex lay her on the bed, gently kissing and undressing her; she knew this was what Alex needed. Nikki patted the bed next to her giving her the seductive smile that always got her going. Alex took care to be very gentle with her, bordering on worshipping her.

As they slowly made love that night, Alex's mind wandered. Later she lay awake for several hours, her mind reeling from the day's events. Only once before had she been so out of control that she didn't realize what she was doing.

Alex told herself she knew when to walk away. She knew when she was unable to control her temper. She knew the signs. Not being able to sleep, Alex went to the other room to check some files.

Why didn't I walk away? What in the hell is going on with me? I have a wonderful lover, the job is going great, we've almost caught the bastard who shot me. We could close the case. So why did I lose it?

Not having any easy answers for herself, she went back to work on the files.

†

Alex did everything within her power during the next several days to make it up to Nikki, who still insisted it was no one's fault and that it was just an accident. Alex prepared her wonderful dinners every night, brought home flowers for her and made plans for them to get away for their anniversary. Nikki had always wanted to go to New York City to see a Broadway show. Alex made reservations at a hotel that Scott recommended then bought tickets to several shows.

Two days after the incident, she confessed to Scott what she had done. Alex thought for sure he was going to lay her out cold. Instead, they'd had another one of their long intense conversations on the issues of life. He knew better than to go off on her; it would have done no good. He was hoping talking it through with her would make her look at it from the outside in. If she did that, Scott was sure

Alex would see how she was acting was wrong. He was afraid for both of them if Alex kept on the way she was going.

✝

Upon Nikki's arrival at work Monday morning, Liz waited at her office door. Seeing the bruise on Nikki's forehead, she became concerned for her friend. She knew Alex was upset about something on Saturday when she'd been there, but didn't think this would be the result. Nikki motioned her into her office and Liz closed the door behind her.

Sitting in the leather chair in front of Nikki's desk, Liz waited for Nikki to be settled. "Nikki, what's going on? What happened to your head? Did Alex do this?"

Nikki put her hand up to stop the barrage of questions from Liz. She connected and booted up her laptop before dealing with her friend. She knew this would happen. Nikki was a little peeved at Liz.

"You know what, Liz? People always assume its spousal abuse, never just an accident. Why do we always assume the worst in people?"

Luckily, Liz couldn't see the bruises on her arm from where Alex had squeezed too hard. *Damn. I really don't have time to deal with this crap first thing this morning. I have to finalize this project before ten.*

"Liz, nothing is going on. I tripped over the chair in the kitchen and hit my head on the front of the cabinet, that is all, nothing more to it." Nikki was hoping that this would close the subject. She should have known better. Liz wouldn't let go of it that easily.

"Nikki, I like to think we're good friends. You can tell me anything at all. I would never judge either of you. I know Alex was in a bad mood Saturday night and that she had quite a bit to drink. Did things maybe get a little out of hand? Did she hit you or maybe push you? Maybe she wanted sex and you didn't?"

Nikki was getting a little upset. Why couldn't Liz just let it go? *Damn it!*

"Liz, we're closer than sisters and I've come to love you dearly." Nikki paused, opening a couple of programs on her computer. "Nothing happened. Yes, she was a little drunk, but she would never hurt me. It was an accident. I backed up into the chair and fell over it, pure and simple. Sorry, but my life is kinda boring. Things like that only happen in trashy novels and movies of the week. Now, I know you have to get going on payroll and I have to get this project finalized or both of our asses will be toast."

Right on cue, Mark knocked on Nikki's door. Moaning, all she could think was here came round two of the inquisition.

"Saved by the knock, for now. Call me when you're ready for lunch." Liz opened the door to find Mark on the other side.

"Morning Mark, good weekend? Get a little golf in? Eat a little seafood?"

Mark laughed at Liz's remarks, knowing he looked like a baked lobster.

"Go ahead, Liz, yuck it up." He play-punched her in the arm. "I forgot the sunscreen and didn't really think I would burn so much since it was a little cloudy yesterday. Nikki, is the project done?"

Liz took that opportunity to sneak out before he could see the hickey on her neck and return the harassment.

Mark looked closer at Nikki. "Who the hell clocked you, girl? It looks like they got you good. Did you go to one of those leather bars and some big girl get out of hand?"

Her boss had a wicked sense of humor. Nikki could only guess what was coming next. She did know though that it would be outlandish at the least. She wasn't disappointed.

He laughed, amused at himself. "I know, some big bad-ass butch of a woman came on to you in the bar and Alex went to set her straight, so to speak, and you got in the way. Am I anywhere near base here? Oh wait, I'm sure I can come up with another good one. Maybe she caught Ms. Butch with her hands on you and lost it. Or maybe just the opposite, I could picture Alex liking to watch. Then she decided to join you and Ms. Butch decided she didn't want to share you."

He sat in the chair Liz had just vacated, waiting for Nikki's explanation.

Nikki rolled her eyes, laughing at him. "Geez, you guys are so bad. Where the hell do you come up with some of that crap? Get your mind out of the gutter. Do the two of you always assume the worst? I tripped backwards over a stool in the kitchen and hit my head. That's all, nothing more. Now, if we're all done grilling me for the morning, can we get down to business? I have the project finalized and just want to examine it one more time." Nikki sent the job to her printer, which started spitting out page after page of the presentation.

She looked at him again in astonishment. "Good Lord, a three way…what a line from a porno movie." Nikki shook her head in disbelief.

"Oh come on, you can't blame a guy for coming up with a really great scenario that sounds much better than the reality of just tripping over a chair."

Mark became serious. "So… is that what really happened, you tripped and fell?" Even though he joked, he had a hunch there was more to it than what Nikki was saying.

From the first moment Mark laid eyes on Nikki he knew she had potential. That was why he hired her on the spot. He didn't want anyone else to get their hands on her talent. Not only did she have an eye for detail and finesse with working within the budget, but she was also great with people. Everyone loved her and she was already known in the advertising community. That to him was the greatest bonus. He knew the acquisition of this woman was one of the best business moves he had ever made.

Nikki stood by the printer, looking at the printouts as they came out. "Yes, that is exactly what happened. As I told Liz, this is not one of those trashy novels she reads. Geez, how does Janet put up with you? Does she let you get away with this crap at home? Somehow I don't think so and that's why you pull it all here."

She set the first printout of the project on her desk. Being the perfectionist she was, Nikki started to go through it once more.

Mark knew when he was beaten. Nikki was a great sparring partner for his mind. She learned within her first week how to keep him in line and did so with Janet's full blessing.

"Okay, I know when I'm beaten. I'll be in my office. I have a couple of calls to make. Then we'll meet on this before the presentation. Yell if you need anything."

"I'll be ready in about thirty minutes. You wanted ten copies correct?" Mark nodded as he walked out the door, closing it behind him.

Nikki was unable to meet up with Liz for lunch. Her promotion ideas had been received so well with the client that he took her, Mark, and her staff to lunch, which turned into an all-day affair.

†

A week before their anniversary, Nikki nervously watched the eleven o'clock news, waiting to hear from Alex. When she was going to be very late, she always called. Dinnertime had long since passed with still no word from Alex.

Nikki had even gone as far as to call Scott. She didn't want Alex to think she was checking up on her but she was worried. Alex was more than five hours late and even Scott had no idea where she was. She could hear worry in his voice as well.

Nikki continued to wait by the phone — not knowing that Alex sat only a block away. She couldn't bring herself to go home yet. Sitting in the truck with her head on the steering wheel, a deadly headache bordering on a migraine thumped inside her skull. Her head might not have been so bad had she not pounded it on the side of the truck repeatedly before she got in.

Alex couldn't believe what she had done. Did she really betray the person she loved most in the world? Did she lie to Scott when he called her wondering where she was? Could her existence get any worse? She couldn't understand how she had ended up at this place in her life. Nikki would never forgive her for this.

"As well, she shouldn't. I'm a complete fuck-up," she said aloud

Alex's phone startled her. She retrieved it from the passenger's side floor, where she had thrown it earlier. "Shit! Now who?" She looked at the caller id. "What!" Alex barked into the receiver.

"Where are you? Nikki just called me again. Alex, what's going on? Tell me where you are and I'll meet you."

She could hear Scott's frustration echoing in his words.

"I fucked up."

That was all Scott needed to hear. He knew what she meant. He'd seen it coming and could do nothing to stop it. In order for Alex to learn from her mistakes, she would have to hit rock bottom. Scott could only guide her in the right direction.

In his heart, Scott knew he would be there for her, but Alex's penance was a price to be paid all on her own. Nothing he would say or do would matter until Alex understood the repercussions of what she did. She could do one of two things; confess to Nikki and beg forgiveness, or lie. He prayed that she wouldn't lie. He vowed to himself he would not lie for her, neither would he tell Nikki. That was for Alex alone to do.

The silence was deafening. It startled Alex when Scott finally spoke. "Meet me at Peach's and call Nikki. Please." What she heard in his voice shook her.

She sighed. "I'll be there in five."

Scott found her already at a table with two beers sitting in front of her. "One of those better be mine, woman." Sitting across from her, he snagged one of the beers, downing almost half of it in one gulp.

"The red head, right?"

Alex nodded, her head hanging low. She was unable to look Scott in the eyes, afraid to see her shame reflected back at her.

"Ah shit, Alex, I'd have to say you've hit rock bottom. I'm not going to lecture you or anything of the sort. I am going to remind you that you have a choice to make. Do you tell her and live with the outcome or do you lie to her? My friend, I'll tell you one thing, if you lie to her she will find out. I do promise you, however, that I will not be the one to tell her. Alex, go home and talk to her, she'll forgive you. Maybe not for some time, but she loves you. There. I said my peace."

He raised his empty beer to signal Joe to bring them another round.

After Joe left from bringing the fresh bottles, Alex looked up at Scott. He saw the tears on her face. Scott knew Alex never cried. He saw shame and self-hatred in her eyes. "If I tell her she'll leave me. I'll die without her. I don't know why I did it. I knew it was wrong. I knew I should've said no, turned around and went home to Nikki. You have to believe me. This is the first time I've cheated on her and it will be the only time, I swear to you, Scott."

Scott set his beer on the table, picking at the label for a moment while contemplating what to say next. He looked around the bar, seeing only a few patrons, knowing the pouring rain was keeping them home.

Turning back to Alex, he pinned her to her chair with a look on his face that she had only seen a few times before, but never aimed at her. "I'm not the one that you need to be begging to. She's sitting at home terrified that something has happened to you. She's terrified that you're lying somewhere with a bullet in you or worse…on a slab. Have you decided what you are going to do? This is going to be the biggest decision you've ever had to make. Have you decided to face it or to hide from it?"

"I've been driving around for the past couple of hours not knowing what to do. Knowing I couldn't go home and face Nikki. I finally found myself close to home, pulled off the road and parked for a while to think. I can't tell her, Scott, I just can't. She'll leave me. What do you want me to do? Walk in and say, 'sorry babe I was late because I was fucking a red head from the fifty third and I lost track of time. Didn't realize I was going to be late for dinner.' Would that be okay? I really don't think so. God, Scott, I fucked-up really bad this time."

She motioned to Joe for another round.

Scott yelled to Joe to cancel that order. Turning to his friend, he looked deadly serious. "Alex, I'm your friend and always will be no matter what you decide. I, however, had better get home before Tessa starts in on me. What are you going to do?"

He stood, pushing the chair back.

"I truly don't know. I'll figure it out on the way home. Now get your ass home before Tessa has mine in a sling too. I'll talk to you tomorrow, bud."

They both threw some bills on the table and walked out the door.

A nervous Alex pulled into the driveway fifteen minutes later. She was met at the door by a very worried lover. Nikki inspected her from head to toe to make sure she was had no more holes in her than she left with that morning.

Nikki had been so terrified that something had happened to Alex that she thought she was going to crawl out of her skin. Alex had finally called, apologizing that she ran into an old colleague and they had lost track of time.

Nikki wrapped her arms around Alex's neck and buried her face in her hair.

Alex could feel her lover shaking.

"Oh God, I was so afraid. I thought something had happened. I was so worried when you didn't come home or didn't call." Nikki hung onto Alex as if her life depended on it.

Alex's empty stomach picked that moment to growl, causing Nikki to laugh. "Why don't you go take a shower, you kind of smell like a bar and God only knows what else? I'll go reheat dinner for you, while you get the stink off you."

"Ah yeah, we had a couple of beers. I guess I do need a shower. I'll be back in a few." She kissed Nikki on the lips. "I love you, babe."

"I love you too, now go." Nikki returned to the kitchen to warm Alex's dinner. Then it hit her.

"That smell, it smelled like... No, it couldn't have been. Could it have? It smelled like sex. No. She wouldn't. Alex loves me."

Alex walked into the kitchen to find Nikki staring off into space. Walking up behind her, she put her arms around Nikki and kissed her on the neck. "Hey baby, penny for your thoughts." She kissed her again. She felt Nikki's body tense in her arms. Alex turned Nikki around in her arms so they were face to face.

"What's wrong, babe?" Alex's heart started pounding, seeing the look in Nikki's eyes. A million jumbled thoughts entered her mind at once.

"Nikki?" Fear of a different kind coursed through Alex. Her inner voice that kept telling her not to do it, screamed at her. Nikki knew.

"Alex, what's going on? What aren't you telling me?" She slowly pulled away from Alex so she could see her face better. "And why do you smell like a bar?"

Alex tried turning away from her, ashamed at what she had done.

"Alex…" Nikki hesitated, "did I do something wrong?"

She let go of Alex and backed away.

That smell…she knew what it was. Alex had smelled like sex. Nikki wondered what she had done that made Alex look somewhere else. All the inadequacies came pouring back into every cell of Nikki's body. She once more felt she wasn't good enough for someone like Alex. She turned toward the kitchen. "Your dinner is ready, why don't you eat it while it's hot?"

"Nikki, I…"

Nikki was already in the kitchen, unable to hear her.

Alex stood rooted to the spot. Nikki's actions all but confirmed to Alex that her lover knew what she had done. Alex had done the one thing she never wanted to do. She hurt her and

Nikki thought it was something she had done. Alex followed Nikki to the kitchen.

She looked away from Alex. "Your dinner is getting cold. I know you don't like cold food."

Alex crossed the kitchen and stood next to her.

"Nikki, please—"

Nikki cut her off, "No it's okay. I understand."

Alex was frustrated. A part of her wanted Nikki to call her out on it. Then it would all be in the open. On the other hand, she just wanted it all forgotten and locked away. Primarily, though, she was upset with Nikki just assuming anything without them talking.

She let her anger at herself fester into anger at Nikki. "What do you mean, you understand? Understand what? Please clarify that a little, will you?"

Without realizing it, she had moved her body within an inch of Nikki's. She grasped Nikki's forearm.

Nikki felt a little afraid. She, however, knew she had to say something. "We agreed to hide nothing from one another." Nikki laid her heart on the table. "What I understand is that you have needs that maybe I can't fill. That you would look elsewhere and maybe we really don't belong together, that I—"

Nikki never saw it coming. The hand hit her face so fast it was like lightening striking. She really wasn't sure it had happened until her cheek started to throb. She stood riveted to the spot.

Alex stared back at her, not believing what she had done either. She opened her mouth several times. Nothing came out. She had broken her oath to Nikki that she would never knowingly cause her pain.

"You promised." Nikki turned to walk away.

"Nikki…you belong to me. Do not ever doubt that for a moment." She saw the angry red mark rising on Nikki's cheek. Alex's shame surfaced, kicking her anger aside.

"Nikki, don't please. I need…I would never…Fuck!" She ran after Nikki to the bedroom.

"Please, baby. I'm sorry. I would never hurt you. I'm just so stressed right now. I know it's no excuse. I have none. Please let me talk to you. I love you. You are my life and my world. It hurt that you would jump to conclusions without letting me have my say. Please baby. Can we sit and talk for a while?"

Alex stood in the bedroom doorway as if pleading for her life. The long moments before Nikki nodded her head yes seemed like hours to Alex. Almost afraid to approach her, she slowly walked into the room.

Nikki sat on the bed, unable to look at Alex and waited for Alex to sit next to her. She was so quiet Alex almost didn't hear her. "Okay, let's talk. Why did you smell like sex when you came in?"

Nikki finally looked up at her.

Alex saw pain in her eyes…pain she had put there.

†

There comes a split moment in every human's life where they must choose a path. One will lead them home, the other to their own private hell. The few who chose the latter of the two courses see it as the only way.

Alex had arrived at that moment. She made her choice. One she would have to live with. She neglected to remember though that it would affect all of those around her… those who loved her, the ones that cared more about her than themselves. In that split moment, Alex made her choice. She chose to lie. What she decided to ignore was that the fates always had a way of returning it tenfold.

†

"Baby, I'm sorry I worried you. It's not what you're thinking though. Johnny called me and we kinda met up at Kat's."

Nikki knew where and what it was. What she could not grasp was why would Alex go in a strip club to visit with an old friend?

Alex sat, slowly inching her way toward Nikki. "Well, time kind of got away from us. I was telling him all about you and how wonderful things are now, when this girl came onto the stage that was a dead ringer for you. Watching her strip, then

292

touch herself was almost more than I could take. Then when she came to the table in front of us… well, I kind of had to leave. I sat in the truck for a while, just about jumping out of my skin. The only thing I could think of was coming home and taking you. I couldn't do that to you, so I kind of…well…I made myself feel better."

Nikki felt ashamed that she had thought Alex cheated on her. She could understand why Alex didn't want to come home and use her as a sexual tool.

Nikki took Alex's hands. "I'm sorry love, so sorry. I should never have doubted you. You could've come home, I would've understood…."

Nikki leaned in to kiss her. It started gentle then turned raw with hunger. She spent the rest of the night and into the morning satisfying Alex's cravings, giving of herself and asking for nothing in return. Nikki wanted to make sure Alex always knew to come home.

✝

A ringing broke through Alex's sex induced slumber. She heard Nikki whisper to the caller, then the phone hitting the floor and a small shriek. Alex sat bolt upright in bed, turning to find the source of the commotion. Nikki's body shook as she rocked to and fro.

"Baby, what's wrong?"

Nikki couldn't think, couldn't form the words.

Alex drew her into her arms. Rubbing circles on her back with the palm of her hand, Alex tried to calm her.

Nikki, unable to control it, started to sob.

"Your parent's, car…."

Alex knew….

About the Author

Alane Hotchkin

If anyone knows where the birthplace of oil is in North America you will know exactly where I am talking about. I was born in Oil City, PA and later lived in Pittsburgh. You say do not know where Oil City is. Well imagine a tiny town population "two" directly between Pittsburgh & Erie, PA. I grew up with family always around (mostly male) and all with wicked senses of humor. My one cousin one day decided to see if his father's (my uncle) car would float in the retention pond.

Okay, so now you also know where I got my sense of humor. My earliest childhood memory is driving to the store with my favorite uncle to buy his cigarettes & booze in his HUGE Cadillac with the top down, while listening to an eight track of Dolly Pardon's Coat of Many Colors and so a little girl's education was started. <LOL>

Side Note: Finally, in 2005, I had to admit to myself and unwillingly to others that well....I'm a country hick even though all my life I tried to be a city girl. <LOL>

Other Books from Affinity eBook Press

*

Till There Was You
S. Anne Gardner

Julia is a woman used to power and is not afraid to use it or impose her will to get her way. She appears to have the world but a part of her is empty and cold as a frozen tundra. Julia rides in the mornings to clear her head and to make plans for what she is about to set in motion.

Theodora, known as Teddy, is trying to put together a marriage filled with uncertainties. She felt once upon a time that she would have a great love but that has eluded her.

One morning these two women meet and from the first instance, it is explosive. The attraction is undeniable, the fears very real and the end without question will change them both forever.

*

Nocturnes
JD Glass

From acclaimed author, JD Glass, and featuring some of her most loved characters. Nocturnes is a collection of events and adventures, from the sensual dreamscape of the deepest love, to the brooding intensity of desire.no matter what.

*

Denial
Jackie Kennedy

Time spent in Somalia has Doctor Celeste Cameron accustomed to living and working in a war zone. Coming back home to America, Celeste is glad to see the end of the peril she's been in—or so she thinks.

Danger seems to follow Celeste and she finds it in the shape of Amy. What Celeste feels for Amy scares her more than anything she has faced in war zones.

Amy has the same feelings, but is in denial and vows to marry Josh, Celeste's twin brother, no matter what.

When fate brings them together again, will they give in to their mutual attraction or will they once again deny what they feel.

*

In Name Only
JM Dragon
Sequel to The Fix-it Girl

Can an agreement forged out of necessity actually work?

*

'55 Ford
Erin O'Reilly

Andrea McBride, the author of four books, wants to find someone to restore an old '55 Ford truck that she inherited in a real estate purchase. She will only settle for the best and finds RJ Whittaker who many proclaim to be the best restorer among millions.

*

Desert Heat
Dannie Marsden

For Luce Diamond, an undercover policewoman, her life is in shambles. Her longtime lover left her and an automobile accident that resulted in a child's death haunts her.

*

An Affair of Love
S. Anne Gardner

From a dark past, a forbidden love, a secret comes. Among the confusion and the chaos of an unwanted reality, two women find something they neither want nor can deny.

*

Journey to Her Heart
KB Belmar

The poems and short stories in this book are very personal to me. They are an emotional journey, in which my heart has given me words to express my feelings. They are words that came from what started as an attraction and ended in love. In these words, it is my hope that others may find they can relate to these feelings.

*

Taming the Wolff
Del Robertson

ONLY ONE WOMAN...
HAS THE POWER...
TO TAME THE WOLFF...

*

Private Dancer
TJ Vertigo

Reece Corbett grew up on the mean streets on New York City, abused, used and in trouble with the law.

Faith Ashford grew up wealthy, with all the creature comforts that money provides. When they meet fireworks begin

*

Miriam and Esther
Sherry Barker

Miriam thought her life would play out in the bustling metropolis of Dallas, but after a life changing accident, she moves to the small town of Cool Lake, Texas to get her head on straight and regain her senses.

*

McKee
A.C. Henley

Private Investigator Quinlan McKee has returned to Los Angeles after a three-year absence, only to find herself embroiled in a world of child slavery and police corruption.

*

The Epitaph
Ali Spooner

A college student, Pepper Monroe, is in search of ideas for a history project. Her search takes her a small country cemetery and an unusual epitaph captures her imagination. A retired groundskeeper observes her interest in the particular headstone and strikes up a conversation with the young woman. The story he shares with her of the lingering racial hatred after the emancipation and the plight of one

family provides her a heartrending story for her
project.

*

Paradox of Love
JM Dragon & Erin O'Reilly

Parker Davis's car limped its way into Portsmouth. It was just another city. The major repairs to her vehicle, force her to stay where she was and find employment—the police department.

Olivia Santos lived for her work as a police officer, following a family tradition.. The only thing that she placed above her police work was the love she had for her only living relative—her brother-an undercover cop.

When Parker and Olivia meet at a social function, there is an immediate attraction, which starts them on a road of passionate, unquenchable love. What happens will reflect on their future like an indelible stain forever.

E-Books, Print, Free e-books
Visit our website for more publications available
online.

www.affinityebooks.com

Affinity E-Book Press NZ Ltd

Canterbury, New Zealand

Registered Company 2517228